MW00782553

Tate

THE TEMPTATION SERIES V

ELLA FRANK

Copyright © 2017 by Ella Frank
www.ellafrank.com

ISBN: 9781635762129

Cover Design: Shanoff Formats
Cover Photographer: Fred Goudon
Cover Model: Clément Becq

No part of this book may be reproduced or transmitted in any form or by any means, electronic or mechanical, including photocopying, recording, or by any information storage and retrieval system without the written permission of the author, except for the use of brief quotations in a book review.
This book is a work of fiction. Names, characters, places, and incidents either are products of the author's imagination or are used fictitiously. Any resemblance to actual persons, living or dead, events, or locales is entirely coincidental.

Dedication

To Tate,

From the very beginning I had a plan for my life.
But it wasn't until we met that I knew it was you.

~Logan.

Part One

Change: To make the future course of something different from what it is or from what it would be if left alone.

Chapter One

IT WAS STRANGE how a life could change in the blink of an eye. How someone's perception of things could alter in a nanosecond due to one look or word depending on the mood or the timing, or even the person they were with. And sometimes, when that happened, there was no explaining why. It just…happened.

Well, that was what Logan Mitchell had been telling himself for the past month, ever since he and Tate had returned home from New Buffalo, where he'd had one of those life-changing moments.

Yes, life-changing. That was about the only way he could sum it up. *Or mind-altering. Maybe even some kind of physical metamorphosis?* And that wasn't even him being dramatic, Logan thought, as he heard the shower in the en suite turn on.

No. This was apparently what happened after one was blindsided by a realization he'd never thought he would entertain in his life. A realization brought into sharp clarity by the man behind that bathroom door.

William Tate Morrison.

God, just his name alone made Logan's body

undergo an immediate reaction. Whether it be a ridiculous smile on his face at the mention of it, or the urge to slide his damn hand between his legs because he wanted to groan it out loud. The person who belonged to that name had managed to completely alter what Logan had always assumed would be the trajectory of his life. And this past trip to the cabin had been the biggest shift of all.

It was a cosmic fucking shift of epic proportions that had turned his entire world, and him, on his ass. And all because of one little word that had popped into his head and would not leave—marriage.

As if that wasn't alarming enough, every time he found himself alone in his office lately, he was about two steps away from doodling his and Tate's name on a notepad with *4 Ever* underneath, surrounded by a heart.

Shit, he was really starting to worry over his state of mind, because for the life of him he couldn't work out what the hell had caused this sudden change in him. And there had to be a reason for it. *Right?*

"Logan?" Tate's voice filtered into the bedroom where he'd left him around ten minutes ago, and Logan tried to shove aside his current thoughts and replace them with more neutral ones, because that was another thing he was getting really great at. Not hiding the fact that his brain was twenty million miles away. He hadn't missed Tate's questioning looks lately, but luckily they'd had so much else going on in the past month that he'd been able to hide this particular bit of crazy under all of the other. "You better not have fallen back asleep out there."

Logan stretched under the sheets as the door opened and steam billowed into their bedroom, and just like that, any worry he'd been having vanished at the sight of Tate wrapped in a navy-blue towel and nothing else.

Shoving aside the sheet, Logan was on his feet and crossing over to where Tate was rubbing his damp curls, and when Logan stopped opposite him, Tate paused to greet him. "Mornin'."

"Good morning," Logan said, placing a hand on Tate's chest as he kissed him. "You're up before me. Something important happening today that I should know about?" He was only joking, of course, because while he'd been lying in bed thinking about the giant distraction that wouldn't leave *his* head, there was a much more immediate life-changing event that was already here. A huge change that had already been signed and set in motion. Brought to fruition. And that was about to happen right now. Today.

Tate's lips split into a wide grin that was downright contagious. "Hmm... I don't know. Maybe. But if you don't take your hands off me and get your fine ass in the shower, we'll never find out, will we?"

Logan flirted his fingers down the light dusting of Tate's treasure trail. "You should've woken me. That way we'd both be finished with our shower and be on our way already."

"Sure we would've," Tate said as he resumed rubbing the towel over the back of his head. "If I'd woken

you, we would still be *in* the shower and would more than
likely miss our appointment. Don't even pretend otherwise."

Logan's fingers slipped behind the towel, which he
gripped and then asked, "Since when have you ever cared
about being on time?"

"Since today. Plus, you've been sleeping like shit
lately, so I figured I'd give you an extra ten minutes where
you weren't tossing and turning."

Well, hell, Logan thought. Guess Tate was paying
closer attention than he'd thought. "Just a lot going on with
work renovations and—"

"I figured. But you need to find a way to start
unwinding at night." Tate brought two fingers up and
gently pushed them to the middle of Logan's forehead.
"Turn off that big brain of yours."

If only it was that easy. "I can try and do that," Logan
said, and then he tugged the towel from Tate's hips and
lowered his gaze down his naked body. "As long as you
promise to help by turning on something else that's big of
mine instead."

"I'm sure I could work something out," Tate told
him, and when Logan dropped the material and reached for
him, Tate took a step back and added, "Later." He then
pointed to the shower and said, "Go. We have to be across
town in an hour."

Logan arched an eyebrow at the order but finally
gave in. "Fine. I'm going. But for the record, this better be
the only time you ever tell me to go away while standing in

front of me hard and naked, or I might develop a complex."

"I'm hard because *you're* naked. How is that giving you a complex? Now get in the shower. You've got ten minutes."

Logan gave in to the urge to give Tate one more thorough perusal, and then, without another word, headed into the bathroom. As the door shut behind Tate and the steam from the shower started to fill the stall, Logan looked at the glass doors, *and yeah,* had to hold back that absurd urge from earlier.

There would be no hearts left on the clear panes of their shower this morning. No *4 Evers* underneath it either. But damn if he wasn't tempted by that bossy fucker who'd just ordered him in there like a petulant child.

Christ, he was totally sunk when it came to William Tate Morrison.

* * *

TATE TOSSED THE towel across the chair that sat in the corner of their bedroom and snagged a pair of briefs and faded jeans out of the closet. The sound of the running water had a grin playing on his lips as he pictured Logan grumbling the entire way through his shower. But not even his sexy ass was going to send Tate off course today. They had too much to do, and he was so damn amped up about where they were headed this morning that he was surprised he hadn't spent the night the same way Logan had—tossing and turning.

Poor guy. Logan had so much on his plate right now, between the renovations at work and their own lives, that Tate was glad they were at least going to be able to cross one thing off that list today.

Ever since they'd returned from their weekend at the cabin, it felt as though their life had been in overdrive. Ironic, really, considering the two of them had come to the conclusion they wanted to scale back on things while away on that very trip. The thing was, though, they weren't busy separately—they were busy rearranging *their* lives. It just somehow happened that once they'd started that ball rolling, it had picked up momentum and tumbled along much quicker than either of them ever expected. *In a good way. But an insanely fast way,* Tate thought, as he pulled out a white t-shirt to tug over his head before grabbing a grey linen button-up and shrugging it on, leaving it to hang open.

With his boots and socks in hand, he made his way out of the bedroom and into the living room of the condo that was currently littered wall to wall with sturdy moving boxes that were either halfway full or sitting empty ready to be packed. There was a giant roll of bubble wrap propped up by the kitchen island, and across the black marble counter were rolls of tape, a pair of scissors, and a couple of Stanley knives. Oh, and the four empty beer bottles they'd left there after they'd finished their initial rounds of prepacking the night before.

Tate wandered over to one of the recliners and

dropped his boots on the floor before hunting down his cell phone, which he'd left by the coffee machine last night to charge. He had a quick call he needed to make this morning, but before he did, he checked for any messages he might have missed. When the only one he saw was from his father confirming the time for tomorrow's dinner with Jill, he grimaced.

Dad: Six o'clock work for you guys? If so, see you then. Let me know if you need to change anything.

Tate swallowed around the lump in his throat as he read the text three more times than necessary. *Yeah, okay.* He was kind of guilty of having put that off. But they'd been busy, and, well, he'd discovered he needed a little more time to wrap his head around the idea of sitting down and stomaching a meal in that house again with Jill.

It was probably stupid, but even though his father had gone out of his way these last few years to make that place as welcoming as possible, the idea of seeing his sister there definitely impacted the sense of security he'd come to enjoy under that roof again.

Knowing he could no longer put it off, Tate shot back a quick reply to let his father know that that was fine, and made a promise to himself that he meant it. Then he put the phone down to grab Logan's traveler's mug and fill it for him so he'd have some when they were finally ready to go. He also grabbed two breakfast bars and a glass of juice for himself, before he picked his phone back up and scrolled through the contacts for the number he was looking for.

Once he had it on his screen, he listened for the shower to make sure it was still running, took a bite of his bar, and then hit call.

Taking up a seat in the recliner, Tate lounged back and rested his ankle on his knee as he waited for the person at the other end to pick up. It didn't take long, and then Cole's voice was coming through the speaker.

"Hey, Tate. You're up early for a Saturday. I thought only people with kids didn't sleep in on the weekend."

Tate laughed as he heard the sound of small voices in the background. "Hey yourself. And you would be right any other weekend."

"Oh, that's right. It's the big day over there today, isn't it?"

"Big weekend in general," Tate said, and took a sip of his juice. "I don't think we have a minute to spare over the next two days."

"That's what Logan was telling me. You guys are going to be exhausted come Monday."

Tate thought of the next forty-eight hours and didn't disagree. "Don't be surprised if he calls in."

"Yeah, right," Cole said. "Josh is taking us on a walk-through of where our new offices are going to be. Do you really think Logan is going to sit out on that while Priest and I get first dibs on the choices available?"

Hell no, he didn't. There wasn't a chance Logan would miss that. He would likely be there roping off his section before anyone else even arrived. "Yeah, you might have a point."

"Trust me, he's been eyeing the specs ever since we started discussing the idea. He'll be there. Even if it's only to say 'that's mine' and then leave."

Tate chuckled over how accurate that statement was. If there was one thing Logan never had trouble expressing, it was what he considered *his*. Something Tate was intimately familiar with. He took another bite of his bar and then shoved that thought aside, determined not to get sidetracked. "How's the Madison clan this morning?"

"The Madison clan is—" There was a loud *clang* and then the phone was muffled as Cole said, "Thomas, how many times have I told you not to ride that scooter in here?" There was a high-pitched "sorry," and then Cole was back. "The Madison clan is trying to make their father old before his time. Sorry about that."

"No problem," Tate said, and smoothed a hand along his leg to rest it on his knee. "But speaking of getting older… While Logan's not around, I wanted to ask you about his birthday."

Cole laughed so loudly at that Tate couldn't help but join in. "You're a brave man saying that in the same vicinity as him."

"He's in the shower. My life is safe."

"For now," Cole said. "But have you forgotten who we're talking about? Logan doesn't *do* birthdays. Well, his own, that is."

Tate hadn't forgotten at all. He'd been battling about

birthday celebrations with Logan for as long as they'd been together. Logan claimed he didn't want to celebrate a day that merely signified he was getting one day closer to grey hair and a retirement home. Tate, however, knew there were other, more personal, reasons behind Logan's adamant refusal to celebrate the day he was born. And after the first year, when he'd put up such a fight about it, Tate had let him off the hook.

Well, not this year. He wanted to do something special for Logan, and he was determined.

"Too bad," Tate said. "He's getting one this year whether he wants it or not."

"Uhh…I don't know if you're brave or stupid," Cole said around a laugh.

"Probably a bit of both. But I'm hoping you will be too."

"Wait. You want me to help you plan a birthday get-together? For Logan?"

Tate's lips twitched at Cole's tone. "I was hoping."

"You do know I have two young children to support and take care of, right? Why would you want to risk the life of their father?"

"Oh, come on," Tate said. "It won't be that bad. I mean, what's the worst thing that could happen?"

"I thought I just told you. My children could wind up fatherless. Why would you want to do that to them, Tate?"

Tate couldn't stop his laughter at Cole's serious tone.

"Okay, well, how about you help me plan it and we'll tell Logan that it was all me?"

There was a pause, and then Cole said, "You have great faith in how much he loves you. You know that, right?"

The comment was said in jest, but Tate *did* have great faith in how much Logan loved him. And he knew that even if Logan got annoyed over this, he'd eventually come around and see that Tate was doing it to celebrate him, not for any other reason.

"I do. Plus, he can never stay mad at me for too long." Tate heard movement coming from the bedroom and got to his feet to put his empty glass in the sink, knowing he had to wrap things up before the man they were discussing emerged. "So, you in?"

Cole sighed. "I suppose. It's your funeral. Just be sure to write down what kind of memorial service you'd like. I feel it's the least I can do."

"You're really worried. Maybe he'll surprise us," Tate said.

"Oh, you poor, delusional man."

"I'll call when I work out more details."

"Okay. Rachel will be all over this when she finds out also. So make sure you keep her name out of it too. I would like my children raised with a mother."

"Mum's the word."

"God help us all," Cole said. "Have a good weekend. Try not to run yourselves ragged."

"Will do. See you guys soon."

"See you, Tate."

Just as Tate ended the call, Logan came out of the bedroom wearing pressed khaki slacks and a white and burgundy checkered shirt that was neatly tucked in at his trim waist, which was surrounded by a caramel-colored belt to match his leather shoes.

Never an item out of place, Tate thought, as Logan fastened his watch exactly where its rightful spot was on his left wrist.

When he came to a stop in the kitchen, Logan looked at him from behind his glasses and said, "Look at that. I have five minutes to spare."

Tate brushed his lips across Logan's, and when he went to pull away, Logan stepped forward and slid his hand around his waist beneath Tate's loose shirt.

"Where do you think you're going? I said I have five *minutes* to spare. Not seconds."

Tate ran his eyes over the handsome face in front of him and said, "You need to eat something before we head out. We have a long day ahead of us. I put your coffee in your mug, and there's a breakfast bar on the counter. You can bring it with us."

Logan's eyes drifted beyond Tate's shoulder to the items and then came back to fasten on his. And the way they softened made Tate's heart warm.

"Thank you. Did you eat?" Logan asked.

"Juice and a bar just a second ago." Tate then

stepped around Logan and headed for the side table in the cluttered foyer. "Let me grab my wallet and keys and we'll get going, yeah?"

"Okay. Oh, and Tate?"

Tate looked over his shoulder to where Logan was now unwrapping his breakfast bar. "Yeah?"

"I'm super fucking excited about today. I just wanted you to know that in case I hadn't said it with everything kind of crazy around here."

Tate shoved his wallet in the back pocket of his jeans as Logan headed over to him with his mug in hand and a grin on his face.

Yeah, there's no question about the love here, Tate thought, and reached for Logan's hand. *Let's hope he remembers that when he wants to kick my ass next month.* And with a smile over that thought, Tate led the two of them out the door of their condo and toward their first appointment of the weekend.

Chapter Two

THE SUN WAS making a valiant effort to stay relevant on the cool October morning, as Logan turned his car onto the picturesque, tree-lined street in the heart of Wicker Park. It was just nearing ten on Saturday, and as his Audi slowly made its way down the narrow road, he turned and looked over at his silent passenger.

Tate was staring out the window at the houses bordering the street with an expression caught somewhere between apprehension and excitement, and Logan understood those feelings well. He still couldn't believe that they were there either.

This was their third trip out to Evergreen Avenue, and today would make everything over the last month official. The beautiful homes with the immaculate yards, covered in a mixture of old growth and new trees, were now going to be a permanent part of their lives. Because, as of yesterday, the two of them had signed the final papers that made number nineteen sixty-six their new home.

"Is it weird that I'm nervous?" Tate's question was the first thing he'd said in the last ten minutes, and though the silence in the car hadn't been an uncomfortable one, the familiar timbre of his voice eased some of Logan's own anxious energy.

"If it is, I guess that makes me weird too."

"Really?" Tate said, and flashed a half-smile.

"Really. It's a big investment. A big change for us." *And not the only one that's been on my mind*, Logan thought, as Tate nodded and returned his focus back out the window as Logan spotted the black iron fence that surrounded their destination.

As he pulled up to the curb, they each sat there and looked at the two-story, all-brick house, which had been built back in 1905 and since been converted into a flawless vintage home—their home.

It really was hard to believe that they'd only discussed this for the first time a little over a month ago, and now here they were about to head inside the place where the newest chapter of their lives would begin. It was nerve-racking but thrilling at the same time, and as Logan pushed open the door, the sound of Tate shoving his shut sent a jolt up his spine.

God, he was jumpy. That had to be that unknown factor, Logan supposed. The feeling that this was the start of something major that he didn't want to fuck up. So, of course, it was accompanied with the usual restlessness and heart palpitations, *right*? Kind of like the other major thing he'd been ruminating over to the point of obsession. He'd never been more distracted in his life.

"You coming?" Tate asked, as he looked over the

roof of the car to where Logan was still standing with his
door wide open. *Shit, distracted is right.*

As Logan shut the car door and came around the
hood, a gust of cool wind slammed into him and had him
shoving his hands into the sports jacket he'd thankfully
remembered on the way out the door. He hopped up onto
the sidewalk and walked over to where Tate stood in front
of the waist-high gate that housed a small mailbox, and
Logan noticed that he too had his hands in the pockets of his
jeans as the wind ruffled his hair.

The chilly blasts of October always seemed to come
on suddenly in Chicago, and were a stark reminder to get
ready for what winter would eventually bring their way. But
for now, they still got some warmth out of the sun overhead.
When Logan stopped beside Tate, he glanced at the path
leading to the front door, and then back to the man beside
him. "You ready to head inside?"

Tate gave the place another once-over and then
grinned. "Yep, sure am."

"Okay, then," Logan said, and unlocked the gate.
"Let's go."

As they made their way up to the front door, a tall
woman in her mid-thirties with sleek black hair flowing past
her shoulders stood on the porch. Cassandra, their real
estate agent, had been a lifesaver over the last month, and
she beamed at the two of them as she waved a set of keys on
her fingers.

"Welcome home, boys."

* * *

TATE REACHED FOR the keys Cassandra held, and as he wrapped his fingers around the brass, he looked back to Logan, who was right behind him peering up at the bay window on the second story.

The breeze had mussed up Logan's hair, and when those blue eyes of his found Tate's and a slow smile curved his lips, Tate knew he'd never forget how Logan looked standing there on the steps of their new home.

Wow. He still couldn't believe they'd done it. Really done it. When they'd first talked about selling the condo, Tate had never actually imagined Logan would want to leave it behind. But he'd surprised the hell out of Tate with his enthusiasm over the idea. It was as though the thought had never occurred to Logan, but once it had, he'd been all in.

As soon as they'd gotten back from their trip, Logan had been emailing him potential areas, homes, crime rates, etcetera, and Tate had to admit it was both amusing and kind of awe-inspiring to watch Logan in research mode. His lawyer liked his facts, that was for sure, and Tate had to hand it to him: Logan had found a spectacular location, where they'd gone through dozens of open houses before they'd finally agreed that this was the one—even if the price tag had made Tate balk until he and Logan had sat down to crunch the numbers and decided they could make it work.

"I believe my job here is done," Cassandra said as she shrugged her black handbag up her arm and stepped outside past the two of them. "If you have any questions at all, please let me know. But everything has been signed and filed, and as of now, you are free to start moving in."

"Thank you," Tate said, as Logan came up the final step.

"Really," Logan agreed, shaking her hand. "You made this such an easy transition."

"It was my pleasure." Cassandra headed around them and down the steps to the path. "Maybe next time I'm downtown I'll visit that bar of yours and you can repay me with a glass of wine."

"That's a deal," Tate said.

"Good. Now let me get out of your hair so you two can enjoy. The place is beautiful." Then she was walking to her car, which Logan had parked behind.

"Well, you have the keys," Logan said. "After you, Mr. Morrison."

Tate unlocked the front door and then stepped over the threshold, and when he heard Logan shut the front door behind him, Tate smiled to himself and moved into the formal living room.

Just like upstairs, there was a large bay window off to the left on the first floor, and a fireplace in the wall that would be perfect during the winter months when the weather dropped below freezing. The polished hardwoods gleamed in welcome as the sun slipped through the front window, and Tate stopped in the center of the room and turned to see Logan leaning with his back up against the front door.

"This feels a little surreal, doesn't it?" Tate asked, as Logan continued to quietly watch him.

Sure, the two of them had lived together for years now, but somehow this felt different. The whole experience of making the decision to do this together, it felt…more. Tate laughed at himself and let his eyes travel around the empty space, and wondered how it would look in two months, four, and six, and then let his eyes come back to Logan.

Where Tate was busy marveling over the fact that this unbelievable place was now theirs, he found Logan's stare intent upon him. *Not* their surroundings. The contemplative expression on Logan's face was one Tate had seen a lot recently when Logan hadn't realized he was watching. But Tate wasn't worried about it. He'd just chalked it up to the same distraction and jitters he'd been having over this huge step they'd just made. Like Logan had said in the car, this was a big change for them.

"I can't believe it's really ours," Tate said. The size alone was going to take some getting used to.

Logan pushed off the door and wandered over to where he stood, and placed a palm on Tate's chest as he finally spoke. "I know. It hasn't quite sunk in yet."

Tate brought a hand up and placed it over Logan's as he looked around again. "It's *huge*."

When Logan laughed, Tate spotted the mischievous

sparkle in his eyes and grinned.

"It never fails to amaze me how hot those two words sound coming out of your mouth," Logan said. "Even in reference to our house."

Tate took Logan's hand, tugging him out of the living room. "Come on. I want to look around now that we finally have the place to ourselves."

He led them past a white staircase and into the kitchen outfitted with a sleek island counter, dark wooden cabinetry, and stainless steel appliances. There were two sliding doors off to the right, which housed the perfect office space for Logan and already had beautiful built-in bookshelves, and, at the very end of the home, near the back door, was a small eating area.

The space was completely devoid of furnishings for now, but as they'd walked through the home over the last few visits, the two of them had discussed exactly how they'd seen the place coming together.

Tate came to a stop at the glass back door and looked out to the backyard, where there was a stone fire pit and barbecue, and couldn't help the total fucking rush of pleasure that this was his and Logan's home. One that *they* had chosen together for themselves. Damn, but they'd come a long way.

As he stood there, Logan came up behind him and wrapped his arms around his waist. And when he rested his chin on Tate's shoulder, Tate turned his head and kissed his cheek.

"Still like it?" Logan asked.

Tate turned in Logan's arms and knew he had to have the goofiest smile on his face ever. "*Like* isn't a strong enough word."

Logan returned his grin, and Tate was pleased to note his was just as boyish, just as silly, with their shared enthusiasm. "I know exactly how you feel. It's almost...I don't know...a rush to think that it's ours. Kind of like being high."

Tate couldn't help but laugh at that, because Logan had just zeroed in on the exact thought he'd been having. "Know that feeling well, do you?"

Logan waggled his eyebrows. "Not from anything chemical or herbal," he said, and then connected their lips lightly. "But when I'm inside you I feel fucking euphoric, and this has to be close to that feeling. Maybe a distant second."

Tate nipped at Logan's lip and then walked him backward until his ass hit the end of the counter in their new kitchen. "A distant second, huh?"

Logan's eyes narrowed a fraction, but that grin of his remained as he nodded.

"What about when *I'm* inside of *you*?" Tate asked, and he didn't miss the way Logan shifted his lower body so their hips were now connected.

"Oh... You're right," Logan said as his eyes dropped to Tate's mouth. "Nothing comes anywhere close to either of those two things. So maybe a distant third. What the fuck was I thinking?"

"I don't know." Tate snaked one of his hands down between them to massage his flattened palm over the ridge behind Logan's zipper. "But maybe we need to refresh your memory. Lots of new rooms here to break in." As Logan's eyes drifted shut, Tate curled his fingers around the now prominent bulge, causing a groan to slip free of Logan. "What do you say? Want to check out our new bedroom for a minute or two?"

As Logan took hold of either side of Tate's shirt, he ground himself against Tate's hand. "As much as I'd like that, have you forgotten we have to— *Ahh*," Logan said, when Tate lowered his head and kissed the patch of skin just beneath his open collar.

"Have to...?" Tate continued to palm Logan's erection and gently bite and nuzzle his way up and down his neck.

Logan's ragged breathing made Tate's pulse race, and when he sucked the skin hard enough to leave a bruise, Logan shuddered and turned his head so they were eye to eye. The strain on Logan's face made it obvious he was making an effort to behave himself, which amused Tate, and also made him more determined than ever to sway him.

"We have to be somewhere in thirty minutes," Logan managed. "We don't have time for—"

Tate's fingers at the button of Logan's pants cut him off mid-sentence. "Time for what?"

Logan wrapped one of his hands around Tate's wrist,

stilling him. "We said we'd meet him at eleven. And he's always early."

Tate unbuckled Logan's belt and eyed him boldly. "Good thing I've never been worried about running late. But since you're so worried, we don't have to go upstairs to our new bedroom. We can start right here in the kitchen. That should buy us some time. Ten minutes?"

"Tate…" Logan said, but there was little to no resistance in his tone as Tate unbuttoned his slacks and unzipped him.

"Let me welcome you to our new home." Tate slipped his hand inside Logan's briefs, and his own cock reacted to the hot throb of Logan's in his hand.

"Jesus," Logan muttered, but when he finally released Tate's shirt to brace his hands on the counter behind him, Tate knew he had him. "Ten minutes, you say?"

"Yeah… But I bet you don't last five," Tate said, and dropped to his knees.

As he yanked Logan's briefs and pants to mid-thigh, Logan shoved his fingers through his hair and angled Tate's face up so he could look down at him. Tate licked his lips at the flush now staining Logan's cheeks, and had to bite back a groan when Logan used his other hand to guide his cock along the seam of his mouth.

"Well, then, that'll give you five minutes to make sure I'm all cleaned up and presentable afterwards. Won't it?"

Even though Logan's words were stated as a

question, no answer was required. Both he and Logan knew the second Tate had him in his mouth he wasn't going to let him go anywhere until he swallowed any and all evidence of what they were about to do, and his eyes must've relayed that loud and clear, because all Tate heard before Logan slipped between his lips was, "Better hurry, we're down to nine."

As it turned out, they only needed seven.

Then they were back in Logan's car, more or less presentable, if Tate didn't count his raging hard-on, heading across town to their eleven o'clock meeting.

Chapter Three

"IS HE HERE?" Logan scanned the handful of customers seated in The Popped Cherry for the early morning lunch they opened for on the weekends, as he waited for an answer from their new bar manager, who'd just come to a stop at the end of the counter.

Robbie Bianchi, dressed smartly in his work attire, stood opposite them and indicated with a tilt of his head the booths on the opposite side of the establishment. "He sat over in the other section, thank God. Got here around fifteen minutes ago."

"Of course he did," Logan said, and shot a pointed looked in Tate's direction. "I told you. He's always early."

"We're only a few minutes late. Stop worrying. I'm sure he doesn't even care."

Robbie wiped down the bar and shrugged. "I don't know about that. He was about as happy as a grizzly bear when he got here, and has been scowling ever since."

"Why?" Logan said. "What did you say to him?"

A flash of concern crossed Robbie's features for a millisecond until Logan's lips curved and Robbie let his indignation come to the surface instead. "Nothing. I sent Bianca to take his order. The less I have to do with that man, the better for all of us."

Logan arched an eyebrow at Robbie's tone. "That *man* pulled off a miracle when he got your cousin out of a jail sentence. I'd think you could finally admit there was some merit to his way of doing things."

Robbie made an inelegant sound. "Please, the last thing I'd ever do is give *him* that kind of satisfaction."

"But you'd be open to other forms?" Logan said. "Good to know. Maybe that'll cheer him up."

Robbie gave him a droll look, and then flicked his gaze in Tate's direction. "Can you please get him out of my face?"

Tate took hold of Logan's elbow and nodded. "You got it. Everything else going okay in here today?"

"Until about fifteen minutes ago, just peachy."

As Tate tugged on Logan's arm, Logan said, "You used to be such a cheery young man."

"Yeah? Well, you only used to see me five minutes out of a day. Maybe I wasn't so cheery when you weren't around."

"Aww," Logan said. "You missed me when I left. That's really sweet. And borderline stalkerish. We did do a background check on him, right, Tate?"

"Oh my God." Robbie rolled his eyes. "Go away, please."

As they left the bar, Tate tsked Logan. "Is there a reason you continue to harass him so much?"

"Other than the pure enjoyment I get out of it? Not

really," Logan said, as they wove their way through some people entering the front door.

As they headed around the corner, Logan spotted the man they were there to meet sitting in the far booth with his head bent down over his phone, *and yeah, okay,* he did have a surly expression on his face. "You don't happen to have any honey out the back anywhere, do you? I hear that's what bears like."

"Huh?"

"Robbie's right. Maybe it was a bumpy flight," Logan muttered. "He does *not* look happy."

* * *

TATE FOLLOWED LOGAN'S lead as they headed over to where the newest partner of Mitchell & Madison sat glaring at whatever he was reading on his phone. *Joel Priestley.*

Tate was still trying to work the guy out. He'd met with him a couple of times now. Once at the office, and once at a partners' dinner with Cole, Rachel, and Logan, and still he didn't have a great read on him. That was unusual for him, given his chosen profession, and one he usually took great pride in being able to do well—but not with this guy.

Priest, as Logan and Cole called him, was a difficult one to figure out and get to know—whenever he opened his mouth to speak, it was always done with purpose and as few syllables as possible.

"Well, there he is," Logan said. "The L.A. transplant.

No need to frown so hard, Priest. We're not that late."

Priest glanced up from whatever he'd been reading, but even after he'd ascertained who'd addressed him, the tight-lipped expression he sported didn't waver.

Yeah, Tate thought. *There'll be no "so good to see you two again" coming from this guy.*

As they slid in the opposite side of the booth, Priest sat back in his seat and rested an arm across the table, absently spinning the phone, which he'd flipped over so it sat facedown in front of him.

"The only time I'd be frowning over you being late, Mitchell, is if I were here to date you or fuck you," Priest said matter-of-factly. "Which we all know I'm not." Tate then watched his eyes drop down to Logan's open collar. "Nice bruise."

Logan looked down, but, clearly unable to see what Priest was seeing, opted for rearranging the collar of his shirt instead. Tate didn't even raise an eyebrow. He wasn't about to deny what had made them late. He merely smirked, pretty damn pleased with himself.

Priest was a smart guy, and one thing that Tate *had* learned from their first meeting was that he was stealthy like a sniper. One who aimed-and-fired with no warning at all. He balanced Logan out in that way, because while Logan was whip smart, he was a direct hitter, the one whose intentions were always crystal clear. With Priest you didn't know he was there until he was gone, having done exactly what he came to do.

"I always love finding out new things about friends. Don't you, Tate?" Logan said, never one to be easily shocked or offended. "Have to say, though, Priest, didn't know you swung our particular way."

"I don't *swing*, period," Priest said. "Not my scene."

"Now there's a shocker." Tate laughed, and it wasn't lost on him that Priest had neither confirmed nor denied the part about *whom* he didn't swing with.

"Yeah, that seems about right," Logan said, shifting toward Tate. Then he draped a proprietary arm across the back of Tate's shoulders. "I bet you didn't play well with others as a child, either. Did you?"

Priest looked between the two of them, his eyes narrowing on Logan's arm. "As if you did."

Logan chuckled, and Tate couldn't help but join him. "Now that's where you're wrong," Tate said. "He played very well with others for a long time. Maybe a little *too* well."

Priest sized Logan up. "Now that does surprise me."

Tate, curious as to Priest's way of thinking, cocked his head to the side. "Really?"

"Really," Priest said. "He's the most settled one sitting at this table. I can't imagine him playing the field at all. He likes the one-on-one too much."

At that little analysis, Tate's jaw almost hit the table, and then he let out a raucous laugh. When Logan's fingers tugged on his hair in response, Tate looked over at him and wiped a tear away from his eye.

"You okay there?" Logan asked.

Tate tried to bank his hilarity, but he was still trying to wrap his brain around what Priest had said. *Maybe the guy isn't so smart.* How anyone could look at Logan and think he couldn't, and hadn't, gotten anyone he wanted was baffling to him. *Hell, he'd even gotten me, the straight guy.*

"I feel like I should be somewhat insulted by your reaction," Logan said, but his grin made it obvious he was amused not offended.

"Sorry," Tate said around a laugh. "That was just…unexpected."

"Well, since you knew me *before* I met you, I suppose I have no wiggle room, do I?"

"Not even a little," Tate said, grinning. But when Logan's vibrant eyes took on that thoughtful light he'd had more often of late, Tate found himself caught in that stare a little longer than felt normal under the current circumstances.

It wasn't until Priest spoke up again that Tate even remembered he was at the table with them.

"Okay. So when are you two going to get the hell out of my new condo so I can move in?"

*　*　*

LOGAN WAS FINDING it difficult to concentrate on anything other than Tate as he sat there transfixed by his profile. Tate had rounded back to Priest when he'd asked his question about their moving situation, but Logan was still getting over the one-two punch his newest business partner had just landed with his offhand comment—*He's the most settled one sitting at this table… He likes the one-on-one too much*—which had left Logan wondering how in the hell Priest had picked up on that.

It was true, of course. He *was* happy not playing the field now that he had Tate. But the no-nonsense way Priest had delivered his assessment made it sound as though a monogamous relationship was something Logan had been in search of his entire life.

Bet he wouldn't think that if he knew how much the prospect of that very notion is messing with me lately. Or is it? Jesus. The guy was fucking with his head now, and when Logan looked across at Priest, he saw his eyes crease, as though he knew exactly what Logan was thinking. *Perceptive asshole.*

"About two weeks should do it. Right, Logan?" Tate's voice caught Logan's attention, giving him an excuse to look away from Priest, which he immediately took advantage of.

"Yes. I think that should be good. Then it's all yours. That okay with you?"

"That works," Priest said. "Any more than two weeks in a hotel and it feels like the walls are closing in. I start to get antsy."

"Can't have that," Logan said. "Don't want you running back to the West Coast before you prove your worth."

"I already proved that, or I wouldn't be sitting here." Priest spun his phone on top of the table again. "But if you want me to continue doing so, make sure your ass is out in two weeks. I need my space and privacy if you expect me to work on all cylinders. I'm no good to anyone when I don't get it."

It was an interesting way to phrase things, but before Logan could say so, Tate spoke up. "You're a peculiar guy. You do know that, right?"

A slow curve morphed the corner of Priest's lips, and he gave a nod. "I do know that. Thank you."

"Right," Logan said, and brought his hand down to rap his knuckles on the table. "I don't know about you two, but I want a drink." *More like* need *one.*

"I could go with one too," Tate agreed, and then looked out of the booth to Robbie and waved. When Robbie looked their way, Logan saw Priest snatch up his phone and slide out of the booth, and wasn't surprised in the slightest.

"I'm going to pass. It's been a long day with the early flight, and I've yet to check in."

It was now Logan's turn to size up the man shrugging into his jacket. *Long day my ass.*

He didn't know jack shit about Priest's private life, not even if he had one he'd left behind. But one thing Logan knew for certain was that the dislike Robbie felt toward Priest was returned tenfold. And that was the only reason he was leaving to go back to his cramped hotel room.

"Don't let us hold you up," Logan said, aiming an arrogant smile in Priest's direction as Tate sat back and looked up at the man. And then, because he felt he owed Priest a final jab for so perfectly getting under his skin earlier, Logan made sure to add, "We wouldn't want you to get *antsy*."

Just as Logan predicted, Priest's brow furrowed, and Logan raised his hand to give a quick wave. "See you Monday, Priest."

"Until then, Mitchell. Tate."

"See you soon," Tate said, and without another word, Priest left the bar.

* * *

"THAT GUY IS..." Tate thought over his words and then ended, "Interesting."

"That he is," Logan said, shaking his head.

"I never actually thought I'd meet anyone more direct than you, but..." When one of Logan's eyebrows arched, Tate continued, "He definitely gives you a run for your money."

Logan pulled his phone out of his pocket. "You wouldn't be wrong. But that's what makes him so effective. I don't think anything could shock him." As he turned on the camera in his phone, Tate watched Logan flip the screen so his face was on it, and then he reached up and pulled aside the collar of his shirt. When he spotted the mark Tate had left on his neck, Logan aimed narrowed eyes Tate's way. "Not even a huge bruise on my neck, apparently. Good job, Morrison."

Tate's eyes lowered to the purplish mark marring the skin, and he felt an immediate flood of possessiveness. *Hmm, I did do a good job. Mine,* he thought. "I didn't hear you complaining at the time."

Logan's gaze smoldered at the reminder, and just as he was about to speak, Robbie arrived at their table.

"What can I get for— *Holy shit,* look at your neck."

Tate brought a hand up to muffle a laugh, while Logan switched off his phone and shrugged his shirt back in place. It managed to cover the bruise now that Tate was looking, but when Logan shifted in *just* the wrong direction, that shirt of his spread wide and, *oh yeah,* there was his stamp of ownership.

"Jesus," Logan said. "Am I going to have to button this thing all the way to my throat?"

Robbie's eyes moved between the two of them, but then finally skidded to a stop on Tate. "Wow. Who would've guessed you had *that* in you."

Logan sighed beside him, and Tate, feeling particularly proud of himself, gave Robbie an arrogant look. "Trust me. You haven't guessed the half of what's been in me—"

"Tate," Logan said, whipping his head in his direction. But Tate just laughed. He was having too good of a day, and Robbie was around them often enough now that there was no point in always censoring himself.

At first, Tate had been overly careful about what came out of his mouth in regard to him and Logan around his new bar manager. But damn it was getting exhausting, and hadn't one of the biggest draws of hiring Robbie been that he'd be comfortable in this place of business? Plus, with Logan, it was close to impossible to keep talk of sex out of the equation, and it wasn't like Robbie would ever judge one way or another.

So, yeah, it's time to just settle in and be myself, Tate thought. "Stop acting so shocked," he said to Logan. "You know it's true, and it's not like you've never left a mark on me."

"Well," Logan said, relaxing back in his chair and stretching his arm back out behind Tate's shoulders. "I guess I've been told."

"I would say *so*," Robbie finally said, and then he aimed an interested look in Tate's direction. "By the way. This conversation just totally put you in his league."

Tate eyed Robbie, wondering *what* exactly he meant by that.

"Anyone that can boss him around has to be smokin' hot in the bedroom. Add in the fact you're *clearly* an animal," Robbie said, his eyes once again going to Logan's neck, "and sorry, Logan, suddenly you're not the sexiest owner of this bar."

Logan scoffed, and Tate felt his fingers weave through the back of his hair as Logan leaned over and

pressed a kiss to his cheek. "Trust me. I'm well aware of
who the sexiest person in this bar is. Now go away and get
us a couple of beers so I can leave a mark of my own on
him."

Tate hummed in the back of his throat and put a
hand on the thigh Logan now had plastered against his, as
Robbie took one last look at the pair of them and then went
to do as he was told.

"Whatever will we do about having such mouthy
employees? Me with Priest. You with him," Logan said, as
he flicked his tongue over Tate's earlobe.

"I was just thinking that Robbie was turning out to
be a close to perfect one for us." Logan pulled back and eyed
him as though he'd lost his mind, and Tate shrugged. "You
have to admit, he's good at following orders."

Logan's gaze drifted beyond the booth to where
Robbie was now heading behind the bar to fetch their
drinks. "He is good at that."

Tate thought about how stressed he'd been over the
prospect of hiring someone new to come in and take
Amelia's place. But the transition between her and Robbie
had been seamless. He'd picked it up faster than they'd
expected, and though he was still finding his footing when it
came to the confidence of being in charge, Tate was starting
to see the sass that had once been such an inherent part of
Robbie reemerge. "He knows us. There are no surprises
there."

"True..."

"And he's...fun," Tate said, surprising himself.

"*Fun?*"

"Yeah. When he's not trying to be something he's not. He's fun. I feel comfortable around him." That brought Tate up short, and he laughed. "God, I can't believe I just said that."

"Neither can I. But I get it." Logan placed his hand over the one Tate still had resting on his leg. "He was the first person to give you that sense of acceptance. He didn't bat an eyelash over the fact that you were with me when we started dating."

"You're right. That's definitely a part of it. Funny how things work out, isn't it?"

"What do you mean?"

"Well," Tate said, "he helped me accept who I was and who I wanted. And now I feel like he has no idea who *he* is anymore."

"Yeah." Logan let out a sigh, and then stroked his fingers down the back of Tate's neck. "I can see your brain working overtime. You're worried about him, aren't you?"

Tate looked over his shoulder toward the bar, and when he saw Robbie headed back in their direction with two bottles in hand, he looked at Logan and said, "I don't know. Maybe a little. I mean, maybe this time I can help him out."

"Gonna pay it forward with Robert Bianchi, huh?"

"Would that be so bad? Lord knows he seems as though he could do with a little guidance in his life."

"You won't hear any argument from me on that.

From the little I've gotten out of him, he's still trying to get his feet back under him. Just make sure he's aware that the *sexiest* bar owner is taken. We both know how incorrigible he is."

"Was," Tate said. "He *was* incorrigible. Now he's—"

"Right *here*..." Logan said, as the man they'd been discussing arrived at their table and put their beers down in front of them.

When both of them looked over at Robbie and plastered what Tate suspected were the fakest smiles imaginable on their faces, Robbie said, "What?"

"Nothing," they said at the same time.

But Robbie wasn't buying that. "You're full of shit. Both of you."

Logan wagged a finger as he reached for the Corona and pushed the lime wedge into the bottle. "See, Tate? What'd I tell you? We're stuck with two new employees who clearly think it's okay to talk back to their bosses. Between him and Priest, I don't know who's worse."

"Uhh, I'm nothing like him," Robbie said, and Tate could tell it took everything in the guy not to say anything more on the subject. "Do you two want any food, or is that it?"

"Nah, this is good," Tate said, and Robbie, *the smart man*, didn't linger. He turned on his heel to walk away, and Tate looked over at Logan. "Maybe we need to have a get-together at our new house when we settle in. Or a game night. We could invite a couple of extra players. A West

Coast transplant and a lost little sheep. It's the friendly thing to do."

Logan let out a loud bark of laughter and took a swig of his beer. "Oh, that's just asking for trouble, Mr. Morrison. I don't know if you're brave or stupid."

Considering that was the second time he'd been told that today, Tate was starting to believe that maybe it was a little bit of both, and *maybe* that was what happened when you were so damn happy.

You became braver than usual. And inexplicably stupid.

Chapter Four

AHH, WHAT A difference a day can make, Logan thought, as he cast a surreptitious glance in Tate's direction the following evening from where he sat in his car in Will Morrison's driveway. He'd just pulled up and parked behind an enormous Dodge pickup truck, and while they both knew they had to get out and head inside, Logan wasn't at all surprised that the two of them were...lingering. "Well, this feels familiar."

Logan tapped his fingers on the steering wheel as he peered out the windshield and up to the wraparound porch of Will's house.

"Yeah," Tate said with a grimace—no further explanation needed. They were both more than aware that for the first time since they'd made the trek to meet Tate's family, they were back to sitting in a car outside of Tate's childhood home with a sense of unease in the air.

But that was the past. That was a long time ago. Since then they'd been back here to the scene of that horrible nightmare and been invited inside by the man who owned the place and welcomed into his life. And today, Logan had to believe, would be different than the first.

He sat back in his seat and reached across the car to run his fingers over Tate's forehead. "Stop scowling. We're not on trial. We're going to dinner."

"Ugh, I know." When Logan went to remove his arm, Tate took hold of his hand and entwined their fingers. "I just hate the thought of rehashing all this past shit. And that's exactly what's going to happen tonight."

Logan studied the worry lines etched around Tate's lips. "Well, yeah. That's what this is about. Clearing the air, right? It's what you want. But...you don't have to do it right now if you aren't ready. I can turn the car around and we can reschedule for some other time."

Tate sighed and let out a shaky breath, and Logan gave him a moment.

When Tate had first asked him about tonight, he'd done so only days after his initial sit-down with Jill, and Logan had sensed that his initial agreement to it all was something Tate hadn't overly thought about until *after* saying yes. Because instead of scheduling the dinner within the following week, as Logan would've assumed, Tate had been dragging his feet on it.

He'd let weeks pass until a month was gone and he had several messages on his phone from his sister wondering if he'd changed his mind. But he hadn't. That wasn't Tate's way. He'd been deliberating over it. Weighing all the pros and cons while trying to work out how everything would eventually play out. And Logan wasn't about to rush him.

Knowing Tate, he had more than likely been trying to wrap his head around what tonight would mean to the both of them, and Logan had been more than willing to let him take his time and do it when he was ready. In fact, he'd been grateful for the opportunity to analyze his *own* feelings about the matter. And he had many when it came to the reappearance of Jill.

Feelings. Questions. Suspicions. First and foremost, why hadn't she reached out before now? She claimed she had a tense relationship with her father, but come on. If you wanted to see someone, you made a fucking effort, *right*?

"Okay. Let's get this over with," Tate said, the sound of his seatbelt unbuckling pulling Logan from his thoughts.

"Okay. Let's."

They got out of the car and met up in front of it, where Logan took Tate's hand in his and brought him in close. "Hang on a minute. Let's see if I can think of a good excuse to get you out of there if you want to leave."

When Tate merely eyed him, his grim expression not changing, Logan became more determined than ever to pull a smile from him.

"How about you say: Logan, I'm a little stiff from all this recent packing with you. I think it's time we headed home."

Tate's lips twitched. "I'm just supposed to work that into a conversation?"

"Hey, if you can't work the word *stiff* into a conversation with me, we have bigger issues to deal with than dinner with your sister."

And just like that, Tate's gorgeous smile lit his entire
face. "You're out of your mind."

"Maybe," Logan said, and then leaned in to kiss
Tate's mouth. "But you're smiling, and that's exactly what I
wanted."

"And you always get what you want."

"Well, yes. This you already know." In a final show
of support, Logan brought their hands up to kiss Tate's
knuckles, and then, without another word, the two of them
headed for the house.

* * *

TATE DIDN'T BOTHER knocking, since he knew his father
would've left the door unlocked for them, and as they
walked inside, he told himself for the hundredth time that
everything was going to be okay. *Yeah, now if I could just
believe it.*

Logan's hand around his was a comfort, though, as
was the warmth of him as he stuck close behind Tate while
they made their way down the narrow hall. He could hear
the sound of voices as they neared the entryway to the
kitchen, and just before he stepped through, he glanced over
his shoulder one last time to Logan, who nodded and gave
him a gentle shove.

Right, it's go time.

Tate squared his shoulders and, without another

second of hesitation, walked out into the open space. His
father was standing on one side of the kitchen island, facing
the other two occupants of the room, who had their backs to
him and Logan. They hadn't yet noticed their arrival, but
when Logan sidled up beside him, Tate's father's eyes
finally rose and came to a halt on them.

Jesus, why am I so damn nervous? It wasn't like his
father was going to cause a commotion over them. But that
didn't mean the other two in the room would be as—

"Tate, Logan," his dad said, a broad grin lighting his
face. "You're here."

He came around the island and headed over toward
them, but Tate was too focused on the other two in the room,
who'd now turned to face them.

Jill had opted for casual today, in jeans and a crimson
lightweight knit top. Her hair, the same color as his own, fell
in soft waves over her shoulders, and she had a half-smile
on her face, as though she wasn't quite sure what kind of
reception she'd get from them. Sam, her husband, hadn't
changed a bit. Sporting his usual faded jeans, flannel over a
tee, and work boots scuffed around the edges, he looked
exactly how Tate remembered him. A real man's man. And
when he reached for Jill's hand in a sign of support, much as
Logan had Tate's outside, Tate couldn't help but wonder for
the umpteenth time just how this was going to go down.

When his father stopped in front of them, Tate finally
tore his attention away from the silent onlookers and
focused on the warm greeting he was getting instead.

What did he say again? Oh, right, just that we're finally here. Get with the program, Morrison. "Yeah," Tate said, kicking his ass in gear. "And we're not even late."

His father gave a chuckle, his eyes going to Logan. "I bet that had more to do with you than him, am I right?"

"You might be," Logan said as he released Tate's hand and reached out to shake his father's. "How you doing tonight, Will?"

"Good. Good," Will said, but then his lips pulled tight and he kind of…winced.

Great, Tate thought. *So things are already awkward. That's just great.* Lowering his voice, he asked, "Did they say something to you, Dad?"

"What? No. No. Nothing like that. It's just a little tense. But we knew it would be, right?"

"I guess."

"It's going to be fine," his dad said, and then turned back to Logan. "Why don't you come on over, son, so Tate can finally introduce you the way he should've been able to that first time around."

At his father's words, Tate looked to Logan, and was jarred out of his thoughts in an instant. He'd been so wrapped up in his own head that he hadn't really thought about how this would be affecting the man beside him. But when he stared into Logan's eyes, he was stunned to find them glistening. Tate wasn't even sure that Logan was aware of it himself, but what his father had just said had clearly rocked Logan to his core.

Logan visibly swallowed. "I'd like that."

Will clapped Logan's shoulder and then nodded. "Good," he said before turning on his heel. "Come on, then, Tate. Let's get the hard part out of the way."

Tate studied Logan for a second without a word, and then Logan blinked, and that vulnerability that had snuck through to the surface vanished behind the usual confidence that lit those eyes.

What is going through his head? Tate really wanted to ask him, but now wasn't the time. So he filed it away and vowed to come back to that as they headed across the tile to where Jill and Sam stood waiting for them.

It was time for show and tell.

* * *

EARLIER, WHEN THEY'D been driving over in the car, several thoughts had been floating around Logan's head in regard to how tonight would go. But never had he expected Will Morrison to stun him with a shock straight to the heart.

Shit. He'd been poised to be the quiet onlooker in the background tonight. The one not to let his emotions get to him as they went through the motions of dealing with whatever Jill did or didn't do. He'd wanted to be that pillar of strength for Tate. That rock, should he need him. But one sentence from Tate's father and suddenly Logan's legs felt as though they'd been kicked out from under him.

Never in a million years would he have suspected

that Will Morrison would be the first man to ever say something remotely fatherly to him and actually *mean* it. But there it was. Just out there, like it was the most natural thing in the world for him to have said. And for someone whose own father had never bothered to acknowledge him, let alone introduce him to anyone, including his own brother, those simple words had meant everything to Logan.

"Jill, Sam. I believe there's someone you have yet to meet," Will said as he moved up to stand beside his daughter.

It was interesting, but not all that surprising, that after everything that had happened between the Morrisons, it was Tate who Will had reconnected with. The two of them were practically cut from the same mold. Tate not only resembled his father, but over the years Logan had also come to realize he possessed the man's capacity for acceptance, directness, and love.

The man standing on the other side of Jill, her husband, Sam, looked much the same as he had the one and only time Logan had ever seen him. *Rugged* was the word that came to mind. He was a big guy, easily six two or three, and broad-shouldered. The exact opposite to himself, Logan thought, and wondered what Sam made of him standing there in his designer jeans, light pink button-up shirt, and speckled grey and white cardigan.

Tate cleared his throat, and if Logan hadn't been so preoccupied, he might've realized how uncomfortable everyone appeared as they faced off with one another.

"Jill, Sam," Tate said, much as his father had, and then he turned toward Logan, and the serious expression on his face morphed into one full of pride. "This is Logan. My boyfriend."

And yep, thank God he's holding my hand, because the legs are threatening again.

When Tate rounded back to the other couple, it was with his head held high and a confidence that had once not been there. And the power of those words right then were so overwhelming in their enormity that time seemed to pause to applaud them.

Jill was the first to step forward and hold her hand out to Logan, and he had to admire the bold way she locked gazes with him. "It's so nice to finally meet you, Logan."

Logan reached for her small palm, and as his engulfed it, he inclined his head ever so slightly. "Likewise."

As they parted ways, Sam ambled forward and thrust his hand out. "Hey there. I'm Sam," he said in a gruff tone that matched his appearance.

Logan gave his hand a robust shake. "Logan. Nice to meet you," was all he managed, but luckily for him, Sam then turned his attention to Tate and held his arms out wide.

"And it's hella good to see you again, man." As Sam moved to take hold of Tate's outstretched hand, Tate was tugged in to a hug and a thump on the back, shocking the shit out of Logan, and apparently Tate, who took a second to loosen up and return the gesture.

When he was released, Sam shoved his hands into

his pockets and said, "I don't know about all you, but I sure as shit could do with a beer."

Logan was positive he must've looked like someone had just pulled the rug out from under him, because out of all the things he'd expected upon walking into this house today, it wasn't that the flannel-wearing, truck-driving *Sam* would be the one to break the ice in the room.

Well, that'll teach me to stereotype.

Will slapped his palm on the kitchen island. "Agreed. Okay. Why don't you all head out to the back patio, and Tate? Start up the fire pit, would you?"

"Sure thing, Dad."

Logan looked at Will. "You need any help?"

He wasn't sure if he was asking to be helpful or merely to give himself some time to process everything that had just happened. But Logan had a feeling Will was onto him, because he shook his head.

"Nope. I'm just fine, son. You four head out and I'll be along in a minute."

Yeah...he's totally onto me.

Jill continued to watch Tate carefully as though she thought he might vanish as she moved into her husband's side and let him lead her toward the back door. Then Tate took Logan's hand and gave him a look that said, *You ready?* And all Logan could think was, *How did the tables turn to where I'm now the one trying to think of an excuse to make a run for it?*

* * *

WITH HIS FINGERS wrapped around Logan's, Tate
directed the two of them out to the covered patio, and then
he let Logan go so he could take up a seat on one of the
outdoor settees while Tate got the fire started.

Out of the corner of his eye, he saw that Jill had taken
a seat beside Sam, so close that she was practically glued to
his side. And Tate knew if *he* was anxious, then she had to
be feeling the nerves tenfold.

Not only was she coming face to face with him, but
she was also dealing with Logan and their father. That was a
hell of a lot of testosterone in one room. Then add in the
strained relationships with all three, and shit, Tate figured
she won when it came to who was the most on edge.

Once Tate had the fire going and went to take a seat,
he caught Jill watching him with a longing look in her eyes,
but she quickly turned away before he could offer up any
kind of acknowledgment. So, without a word, he walked
back to where Logan waited for him.

When he got to the chair, Tate noticed the way his
lawyer had planted his ass in the farthest corner of the seat,
as though he maybe thought Tate would sit at the other end.
But there was no way that was about to happen tonight.

Not here. Not now. Not fucking ever.

Tate took a spot, much like his sister, so he was
plastered to Logan's side, and then he rested his palm on his
thigh and planted one of his ankles on his knees and settled

in.

It was time to get fucking real. *But…where to start?*

"So, uhh, were you guys here long before us?" Tate asked, and then wanted to roll his eyes at himself. *Shit, I sound lame.*

"Nah," Sam said, looking between the two of them. "Got here about ten minutes before you guys showed up."

Right. Okay, then. Next, anyone?

Tate glanced at Logan, who was usually the one he counted on to talk them out of any situation. But for once in his life, Logan looked completely and totally out of his depth. He was staring across the room at the two strangers opposite him and had one arm on the side of the chair. Tate noticed his fingers were gripping it in a way that could either mean he was trying to convince himself to stay, *or* he was thinking about using that hand to propel himself up so he could hightail it out of there, and hell, Tate sure as shit could relate to that feeling.

He smoothed his palm a little up Logan's leg, and when that finally got his attention, Tate offered a smile he hoped was more reassuring than it felt. Then he leaned over and lowered his voice to say the one thing he hoped would break through and relax Logan. "You okay? Or is your back a little *stiff* from all the packing we've been doing lately?"

The minute his words registered, Logan's eyes lit up with the spark Tate had wanted to see, and he knew that whatever followed tonight, as long as Logan was beside him, the two of them would get through it.

Chapter Five

LOGAN COULDN'T HELP the smirk that crept across his mouth at Tate's words, and there was absolutely no way he could stop himself from stealing a kiss—no matter who was watching, *because that charming grin he's flashing at me is too damn tempting to ignore.*

"My back is just fine." Logan brushed his lips over the top of Tate's. "But thank you for asking. I would, however, really love it if your father got out here soon with a *stiff* drink."

When Tate chuckled over their inside joke, nearly all of Logan's tension dissipated. It was obvious Tate didn't care *who* was on the porch with them and what they were witnessing, and Logan wanted to give himself a swift kick in the ass for allowing anybody else's opinion on them to dictate his own response.

What the hell was the matter with him? Since when had he given a shit about what someone else thought? But as he settled back in the seat beside Tate and took his hand, Logan knew.

It was the last time I met this particular woman and it ended in a fucking disaster.

But not now. Not this time. This time would be different. And when Logan looked over at Jill again, he was surprised to see a soft smile playing on her lips. She didn't appear outraged. Didn't appear disgusted, as she once had. In fact, as she looked between Tate and himself, she seemed...pleased.

"So," Tate said, returning his attention to the other two in the room. And when he would've said more, Jill shifted forward on her seat and raised her palm for him to stop talking.

"Please," she said. "Before we go any further tonight, there's something I need to say." When Tate nodded, her gaze flicked to Logan, and she blinked a couple of times, as though trying to gather her nerve. "I owe you an apology," she began, and when she paused, Sam placed a hand on her back, and it seemed his support gave her the strength she needed to continue. "I was horrible to you the first day we met. When I think back to it, I can't believe the way I acted."

Logan remained silent, not knowing what to say. He knew what he wanted to say, something along the lines of *yes, you fucking were.* But he figured if they were going to talk this out, then it needed to be with some modicum of decorum.

"I have no excuse. Not one. There *is* no excuse for the way I behaved. I came into your place of business and acted as though you were beneath me because I couldn't wrap my head around what I was seeing that day."

Logan recalled the exact moment she was referring

to. When she'd burst into his office and found him and Tate in a kiss that not only rocked their world but also turned out to be the catalyst that made Tate's implode upon itself.

"Again, that's no excuse. And I'm not trying to make it one. What *should've* happened that day, what I wished had happened, was that I talked to my brother." Jill let her gaze drift to Tate's, and her mouth tipped down. "I should've gone to him, listened to what he had to say. I should've suggested we go to lunch or something so he could talk to me and tell me what was going on in his life… But I didn't do any of that."

When her words came to an end, Logan tightened his fingers around Tate's and took in a deep breath. He thought about everything he'd ever wanted to say to Jill if given the opportunity, and as he exhaled, Logan decided he just needed to say them. He'd never been one to beat around the bush, and if they were ever going to move past this, if Tate was ever going to have a chance of mending this damaged relationship, then he also had to be honest in his thoughts about Jill's sudden reappearance and acceptance of them.

"No, you didn't." Logan looked at Sam, trying to gauge him and where he stood on all of this. Because while Logan wanted to speak up and say what was on his mind, he didn't relish the idea of getting into a brawl with Jill's husband. But what he saw when their eyes met was non-confrontational. And Logan had a sneaking suspicion the two of them had discussed this very moment and how to handle it before they'd arrived tonight.

Well, here goes nothing. "You were hateful, judgmental, and rude that day."

Tate shifted in the chair beside him, but didn't say anything to stop Logan, so he continued. "If it were only me, maybe that would've made your actions less deplorable. But it wasn't just me that day in my office. It was your brother. And you took something fundamentally important away from him. You took away his choice. His voice. You took away his right to take his time and understand what was going on in *his* life, with no regard whatsoever to how your interference would impact him."

God that felt good to finally get off his chest.

"I know," Jill said, and had the good grace to lower her eyes.

"Do you?" Logan asked. "Do you understand how one kind word from you, one extended olive branch, could've changed all of this? That instead of us sitting here feeling as though there is a giant chasm between us, you could've stepped up four years ago like your father did and come and found your goddamn brother?"

"Logan," Tate said, but before Logan could respond, Jill spoke up.

"No, Tate. Let him talk. He's right. And it's about time he had the opportunity to say what he's feeling."

Logan looked to Tate for guidance. If he saw even the slightest misgivings about him speaking his mind, he would zip it. But when their stares collided, all Logan saw was understanding. A bone-deep understanding that this was his opportunity. The chance to finally put to rest the ugliness of that day and the ones that followed, so they could bury it and move the hell on. And Tate was more than fine with him taking it.

"I guess I'm trying to understand—why now?" Logan asked. "You've had four years to reach out to your dad about Tate, and you didn't. Even after his car accident, you were nowhere to be found. So excuse me if I'm a little bit skeptical about your intentions here."

Jill nodded and scooted to the edge of the seat. "No. Please. I want you to ask me anything. Of course you're skeptical. I would be too." When she paused, Logan waited, knowing she was likely thinking about how she wanted to say whatever it was that was on her mind. Then her eyes cut to Tate and softened. "I've already told this to you, but I think it's imperative that Logan hears it as well." And when her eyes, the same color as Tate's, locked back on to Logan's, she said, "I'm sorry. I know they're only words, and actions are what will back them up. But I have never been sorrier about anything in my life than I am over the way I behaved that first day in your office, the weekend that followed, and every day since then that I didn't reach out and find my brother."

She stopped talking long enough to swipe her tongue over her bottom lip, and then she continued. "You know what it's like to love, Tate. To be loved *by* him…"

Logan's heart clenched at those words, and he allowed himself to look at the man she was referring to, and

Tate was right there staring back at him. His expression telling him that yes, he was loved by him, and that was never going to fucking change.

"He has this way of making you feel as though you're the most important person in his world. And that he'll do anything for you, fight any battle. And he's always been that way. He was my knight. My big brother. And I thought I knew everything about him. Until you."

At those final two words, Logan turned back to Jill and saw her lips crook to the side.

"I was jealous. Stupid, huh?" She gave a self-deprecating laugh. "That day I came to your office to meet up with Diana, I knew Tate would be there. She'd told me they had a meeting. And I thought it would be the perfect time to talk to him for a minute on his own, because the last couple of times I'd seen him here at the house, he'd been distracted. A little off. But he hadn't called to talk to me about it like he normally would, and when I asked him if he was okay, he said he was fine."

Logan raised an eyebrow at Tate.

"You were a lot to deal with," Tate said. "I was processing. Plus, I already told you you're my biggest distraction. Have been since I met you, apparently."

"Apparently," Logan said, and squeezed Tate's thigh. Then, wanting to hear the rest of Jill's explanation, he directed his focus back to her and her husband.

"Diana had been talking about reconnecting with him," she said. "Wanting to maybe try again—"

Logan couldn't help the sound of disbelief that left him at that comment. And it took everything he had to bite his tongue, because *Tate was all mine by that stage. No damn question about it.*

"So when I walked in and saw you and Tate together, I didn't understand what I was seeing. I mean, I understood, but couldn't process what I was seeing. And then I…" She seemed to struggle to find the right word. "Then I acted like a total bitch."

Well, that we can agree on. "Yeah, you did."

Jill smiled at him, a wide grin that stretched across her mouth and transformed her features. And for the first time since he'd met her, he saw the striking resemblance between brother and sister.

"I can't go back and change what I've done. I know that." Jill angled her face toward Tate and became serious. "I also know my relationship with you will never be the same. But ever since the day I left you in the hospital, I have thought of nothing other than how to fix what I knew I had broken. How to approach you. How to possibly say sorry for everything I did and said to you. And the more time that passed, the harder it became, until…well, until I literally ran into you at Mariano's that day and my heart just about stopped."

She looked back at her husband then, and Sam rubbed a hand up her back and nodded. When she turned back to face Tate and Logan, she had tears in her eyes. "I saw you standing there with those two little children—your niece and nephew, right, Logan?"

Logan swallowed. "That's right."

She nodded and bit her lip. "And I thought, *What have you done? You stupid, selfish, ignorant woman. What have you done?* How had I let my brother, my own *brother*, slip away from me? Possibly have children I didn't know about? How had I deprived him from my *own* children? This wonderful man," she said, looking at Tate. "What kind of human being am I?"

She shook her head and wiped her eyes. "A pretty horrible one, I realized. And even the hurt and anger in Tate's eyes that day was nothing compared to the disgust I felt for myself. When I got home that night, I broke down and told Sam everything."

She sat back down beside her husband, and he took her hand in his. "He'd been trying to convince me to reach out for years. But I'd gotten myself into a dark place with it all where I just couldn't work out a way to begin the conversation…"

Logan felt Tate move on the seat beside him, and watched him bring a hand up to rub his face. He was clearly feeling the emotions that were running high in the room. So Logan raised his arm and put it across the back of the chair, letting Tate settle into his side, appreciating the need to find comfort in the other right then. This conversation wasn't an easy one.

"What could I possibly say that would ever make you want to talk to me again?" Jill asked. "And all I could think that night was, what if I never see him again? What if he doesn't call? But…then you did."

Logan stroked the back of Tate's neck, trying to ease the rigid posture he could see there, as Tate slowly nodded and said, "You can thank Logan for that."

"I think there's a lot I have to thank him for," Jill said. "I'm hoping he'll give me the chance."

* * *

TATE LOOKED AT Logan's profile and wished for a split second he had the ability to read his mind, or, for that matter, his facial expression. But right then he had no idea what was running through Logan's head.

There were so many emotions floating in the air that it was hard to decipher which one belonged to whom. But one thing Tate did know was that Jill had definitely given Logan something to think about, because if Logan wasn't convinced she was sincere? If he thought for one second she was anything other than genuine? Then he would have no trouble telling her so, getting up, and leaving.

But Logan wasn't doing that. He was listening. He was hearing her out. And right now, Tate knew he was analyzing everything he'd just heard and trying to decide if he wanted to trust her.

Tate studied Logan's set jaw, serious mouth, and cautious eyes as he sat there all protective, ready to fight to the end for him. That fierce loyalty was so intrinsic in Logan it was almost palpable. Like a shield that wrapped around anyone he loved, and God forbid you mess with that man's property. He'd fuck your shit up.

"I'm willing to be open about it if Tate is," Logan finally said.

Cautious to the very end, Tate thought, as Jill gave a slow nod. "That's all I can ask for," she said.

"Agreed," Logan said. "I would never stand in the way of you getting to know your brother again." Then he turned to Tate. "I want that for him."

Tate reached across then to touch Logan's cheek, and kissed him. "Thank you."

And before Logan could respond, the sound of the back door opening had his gaze shifting, and Tate turning, to see his father coming outside with three beer bottles in one hand, and a tumbler in the other.

Yeah… Not at all suspicious timing there, Dad.

"How you kids getting along out here?" Will asked.

Logan raised an eyebrow. "We're all still alive."

For now, Tate thought.

"Well, that's a good start," his dad said, with an awkward smile.

"I would say so." Logan lowered his eyes to the tumbler. "But that sure would help."

"Right. Right." Will handed Logan the glass and Tate a beer. Then he crossed over to Jill and Sam and handed them both bottles before asking, "And you two? Doing okay?"

Jill looked up at their father and nodded. "Yeah, Dad, we're good. We cleared the air for now. You can relax."

Tate watched his father's shoulders loosen, and then he moved over to the fire pit and rubbed his hands together to warm them, and Tate had to wonder how long the thaw would last.

"In that case," their dad said, "drink up and come inside. It's time for dinner."

A COUPLE OF hours later, a pot roast and several drinks had everyone slightly more comfortable in their skin as they sat around the living room trying to find some common ground.

Their father was a great buffer, Tate thought. He was doing an admirable job of directing the conversation to safe topics, and even though Tate knew he had his own issues he needed to sort out with Jill, he clearly wasn't going to tackle them tonight. He was busy making sure everything remained copacetic between the other four in the room.

Tate told them all about the new house, and Logan complained about packing. They learned that Jill now ran a daycare and Sam still worked in construction. But as conversation continued and Jill began talking about the little house they had lived in ever since they'd been married—something happened.

It wasn't conscious. And it certainly wasn't expected. But as Jill retold a renovation nightmare on what *not* to do when installing your own garden tub, an overwhelming sense of loss hit Tate. So much so that it just about knocked the air out of his lungs. The living room they were all seated in began to feel as though it were closing in on him, and as he tried to focus, he found that he couldn't.

Jesus, what the hell is the matter with me?

But as he sat there on the couch beside Logan, Jill's words started to jumble together until he lost track of them, too busy wondering why this particular topic was causing such a reaction in him.

Maybe it was because he remembered walking through that place when she'd first found it, that the idea they were still there, still the same as they ever were, when he was so completely different, brought to the forefront just how *changed* his life was.

He had no fucking idea. But as Jill continued to talk, Tate's mind began to reel and his heart started to race, until he felt as though his entire equilibrium was off balance…

"Oh, and Cooper and Jonathon. They're so big now—"

At the mention of his nephews' names, that was it. Tate shot up out of his chair so fast that Logan spilled the drink he held in his hand.

"Shit, Tate," he said, grabbing for a napkin on the coffee table to wipe the bottom of the glass. But before anything else could be said, Tate booked it out of the room.

Fuck. Fuck. I need some space. Some fucking air, he thought, as he shoved open the front door and headed out onto the porch. As the screen slapped shut behind him, Tate tugged at the collar of his shirt, suddenly feeling suffocated. When he finally got in a gulp of air, he braced his hands on the railing, let it out on a rush, and shut his eyes.

The stillness of the night mocked him as the blood pounded in his head, and when he heard the door open and shut behind him, he didn't have it in him to turn and see who it was. Honestly, he wasn't sure he was ready to see anyone just then.

As the initial wave of anxiety eased and the soft footfalls of sandals met his ears, he knew before she came up beside him that it was Jill who had followed him outside, and Tate wondered how much convincing of Logan she'd had to do to let her be the one to come find him.

When she came to a stop beside him, he opened his eyes to see her hands resting on the rail by his, but he didn't turn to greet her. Instead, the two of them stood there staring out from their childhood home for the first time in four years.

It was surreal.

"Tate," Jill said so softly he almost missed it. But then she placed a hand on his arm, and he felt his eyes dampen.

Damn it.

"Tate. I want you to know the kids, Cooper and Jonathon, they've missed you terribly. They have no idea what happened."

Tate flinched at the mention of his nephews' names and steeled himself against the fist that took a tight hold of his heart. He actually brought a hand up to rub it against his chest, it ached so damn much.

This right here. *This* pain? *This* loss? *It* was what he'd been dreading tonight.

His nephews. Those innocent boys. They had become ghosts to him. Buried somewhere inside himself, along with the mother he'd never see again. And somewhere in the darkest corners of his mind, he was aware that was why he'd gravitated so heavily to Lila. Thomas, he was a trigger Tate hadn't allowed himself too close to. And while he'd spoken to Logan about Jill and the boys in the past, he'd never quite allowed himself to go there. He hadn't been able to.

The wetness in his eyes wasn't going away anytime soon. So, with a clenched jaw, he finally faced Jill. "How? How do they not know?"

She brought a hand to her mouth, and as tears rolled down her cheeks, Tate knew he was close to losing the same battle.

"They think you went away, overseas for work for a little while."

"Fuck, Jill," he said, and looked away from her, unable now to stop his tears. She stepped in closer to him, but Tate couldn't bear the proximity and backed up.

"I know. There's so much I have to answer for. Sometimes I don't know how I look at myself in the mirror." When Tate said nothing, she whispered, "I want to make this right. They miss you and would love to see you. But I wasn't going to bring them here. Not tonight. This was not a conversation for children."

Tate knew that, and agreed one hundred percent.

"But," Jill said, and then stopped, fiddling with her hands. "What about next weekend?"

Tate gave her an incredulous look, and when he tried to speak, he barely recognized the gravelly tone to his voice. "No. I—"

"Please," she said. "Before you say no, just think about it. We're having a small get-together with some old friends. Some of *your* old friends. People we grew up with."

Tate ran a palm over his face and shook his head. "I don't think so. From past experience, it's the people I grew up with that seem to have the worst reactions."

Jill had the good sense to look ashamed, but then she said something that brought Tate up short. "Just because your family reacted one way, doesn't mean you should write others off without giving them a chance. These people were your friends, and you disappeared from their lives."

"And why do you think that is?" Tate said, defensive and annoyed that she had stumbled onto something he'd never really taken the time to examine closely.

"I know why. I'm just saying that I bet they'd love to see you again."

Tate spun away from her and once again braced his arms on the railing. He didn't want to talk about this. Not anymore.

"You and Logan should come. Think about it. The boys, they'd love it."

Tate swallowed around the lump that seemed to have lodged in his throat. "I'll think about it. But I'm not promising anything."

"Okay then." He heard Jill's footsteps as she headed back to the front door, but before she opened it, she asked, "You ready to come back inside yet?"

"Nah. You go ahead. I'm gonna take a few more minutes out here, then I'll come in."

"You're not going to smoke, are you?"

The question was so out of the blue and indicative of the years between them that had been missed that Tate stumbled over his response. Then he turned around and said, "No. I quit."

"You did?"

Tate nodded. "Four years ago."

A smile crossed Jill's lips, and she indicated with a thumb over her shoulder to inside the house. "That's another thing I have to thank him for, right?"

"Right."

"I like him. He's a straight shooter."

"That he is."

"Okay, I'll see you back inside."

"See you."

And as Jill disappeared inside their father's house, she left him alone with the night and his thoughts, both of which Tate wished he could've escape right then.

Chapter Six

LOGAN'S BEDSIDE LAMP was the only source of illumination in the room as he toed off his shoes and looked across the bed to where Tate sat with his back to him.

Not much had been said on the drive home, and though Tate had insisted he was fine, Logan was under no delusions that the man currently seated on the edge of their mattress staring at his feet was *fine*.

The night had been a rollercoaster of emotions for everyone involved. But for most of the evening, Tate had handled things with a kind of composure Logan was in awe of. He'd been solid and steady, right up until the last hour.

Logan had racked his brain trying to pinpoint the precise moment the tables had turned for Tate. The obvious conclusion was the mention of his nephews' names. *But no,* Logan thought, as he took off his shirt and pants and folded them over the chair in their room, *there was something before that.*

The names—they had been the knife twisting in the wound. But when was the moment it had first been thrust in? He wanted to know. *Needed* to know what had caused his man such pain.

Logan walked around the end of the bed, and as he came up along Tate's side, he raised his head and offered a dejected smile.

"Hey. Sorry," Tate said. "Got lost in my own head there for a minute. Let me get undressed so we can get in bed."

As Tate went to stand, Logan shook his head and reached out to trace the line of his jaw, stopping him. "You want to maybe tell me what's going *on* in your head?"

Tate shut his eyes, and when his thick lashes swept across his cheekbones, Logan couldn't help but brush his thumbs under them.

"Hey?" Logan said, keeping his voice low. "You can talk to me about anything. You know that, don't you?"

Tate didn't look at him, but Logan saw his shoulders rise and then fall as he took in a breath and then let it out. He'd only ever seen Tate like this once before, and it wasn't lost on Logan that it had been in direct relation to his family both times.

It was unnerving. Tate was the steady one between the two of them. The levelheaded one. And to see him so crushed, so unsteady, broke Logan's heart.

Going down to his knees between Tate's feet, Logan sat back on his heels and waited. When Tate finally opened his eyes and Logan saw tears blurring his usually bold gaze, he rose and wrapped his arms around Tate's neck.

"Oh, Tate," he whispered into his hair, and Tate wound his arms around Logan's back and held on as though he were the only thing keeping him grounded. A shudder racked Tate's body, and Logan pressed his lips to his temple, letting him know he was right there and to just let it out.

After the initial wave passed and Tate's fingers loosened, Logan shifted so he could cup either side of Tate's neck and rest their foreheads together. "Feel better?"

Tate nodded and then brought a hand up to swipe his fingers across his wet cheek, and Logan did the same to his other one.

"Want to tell me what that was about?"

"Yeah," Tate finally said. "Just let me go wash my face and get undressed, then we can talk."

"Okay," Logan said, and gently kissed Tate's lips. Then he watched from where he still knelt as Tate got to his feet, stepped around him, and headed into the bathroom, shutting the door in his wake.

* * *

TATE LEANED HIS back against the bathroom door and scrubbed his hands over his face. *Shit. I'm a fucking mess,* he thought, as he pictured Logan's face back there in the bedroom. There'd been a mix of concern and worry swirling in Logan's eyes as he'd looked up at him. And that, on top of everything else he'd been feeling, had become too much.

Tate shoved away from the door and pulled his shirt off, tossing it on the floor as he headed to the sink to splash water on his face. And when he looked at his reflection, the red, swollen eyes were such a foreign sight that he barely recognized himself. Then again, he couldn't remember the last time he'd broken down quite so spectacularly.

He turned the water off and reached for a towel, and once he wiped his face down, he ran a hand through his hair and sighed. Wasn't going to get much better than that tonight, and honestly, he didn't have the energy to care at this point.

Ditching his jeans, he switched off the lights and walked across the bedroom to his side of the bed.

Logan had thankfully turned the lamp off, but with the curtains open, the lights from the surrounding buildings allowed Tate to see the man waiting for him beneath the sheets.

He pulled back the covers, and once he slipped between them, Logan raised an arm, and Tate scooted over until his side was intimately aligned along the length of his. Tate then wrapped an arm across Logan's waist and traced his fingers along the edge of his boxer briefs, and once he rested his head on Logan's chest, he said, "I feel a bit...I don't know, stupid right now."

Logan took his chin in a firm hold and angled his face so he was looking up at him. "Don't you dare feel stupid for how you feel. Not ever."

Tate's lips quirked, and Logan gave him such a stern look that he chuckled. "Okay."

"Good."

"I can't remember the last time I cried this much. My

head hurts."

Logan ran a palm over the back of his curls, and Tate nuzzled into the light smattering of hair on Logan's chest.

"It was an intense night," Logan said.

"Now there's an understatement." Tate let his mind drift to the last part of the evening. The part that had set him off. And he knew that Logan was waiting for him to explain. He wanted to. He was just trying to work out how to say it in a way that wouldn't hurt the man currently wrapped around him. *Because how can it not?*

"Tate?"

"Sorry—"

"Hey, stop apologizing to me. And stop worrying about whatever it is that's keeping you from talking."

Wow. How is it he knows me even better than I know myself?

"Talk to me. Trust me."

"I do," Tate said, and licked his lips. "Okay. I guess you're probably wondering what set me off... I mean, everything was going pretty good for the most part."

"Right. Things at the beginning were a little awkward, but I thought you handled them great. Not only me, but your father and your sister. You were...remarkable, given the circumstances."

"I didn't feel remarkable."

"Are you kidding me? There's no way I could've acted with half the levelheadedness you did under the same circumstances." Logan reached for the fingers Tate had on his waist and interlaced them with his own. Then he brought them to his lips to kiss them. "But then something happened. What was it?"

Tate swallowed as Logan lowered their hands to his chest and waited, and then Tate said, "It was when Jill started talking about her house."

Silence settled in the room. All Tate could hear was the steady *thump thump thump* of Logan's heart, and he knew he needed to give Logan more than that.

"I started thinking about how everything in her life was exactly the same as it was four years ago, you know. Her and Sam. The kids. The house I helped her talk him into buying, even though it was a renovation nightmare. And then I thought about my life and how it's totally—" Tate stopped abruptly, not actually understanding his own thoughts, let alone being able to say them out loud. But Logan, being as intuitive as he was, finished for him.

"Different? Your life is totally different to what it was."

Tate quickly looked up at him to check what Logan's reaction was to that, and when all he saw was a curious expression, he nodded. "Yes. But not in a bad way."

"Okay."

"I told you it was stupid. I can't explain it, because it doesn't even make sense to me. But all I could think about was how unfair it was that her life had just gone along the same way it always had, and mine, it just...it just...blew the fuck up."

Tate pushed up on his arm then and looked down at Logan, who was still watching him with a pensive expression.

"Did you know she told the kids I moved overseas for work? *Overseas.* That was how she explained I was gone. What would she have told them if she never ran into me again? That I never came back? That I *died* there?" Tate ran a hand through his hair. "I don't know. I wanted to be cool with her coming back into our lives, and I was. I *am*. But when she started talking about all that shit, my head started spinning, and all I could think about was how unfair it was that *my* life was the one that had to change. That I was the one who lost fucking everything. And I guess I just hadn't allowed myself to really think about it until then."

* * *

WOW...

LOGAN WASN'T sure what he'd expected to hear when Tate had started talking, but *that* had certainly not been it. And he wasn't quite sure how to take Tate's words in and process them.

He knew how he *should* take them. This wasn't about him. It was about Tate and the family he'd left behind. But it still hurt to hear him talk about all that he'd lost, when Logan had always assumed Tate was happy and fulfilled with the family they had created between them. *Another good reason to make it formal. Official.*

But first things first. He wanted to talk this out with Tate. He was obviously still reeling from the onslaught of memories that had inundated him tonight.

Spinning. That was the word Tate had used. *And why wouldn't he be?*

Over the past years, Tate had perfectly adapted to the new life he'd chosen to live. But in one night he'd been yanked out of that world and been reminded of the one he'd left behind, and Logan would do anything in his power to help him get through the heartache he was so clearly experiencing right now.

"I didn't know that about Cooper and Jonathon. On one hand, at least Jill had the good sense not to poison them against you because of her own prejudices," Logan said, and traced a finger down Tate's jawline. "But on the other, I understand your reaction now that I know what you were thinking."

Tate lowered his eyes, but Logan tilted his chin up, not allowing him to hide. "It's okay to feel what you're feeling, Tate. It doesn't lessen what we have that you miss your old life, your family. That you mourn the loss of it."

"Then why does it make me feel so fucking shitty?"

Logan was about to tell him it was because he was a good guy, but Tate took his ability to speak from him with a single sentence.

"I feel like I'm betraying you by feeling this way."

Before he even consciously thought it, Logan was moving. He pushed up from the bed and gently rolled Tate to his back. With a hand on each of Tate's wrists, Logan pinned them by his head as he stared down at the serious expression now etched into every line of Tate's solemn face. "I don't ever want to hear you say that to me again."

"But—"

"You are not betraying me. If anything, you'd be betraying yourself if you didn't allow yourself to experience what you're feeling. You've been holding on to this for too damn long, Tate." When Tate's Adam's apple bobbed, Logan released one of his wrists and drew his fingertips over it. "And I feel guilty for letting you." As Tate's eyes narrowed, Logan nodded. "That's right. You don't get to corner the market on feeling shitty tonight. How did I miss this with you?"

"You didn't—"

"I did," Logan said. "Just because you didn't talk about it, about them, didn't mean I shouldn't have asked more questions." He stroked his fingers across the curls sweeping Tate's forehead. "I hate that I didn't."

"Logan. Stop." Tate stroked his free hand along the stubble of Logan's cheek. "We're talking about it now. I obviously wasn't ready before anyway."

"And are you now?"

Tate swept his thumb over Logan's lower lip. "Honestly? I don't know. She asked me if we want to go to a get-together at their house next weekend with a small group of my old friends. The kids would be there too, but..."

But you're scared, Logan wanted to say, and

understood the trepidation he could see in Tate's eyes. He was terrified of once again being rejected by his family. But Logan wasn't going to put words in Tate's mouth.

"I guess I'm just worried about how they'll react to me. To us. My nephews, that is. I hate that I even said that."

And I love it, Logan thought. *Because you're always honest with me. Even when it's the hardest thing to say.* "Then how about you just think on it? Let it sit with you and then make a decision. There's no rush. It's entirely up to you."

When Logan released Tate's other wrist so he could take either side of his face and kiss him, Tate lowered his arms and wrapped them around his waist.

Logan closed his eyes and lost himself in the purity of the moment, and when it was over, he raised his head, fully planning to say goodnight so Tate could get some rest. But Tate's fingers slid to his lower back, and he whispered, "Make love to me."

And there was no way Logan would deny such a heartfelt request.

Chapter Seven

EXPOSED...

THAT WAS how Tate felt as he lay beneath Logan right then. *Cut open and exposed.* But as Logan's gaze roamed over him he welcomed the feeling knowing that Logan was the only person who'd be able to ease his mind tonight.

"Close your eyes," Logan said, as if he knew exactly what was running through Tate's mind.

Doing as he was told, Tate shut them, and when Logan's lips ghosted over the base of his throat, he sucked in a tremulous breath.

"The only things I want you to concentrate on for the rest of the night are my hands, my voice, and the way your body responds to mine. Everything else we can come back to tomorrow. Nod if that works for you."

Logan's words were downright hypnotizing, and had Tate's eyes fluttering open.

"Uh ah." Logan was hovering so close that his breath teased against Tate's lips. "I said to close your eyes."

Tate bit his lip and let his eyelids lower once more, and then Logan repeated his earlier order. "Nod if that works for you."

Tate nodded.

"Okay. Now put your arms over your head. Fingers under the headboard."

With his eyes shut and Logan between his legs, Tate obeyed without question. He *wanted* this. *Needed* it with every fiber of his being. And as he raised his arms and did as he was instructed, Logan began to move atop him.

Soft lips trailed along his collarbone to the base of his throat, then a gentle flick of Logan's tongue across his Adam's apple had Tate's fingers flexing against the back of the headboard.

He pressed his head into the pillow as Logan began to kiss his way down the center of his chest, and then he gently scraped his teeth over Tate's left pec. Tate moaned against the sensation, and when the tip of Logan's tongue circled his nipple, he bowed up from the mattress, wanting to get closer to Logan's mouth—but he was denied.

The sound of his ragged breathing was the only noise that could be heard in their room as Logan placed a hand on his abs and held him still, his message clear: *You're still struggling... Still thinking too much. Let go...*

The physical statement was as tangible as if Logan had said the words out loud. But Tate couldn't seem to stop himself from moving under him, and just when he was about to open his eyes and beg Logan to put his lips on him, the hot heat of Logan's mouth was there, cutting off Tate's pleas as Logan glided a hand down beneath the edge of his briefs.

Tate arched his hips, as Logan moved from between his legs to the side of him, and he couldn't find it in him to complain this time when Logan's mouth left him so he could remove the final scrap of fabric from his body.

Now, completely naked and stretched out on their bed, Tate lay with his eyes shut and his arms where he'd been told to put them, and finally felt the stress of the night leave as he gave himself over to whatever Logan felt he needed.

* * *

LOGAN KNELT BY Tate's feet and took a second to enjoy the gorgeous man sprawled out on their sheets. Tate's legs were slightly parted and his thighs bunched every now and then as he unintentionally shifted his hips, seeking some kind of contact or physical caress for that beautiful, thick cock that was flushed and fully erect. His torso was all lean and tanned, and his biceps flexed as he gripped the headboard. And it took everything Logan had to climb off the bed to get the lube and remove his own briefs.

When he returned to his spot, kneeling at the end of the mattress, Logan unsnapped the bottle he held, and it was as though the sound had a direct link to Tate's entire body. He groaned and then he thrust his hips up off the bed, and *damn,* he was breathtaking.

Logan poured some of the liquid into his palm and stroked his erection as he watched, and as a hum of pleasure left him, Tate heard the sound and widened his legs further, rolling his hips up again.

Logan caught sight of the pre-cum leaving a glistening trail on Tate's lower abdomen, and worked his length a little faster. It was one of the most sensual sights he'd ever seen. Tate was totally getting off merely by what he was hearing and imagining.

Logan wasn't touching him. And Tate's hands still had a firm grip on the base of the headboard. Yet with every grunt and panting breath that left Logan, Tate reacted as though Logan were already inside of him.

"Lick your lips for me," Logan said, as his gaze locked on to that face he loved. Tate's eyes were shut, so his lashes kissed the tops of his cheekbones. But with the two-day-old stubble he was sporting and his riot of curls spread all over the pillow, he looked disheveled. And when he swiped his tongue over his lips, Logan knew he was the exact kind of disarray that he wanted to get into.

"Again," Logan said, and this time when Tate's tongue came out to glide across that luscious mouth of his, Logan was down over the top of him, replacing Tate's tongue with his own. He dove into Tate's mouth like a starving man, and the greedy way Tate sucked on him told Logan that he wasn't the only one who was hungry.

He wedged himself between Tate's thighs, and when their hips aligned and their cocks grazed alongside the other, Tate tore his mouth free and craned his head back. With his cheeks flushed Tate looked breathtaking, as he used his hold on the headboard to propel himself up and rub his lower body against Logan's, and Logan planted a hand on either side of him and started to grind his pelvis over the top of him.

Tate clamped his teeth into his bottom lip, and Logan moved down to his forearms so he could burrow his nose into the crook of his neck. He shut his eyes and tried to calm his thudding heart, and once he got himself under some kind of control, he kissed Tate's temple and said, "You are so fucking beautiful."

Tate turned his head on the pillow, and when his eyes lazily opened, the blissful expression swirling in them had Logan connecting their mouths in a kiss he felt in the deepest parts of his soul.

This right here, he thought. *This ability he has to make me forget that anything in the world but him exists... That's why he's going to be mine.*

As Logan pulled away, he trailed his fingers down Tate's side to his thigh, then slid his palm to the underside of his leg and, without any urging, Tate moved it up and over his hip.

"Yes. Just like that," Logan said, as Tate brought his hands down now to smooth them along his ribs. Logan then began to slowly rock his hips in a way that had his own control perilously close to the edge from the sheer pleasure the connection brought.

As the undersides of their cocks ground against each other, the groans of desire that filled the room were reverent, as was the steady way they each held the other's gaze.

Tate's hands were all over him. His sides. His lower back. His ass. And when his fingers slipped between Logan's cheeks and pulled him flush against him, Logan leaned down and gently kissed his jaw. "You feel incredible under me. Like a dream." Tate's breath caught, and when Logan raised his head, he whispered, "I love you."

* * *

TATE'S EYES BLURRED on Logan's face, and he blinked, trying to clear them. He hadn't spoken since Logan had told him to close his eyes, and as he tried to find his voice now, it was difficult.

"I love you too," he managed, and noted how raspy and broken it sounded. He'd never been more emotional in his life as he melted under Logan's touch, and when Logan's breath washed over him, Tate's entire body trembled.

There was something going on here tonight. He could sense it in the air. Not only for him, but he could've sworn there was something in Logan's eyes that he'd never seen before.

Or maybe that's just me projecting, Tate thought. He'd had a long night, and with the careful way Logan was handling him... *Is it any wonder I'm falling apart?*

Logan was systematically erasing every thought in his head and replacing it with his touch, his voice, his sheer presence—and Tate loved it.

With his legs wrapped around Logan, Tate moved his hands lower and increased the pressure, urging Logan to do more, needing him to. And as if they were of one mind tonight, Logan slipped a hand down between them and wrapped it around their straining shafts, making Tate's breath leave him in a rush as Logan leisurely stroked the two of them and continued to obliterate him one kiss at a time.

It was all too much. And not nearly enough. But when Logan's fingers found their way to his back entrance, Tate knew he'd wait for whatever he had in mind, no matter what. He wanted to feel Logan inside him tonight. Wanted to be taken by the man who owned him. Possessed him. Loved him in ways he never imagined possible for one person to love another. So Tate hitched his leg further up Logan's hip to his waist, opening himself for him, and Logan's finger was right there pushing inside.

As his eyes fell shut, Tate pushed up off the mattress, wanting to get closer, and then he heard Logan say, "Perfect," right before his mouth was taken and one finger became two, then three, until Tate was positive Logan was on a mission to destroy any and all ability he had to think. Then, when those skilled fingers vanished and he felt the broad head of Logan's cock entering him, it was all over.

Tate felt as though he were having some kind of out-of-body experience as Logan's fingers wove through his hair and began a delicious rhythm that seemed in tune with the beat of their hearts.

Caught up in the maelstrom of passion, Tate wound himself around Logan and held on to him, trusting him to get them through to the other side in one piece. And as he surrendered to the man and the moment completely, anything other than the two of them faded from Tate's world until all he knew, and needed to know, was Logan.

* * *

AS LOGAN LOST himself to the man unraveling for him, he no longer had any doubt as to why Tate was the one who'd made such a monumental impact on his life.

It was this right here. This connection. This trust Tate was exhibiting in him. It had been there from the very beginning with them. And as Tate's fingers clutched at his back as though he were the only thing keeping him from flying apart, it made Logan want to be that person for him for the rest of his life.

"Tate," Logan said, and then groaned at the exquisite way Tate's body responded to his voice, his narrow channel tightening around his cock.

Logan trailed his fingers across Tate's brow, pushing his sweaty curls from his forehead, and when Tate opened his eyes, he had the glassy look of someone completely immersed in the ecstasy he was experiencing.

"Time to let go for me, gorgeous." As the words left Logan's lips, Tate's parted and an unsteady breath escaped him.

"That's it," Logan said as he began to pick up his pace. He ran the back of his fingers down the side of Tate's cheek, before he reached between them and started to stroke Tate's erection again.

With their eyes locked, Logan marveled at every nuance, every flicker of emotion pulling at Tate, and when a lone tear fell from those beautiful brown eyes to roll down his cheek, Logan pressed a kiss to it. "It's okay. Let go."

"Logan…" Tate said as though he were in a daze, and it was so faint that Logan barely caught it as Tate crossed his arms over his back and held on as he thrust his hips up off the bed and moaned.

The intimacy of the moment, the night, was something Logan didn't want to ever end, as the two of them lost themselves in the rapture of a union that was more powerful than they'd ever experienced before.

Chapter Eight

THE SUN ON his face and a strong arm wrapped around his waist was what Tate woke to the following morning. He cracked his eyes open to see that the curtains were exactly how they'd been the night before, and though the bedroom was now awash in sunlight, the safety of the silence that greeted him had a content sigh leaving his lips.

"Good morning." Logan's voice was soft as it drifted over his shoulder, and Tate reached for the hand on his stomach, craving the extra contact.

"Morning," he said as he rolled over so he was face to face with the man who'd taken such care with him last night.

Logan had a hand under his cheek where it rested on the pillow, and squeezed the fingers Tate now had wrapped around his, as he asked, "How'd you sleep?"

"Good, I think. I don't remember waking up until now, so…"

"That's good. You needed the rest," Logan said, and then released his hand so he could cup Tate's cheek. "Yesterday was—"

"Intense?"

Logan swept his thumb over Tate's lips. "That's one word. Unexpected is another."

Tate nodded, understanding what Logan meant. He highly doubted Logan had anticipated him having a breakdown after the dinner with Jill. Hell, he'd been the one who'd told Logan they should do it and it would all be fine. *Yeah, and look how that turned out.* "About that. Last night, when we got home. I'm sorry—"

"Hey. Hey," Logan said. "That's not what I'm looking for here. I don't want an apology. I want to know if you're okay."

With Logan's attention fixated on him, Tate could see the stress in his eyes, and Tate hated that he'd put it there. "Yeah. I'm okay. It was just…" He paused and tried to think of the best way to put into words what he'd been feeling last night. "It was a lot to take in. More than I expected. I figured it would be dinner, we'd talk and get shit off our chest, and then we'd go home. But…" Tate shrugged. Logan didn't speak, though—he was waiting for him to finish. "Some of the things she said to me outside, they cut deep. About how I hadn't given the people in my life a chance to know the new me. I didn't realize how much I'd, I don't know, cut people out. Kind of buried them and moved on."

Logan's eyes narrowed a fraction as he placed a hand on the sheet covering Tate's hip. "You went through a lot back then. You were dealing with your family. Then your accident. Me." He gave a self-deprecating laugh. "Maybe it was just your way of coping. And after the way your family reacted, no one could blame you for being cautious about who you let into your life."

"That's the thing, though—I didn't let *anyone* in that I knew, did I? Fuck, Logan. How can you not hate me for that?" Tate said, and rolled to his back, realizing that that was one of the things he was most upset about. He'd done exactly what that fucker Christopher Walker had done back in the day. Hadn't he? *Shit,* that thought made him want to be sick.

Logan scooted into his side and took his chin in a firm grip, forcing Tate to look at him, and he wasn't surprised to see annoyance in Logan's eyes. He'd be pissed off at him too.

"Why would I ever hate you?"

Tate's jaw bunched, but Logan held him in place, his hold and stare demanding an answer.

"Because I always thought I was so fucking brave and honest about how I felt for you. Turns out I wasn't so brave, huh?"

"What the hell are you talking about? You were always brave. Always honest," Logan said. "From the very beginning, you owned it."

"But I never once took you around to the people that *I* grew up with. Never introduced you to *my* friends, did I?"

"So the fuck what? You gave up everything to be with me. *Everything,* Tate. Don't think a day goes by that I don't know that. That I don't think about it. If I was a better person, maybe I would've encouraged you to track them all down. But I'm selfish. And the thought of anyone else coming between us or filling your head with bullshit freaked me the hell out back then. So if we're sitting here writing down our transgressions then make sure you add a column for me, I have plenty."

Tate sighed, and Logan raised an eyebrow as if daring Tate to refute him.

"I don't know," Tate finally said. "I don't think you have enough time before work for me to write down all of *your* transgressions."

Logan stroked his fingers over Tate's shoulder and then kissed his cheek. "All I'm saying is stop beating yourself up about things that aren't true. There is enough for you to deal with without worrying about things you don't need to. If, and when, you ever want to meet up with old friends, family, hell, your first kiss—what was her name? Dani Bosley?"

Tate started laughing, which he suspected was Logan's goal. "How do you remember that?"

"I remember everything about you. Don't you know that by now?"

Tate's lips quirked. "That brain of yours is fascinating and slightly terrifying."

"I'm glad you think so, but I'm not done. My point is, if and when you want me to meet them, you tell me, and I'm there. But Tate?"

"Hmm?"

"Never think for one second I have ever thought

anything other than the world of you. Because it wouldn't be true."

Tate's throat choked up at the sincerity of those words, and then he reached for Logan and kissed him hard. "I feel exactly the same way about you."

"You better," Logan said against his mouth.

"I do."

"Good. Then it's safe for me to leave you here this morning? Because I have a new office space to—"

"Claim. Uhh, that's right." Tate nodded. "Yeah, you can go. I'm sure I'll survive fine without you for a few hours."

Logan gave him another kiss and then shoved the sheet aside so he could get out of bed. As he made his way toward the en suite, Tate let his eyes travel over Logan's wide shoulders, trim waist, and tight ass, and then he called out his name. Logan stopped and turned to face him, and Tate kicked off the sheet and crossed over to him.

When he reached him at the door, Tate took Logan's hand in his and grinned, then tugged him inside the bathroom. "I changed my mind. I'm not quite ready to face the day without you yet. Maybe we can reevaluate my state of mind *after* we shower."

* * *

"AHH, THERE HE is," Cole said, as Logan pushed open the door to his office and stepped inside.

With his briefcase in one hand and his coffee in the other, Logan looked over to where his brother stood beside Joel Priestley, who was seated on the three-seater leather couch. "Here I am," he said with a grimace. "As are the two of you."

Cole checked his watch and then frowned. "We were coming to get you to head upstairs. Have to say, we were shocked to find your office empty. I figured you'd be the first here today, or at least be up *there* with your measuring tape."

Logan crossed to his desk, put his briefcase down, and rubbed his fingers across his forehead. God, he was exhausted, mentally and physically. "Who says that's not where I'm coming from?"

"Sherry," Priest said as he got to his feet and slid one of his hands into his pockets.

"Remind me to fire her." Logan took a sip of his coffee and hummed in appreciation. "Or at least reprimand her."

Priest said nothing, merely arched an eyebrow before he headed over to the door to wait for the two brothers.

"Well, if you're quite ready. Do you want to head upstairs, Your Highness?" Cole crossed over to Logan with an expectant look on his face. "Josh should be here soon if he's not waiting on us already." As Cole came to a stop on the opposite side of the desk, he seemed to finally get a good look at Logan, and whatever he saw there had him pausing. His eyes narrowed, and then he looked over his shoulder to

Priest. "Would you give us a minute?"

Priest gave a nod and then reached for the door to shut it. Once it was closed, Cole rounded back to Logan. "What's wrong?"

"Hmm? Nothing's wrong." Logan took another sip of his coffee as Cole crossed his arms over his chest.

"Bullshit."

Logan shook his head. *Fucking Cole and his ability to see right through me.* "Nothing is wrong. I just had a busy weekend getting the house sorted and everything."

"No," Cole said. "If all you had was a busy weekend, you wouldn't look so...so..."

"Oh yes, please finish that sentence. Because if I'm not feeling awesome already, hearing I look like shit is going to help."

"You look stressed. Worried. Not like shit. But you've barely cracked a smile since you walked in that door, and I know you were looking forward to today." Cole came around the desk, and when he reached Logan's side, he said, "Was it the dinner last night? Did something happen? To you? To Tate?"

Logan put his coffee mug down on the desk and brought his hands up to rub them over his face. *Christ,* he hadn't realized just how tense he was until Cole had said something. He'd been trying so hard to keep it together around Tate that he'd barely realized the toll last night and this morning had taken on himself.

"No, Jill was fine. I said all the things I wanted to say

and she sat there and listened. She was apologetic and regretful, and receptive to the two of us in general."

"Okay. Then what's with the frown? You look like someone ran over your cat."

"I don't have a cat. Nor do I want a pussy of any kind." When one of Cole's eyebrows rose, Logan sighed. "I don't know. A few things came up last night, and they..."

"They...?"

"I don't *know*. Rattled Tate, I guess."

Cole moved so he could rest his ass against Logan's desk, and then braced his palms on either side of himself. "I imagine that's pretty normal, given the circumstances. He hasn't spoken to his sister in years. Do you remember when we first met? I was pretty rattled."

Logan cast his eyes in Cole's direction. "You were an asshole."

"*Because* I was rattled. I'd just found out I had a brother."

"Sure. Keep telling yourself that. But that's not the problem here. This isn't so much about Jill as it is about Tate."

Cole quietly contemplated that before saying, "Would you rather I butt out?"

"No. No, it's not that. I'm just trying to work out what I think is going on with him. A lot of old emotions came up last night with his sister. Talk of his nephews, old friends, seeing them again—with me. I don't think he'd really thought about that since he'd left it all behind. And now…"

"Now it's all flooding back in," Cole said.

"Yeah. It's like he's got to come out all over again. And we both know how well that went the first time around."

"Geez. That's got to be rough. One minute you two are buying a house and everything seems right side up, and the next day it gets flipped on its ass."

"No kidding," Logan said.

"So what's the plan?"

"There isn't one yet. We talked some last night and again this morning, but ultimately, it's his decision. He's got this misplaced sense of guilt that he owes me this proper introduction to his friends and family. Like he was hiding me from them or something. But I don't want him doing this for me."

Cole pushed off the desk and faced him with an expression Logan couldn't quite decipher. "Did you ever think that maybe it's not about owing you? Maybe it's about wanting to *give* this to you."

When Logan merely stared at Cole, waiting for further explanation, Cole sighed. "What was the one thing that Chris never did for you? The one thing that asshole denied you at every turn? *Meeting* his friends and family. Tate knows that."

"Oh, come on." Logan gave Cole an incredulous look. "This is nothing like that. *Tate* is nothing like that," he said, his hackles starting to rise.

"I know that. But does he?"

"Of course he does. That's never even crossed my mind. I love Tate. I want to marry him, for God's sake."

"Wait up...what did you just say?"

As soon as the words left Cole's mouth, Logan realized *exactly* what he'd just said.

Fuck. Fuck. Fuck. But there was no way he was able to take it back now, so Logan suddenly took a great interest in the mail Sherry had left in his tray earlier that morning.

"Logan," Cole said, and when Logan continued to avoid eye contact, Cole grabbed his arm. "Did you just say you want to *marry* him?"

Logan looked into Cole's eyes, unable to form a coherent response, but he knew the truth was written all over his face.

As the blood started to ring in his ears and his pulse went haywire, Cole pulled him into a hug and thumped him on the back. And all Logan heard was, "Well. It's about damn time, brother. It's about damn time."

* * *

"*YOO HOO*, EARTH to Tate..." Robbie waved a hand in front of Tate's face where he stood behind the bar with a glass and towel in hand. They were around twenty minutes away from opening, and ever since he'd arrived at The Popped Cherry, he'd been...distracted.

After Logan had left for work, he had dived into the

mammoth task of packing. He'd cranked up the music, grabbed some boxes, and attacked the living room, deciding the busier he was, the less likely he'd sit around and dwell over last night.

But hell if he'd been able to shake it.

Between the night with Jill, his breakdown with Logan, and this morning? Nothing short of a major catastrophe was likely to take his mind off all that was going on with him. Something Robbie had definitely noticed.

"Sorry," Tate said. "What did you say?"

Robbie glanced at the glass in his hand and then nodded at it. "You hoping a genie is going to appear if you rub it long enough?"

Tate rolled his eyes and put the glass on the counter. "Smartass."

"You've been polishing that one for the past ten minutes."

Tate tossed the towel onto the bar beside the glass, and then turned to check out the back shelf to make sure their staples were all stocked enough for the evening ahead. Shit, he needed to get his head on right or he'd be no good to anyone when they opened.

"Hey?" Robbie said as he came up beside Tate. "You okay? You seem a little, I don't know, off tonight."

Tate cast a quick look in Robbie's direction, and when he cocked his head to the side, Tate shrugged.

"Yeah, I'm okay. Just a bit distracted. Lots going on with the new house is all."

"Oh, that's right," Robbie said with a grin. "Settling down out in the 'burbs."

"Wicker Park is hardly the 'burbs."

Robbie placed a hand on his hip and pursed his lips. "True. But still, I saw pictures. It has a little fence and everything."

"A black *iron* fence. There's no white picket shit anywhere. God forbid; Logan would have a coronary."

"Ha. You're probably right. But if anyone could get Logan to do something he didn't want to, it would be you. White picket fences, a parcel of kids, a dog or three?"

Tate immediately screwed his nose up at Robbie's words. The idea of Logan ever doing something he didn't want to for him made him incredibly uncomfortable. And the idea of *changing* Logan horrified him even more. "No way. That's so *not* Logan. Or me, for that matter."

"Fair enough. I'll keep the white picket fences in *my* dreams, then."

"Yeah?"

Robbie's face took on a dreamy quality. "Yeah. One day. I can see it now. A white picket fence, surrounding a little red and white house where a sexy man in nothing but an apron has dinner waiting for me on the stove."

"That's...very specific."

Robbie's eyes widened. "Well, of course it is. If you want something, you've got to visualize it."

"Really?"

"Yep. My nonna always used to say, if you can't see

it in your mind's eye, how are you going to be able to see it when it's right in front of you?"

Okay... So that actually makes sense. "She sounds like a smart woman."

"The smartest." Robbie smiled and then added, "Also the kindest and toughest."

"You're lucky to have her. From what you and Logan have told me, she sounds like one hell of a lady."

"She is. And you're right. I am lucky. I don't know what I would've done without her these last couple of months." Robbie paused, and Tate figured he must've been thinking about his own distractions, before he focused again. "What about you? Your family cool?"

And just like that, Robbie inadvertently reminded Tate of what had been bothering him in the first place. "Yeah, uhh...some of them are."

"Some of them?"

Am I really going to talk to Robbie about this? Tate thought, but as Robbie stood there with an earnest expression on his face, Tate found himself *wanting* to. "Yeah. My dad's a pretty stand-up guy."

"Geez, don't sing his praises too loud. He might hear you."

Tate turned and leaned back against the bar, crossing his ankles. Then he did the same with his arms over his chest. "Well, we've had an interesting relationship over the last few years."

At the serious tone in his voice, Robbie walked across

to the other side of the bar and mirrored Tate's stance. But instead of crossing his arms, he fiddled with a towel he held in his hand as if he was uncertain of his next question. "Because of Logan?"

Tate nodded slowly.

"Your family didn't like that you, uhh…"

"Fell in love with a man?"

"Right."

"You could say that. Last night was the first time Logan met my sister. Well, the first time he'd ever actually had a conversation with her."

"Oh my God." Robbie brought his fingers up to cover his mouth. "No wonder you're a head case today."

A head case… Yeah, that about sums it up.

"Was she horrible to him? Was it awkward?" Robbie asked. "Was Logan horrible to her?"

"No. It was the exact opposite, actually. It went great. She was…apologizing for past behavior."

"Oh, okay. So if it all went well, what's with the frown?"

"Remember your nonna's speech about visualization?" Robbie nodded. "When I first started dating Logan, I visualized taking him home to meet my *very* Catholic family, and all the friends I grew up with. I figured at first they'd freak out, but then, well, then they'd come around and everything would be fine."

Robbie winced. "I assume that didn't happen?"

"No, it didn't. My family disowned me that day.

Kicked me out of the house, and told me not to come back unless it was without Logan. After that, my life changed, and I didn't really think about taking Logan around to my old friends. I was too busy trying to work out how to live my new life." Tate ran a hand through his hair and then gripped the back of his neck. "But I'm starting to think that maybe that was just a good excuse, and that I was a fucking coward."

"Okay, first up," Robbie said, stepping forward with his hands on his hips, "you are *not* a coward. Are you kidding me? Have you forgotten the first time we met at the Daily Grind?"

Hell no, he hadn't. Robbie had been seated opposite Logan flirting outrageously, and Tate had wanted to strangle him. "No. I remember."

Robbie smirked and raised an eyebrow that screamed *exactly*. "There was nothing *cowardly* about the way you looked at me that day. *Or* spoke to me, for that matter. And even though you didn't outright say I was trespassing where I shouldn't be, your attitude sure as shit let me know you already thought of Logan as yours. There was no mistake." Robbie laughed. "God, you were pissed at me."

When Tate stared at him, Robbie reached out and poked him in his forearm.

"All I'm saying is, there was—*is*—nothing cowardly about you. Were you still getting your footing? Yeah. But you made it very clear that day that Logan was yours and I needed to get lost."

Tate finally cracked a smile at that. "You were a little shit that day."

"It's all part of my charm."

"Uh huh."

"But seriously. Why would you ever think that?"

"Think what?"

"That you're a coward, silly."

Tate shrugged. "Oh…I mean, I guess I don't. Not really. It's just my sister wants us to go to this get-together with all my old friends and people I haven't seen for years, and…"

"And?"

"I freaked out about it."

"Umm, after what you just told me about your family, why wouldn't you?" Robbie asked. "Seriously, I had no idea you went through all that."

"Why would you?"

"I don't know. I just assumed you guys were, like, perfect and happy and shit."

"*We* are," Tate said. "And my dad. He came around right after my accident and loves Logan. But I have no contact with my mother at all."

Robbie's expression turned to one of sympathy and understanding. "I'm so sorry that happened to you. *And* to Logan. I was lucky. My family is very understanding; they just don't live close by. But I have friends who've been in similar situations. I also dated, well, you know, my ex-boss. I guess that wasn't really dating, per se. But anyways, he was terrified of his friends and family finding out because of the same reaction you got. Difference is, you were brave. It's so fucking ridiculous that in this day and age people are still so narrow-minded. So judgmental. What should it matter who we love? Who we're attracted to? Pisses me off."

"Pisses me off too," Tate said.

Robbie huffed and then a devious smile quirked his lips. "Then don't let them win."

"Huh?"

"Don't let the ones who have judged you in the past get in your head. Be like you always were with me. Brave and ballsy as ever. Rock up to this thing hand in hand with Logan and show them how happy you are. You were invited, so go."

Jesus, how is it I'm standing in my bar getting life tips from fucking Robbie? "You're right."

"You don't have to sound so shocked, you know." There was a buzzing noise, and then Robbie pulled his phone out of his back pocket. He frowned at whatever he read on the screen before turning it off and aiming a dazzling, but forced, smile in Tate's direction. "I better go get the doors. We open in five."

And as Robbie walked off to do just that, Tate wondered when Robbie was going to take some of his own advice and decide to once again be brave and ballsy.

Chapter Nine

"SO WHEN ARE you going to ask him?" Cole's question was delivered in a hushed voice as he and Logan stood to one side of a taped-off office space, and Priest stood on the other side with Joshua Daniels.

Josh, who owned Creative Construction & Remodeling, was a longtime friend and client of theirs, and also happened to be the husband of Dr. Shelly Monroe. He had just finished walking the three of them off the elevator and showing them where the reception desk would be, and then explained how the glass walls of the new conference room would give the floor an open feeling and still have all the privacy of being soundproof.

Logan loved the openness of it all. Their current setup downstairs was good, but starting to get claustrophobic. With the three of them moving up here along with a few others, it would make for less clutter downstairs and, hopefully, a more productive workspace.

They'd all just come to a stop at the largest of the three office spaces on the floor. With no walls in place yet, just tape extending from the thick column they'd been told would support the interior wall, this was the only office that had a balcony running along one side of it. The very office that Logan had been eyeing.

Yes, this would be real sweet, he thought, letting his eyes wander around the area Josh had marked off. *The question is, how hard am I going to have to fight for it?* He turned to face Cole, and saw the same ridiculous grin he'd had on his face since they'd left Logan's office, gotten in the elevator, and headed up here, and Logan inwardly groaned.

"So...?" Cole asked again. "When are you going to ask him?"

Shit, he's worse than a fucking girl. "Can it, would you?"

If it were possible, Cole's grin got wider, and he kept right on talking. "Does he know? Have you two talked about this?"

"Oh my God." Logan turned so his back was to the other two in the room and pinned Cole with a look that screamed, *Stop talking—now.*

Cole's lips curved. "I'll take that as a no?"

"Take it any fucking way you want. Just zip it. Jesus, when did you get so chatty?"

"When my antiestablishment brother slipped up and said he wanted to get *married.*"

Logan grabbed a hold of Cole's arm and spun him away from the other two. "Would you keep your voice down?" He glanced over his shoulder at Josh and Priest, who were now staring at them. "We'll be right back. Just a little brotherly discussion over who's getting the balcony."

As he rounded back to Cole, Logan shook his head. "You're not going to let this go, are you?" At the *hell no* expression that lit Cole's eyes, Logan sighed. "Fine. Let's see if I can break this down for you in two sentences or less. But then you have to agree to *stop talking* about it. Deal?"

"Deal." Cole clamped his mouth shut.

Logan inhaled and then let it out on a rush, nervous to actually be talking about this for the first time with...well, anyone. "Okay so, no, we haven't talked about it and he doesn't know. And the answer to your *other* question is: I don't know yet." When Cole opened his mouth but then shut it, Logan rolled his eyes. "What? I can see that you're dying to ask something."

As a smile wide enough that it threatened to slide off Cole's face hit, Logan instantly regretted allowing him to speak.

"Can I tell Rachel?"

As if I could stop you. "Would you really keep it from her if I asked you to?"

Cole thought about it for all of a second. "No."

"Figures. Just...I don't know. Keep it to yourselves, okay? I'm still getting used to the idea, and I want—"

"It to be a surprise?" Cole asked, his eyes widening. "Are you going to make it romantic? I could help you plan it. So could Rachel."

"*Oooo*kay. That's enough about that." When Cole went to speak again, Logan held up his finger. "That's it. You promised. And because you're being such a pain in the ass right now, you're going to agree that the office with the balcony is going to be mine."

"What? How is that fair?"

Logan turned around and started back in Josh and Priest's direction, calling over his shoulder, "It isn't. But you're going to give it to me anyway."

When Logan met up with the other two again, Josh looked between him and Cole and asked, "So? Who gets it?"

With a grumble, Cole gestured to Logan with his thumb.

"Somehow, I'm not surprised," Josh said.

"I'm happy to take the middle office." Priest spoke up for the first time, looking between the brothers. "It might be good to separate the two of you as much as possible. And I don't need a big space to work hard."

Logan arched an eyebrow at the not-so-subtle jab. "Neither do I. I just happen to *want* it."

"Is he always this self-indulgent?" Priest asked.

And at the exact same time, Cole and Josh replied, "Yes."

"Duly noted," Priest said.

Logan left Cole's side and walked past the massive pillar and into his new office, heading over to the wide expanse of the windows that flanked both sides of what would soon be all his. He stopped where the windows met in the corner and scanned the surrounding buildings.

It was an impressive view, that was for sure. He could see the Hancock Center and Water Tower Place, and as he continued to scan the area, Logan couldn't help the satisfied smile that crossed his lips. *Damn, my life is real fucking sweet right now.*

New house. New office. Maybe the fates were all coming together to offer him up that ideal moment. The one where everything was just right and was directing him toward that final piece that would make the puzzle complete.

Yes. I like that, Logan thought, as he replayed Cole's words from minutes ago. *When...? Where...? How...?*

It was time to make a plan. It was time to take that final piece and put it where it was supposed to go. And once that was done, then his life would be as close to perfect as possible.

But before all of that, he wanted to show Tate his new kickass office *with* a balcony.

*　*　*

IT HAD JUST turned six when Tate's phone started to vibrate in his back pocket. He'd just finished serving an after-worker a gimlet when he pulled the phone free and saw Logan's name on the screen, so he motioned to Robbie he was stepping out to take the call.

Raising the bar pass, Tate made his way out from behind it and then stepped through the private entrance where he'd be able to talk freely. "I was wondering when I'd hear from you."

"Oh yeah? Missing my voice, were you?"

"Among other things."

"Ooh, I like the sound of that."

"Mhmm. I'm sure you do. But I doubt that's why you called."

"It could be, if you want it to be…" Logan said, and Tate loved the fact that if he did indeed want to take the conversation in that direction, Logan wouldn't hesitate for one damn second.

"Have you forgotten that I'm at work, Mr. Mitchell?"

"No. Because that's the only reason you would have not to be over here standing in what has to be the best office space I have seen in my fucking life."

That smug tone in Logan's voice had Tate laughing as he imagined him in some empty building in his immaculate suit surveying all that was his.

"Is that right? I assume you won the coin toss with Cole for the balcony?"

Logan paused. "Something like that. You've got to see it, Tate. It's incredible. The view alone is…" He trailed off as though he was at a loss for words. "Are you guys busy down there tonight?"

"It's decent, steady." Tate checked his watch. "You going to be there a little longer? I could see if Robbie's okay here and head down there for a tour."

"Yeah?"

"Yeah. Oh, and he's good for Wednesday. You still able to get it off?"

They'd decided they needed to take a day this week to get stuck into packing if they were ever going to get out of the place within the two weeks they'd told Priest. "Yep, already cleared my schedule."

"Awesome. Okay then, give me an hour. If something comes up, I'll call."

Logan hummed. "I'd sure hope so."

Tate reached down and massaged a palm over his dick, which had instantly reacted to that velvety invitation, and then told Logan goodbye before hanging up and heading back inside to find Robbie.

He spotted him down the far end of the bar serving a customer, and when Tate came over, he excused himself and turned to face him. "What's up, boss?"

Tate looked around the bar and saw Bianca out taking orders on one side, and Tim over clearing several of the high-top tables. Then he returned his attention to Robbie. "Do you think you'd be okay if I headed out early tonight?"

Robbie scanned the customers and nodded. "Yeah, I don't see an issue. Monday is never insane, and Alex just got here. She's out back."

"Okay. Well, if you're sure, I'm going to head out. Logan wants to show me the new office space their firm is renovating. He finally got to lay claim to it today."

"Oh yeah. He told me he had to fight it out with his brother and—"

"And Priest," Tate finished for Robbie when he stopped abruptly. "What's with you and him? I know you clashed when he was dealing with your cousin. And sure, he's a bit weird—"

"A bit?" Robbie said, shaking his head. "Now there's an understatement. He's missing a little thing I like to call humanity. Reminds me of a damn robot."

Tate thought about that and had to agree. Priest wasn't the most demonstrative person he'd ever met. "Maybe it's an L.A. thing?"

"Maybe it's an asshole thing."

"Okay. Okay. Fair enough," Tate said. "You sure you'll be okay here?"

"Positive. Now go. Don't let me be the one to stop Logan from showing off for you."

Tate laughed and, with a wave, went upstairs to shower and change before he headed over to check out the newest addition to Mitchell & Madison.

* * *

"STILL HERE?"

LOGAN looked up from his computer to see Cole standing at his door with his briefcase in hand.

"Yeah. You're here late."

Cole winced and walked inside. "I know. I got caught up dealing with a custody case. I hate the ones with babies. Not even a year old and your parents are already fighting over you."

Logan grimaced and sat back in his chair. "That's

rough."

"That it is. Well, don't spend all night here."

"I won't," Logan said, getting out of his chair and coming around the desk. "Tate's coming by. Due any minute now."

At the mention of Tate's name, Cole's eyes sparked and Logan shook his head. "No. I already know what you're thinking. I'm not asking him tonight." Logan chuckled and heard himself say, "I actually like your idea from earlier, though." When his brother frowned, Logan reminded him, "Something romantic."

"Oh yes. I always wished I'd done the grand gesture in a more romantic way for Rachel."

As Logan finally talked out loud about the whole marriage thing, he realized he was kind of excited about it. "Really? How'd you ask her?"

Cole gave him a wolfish grin. "In bed."

Well, I'll be damned. "You did not."

"I did. She thought I was crazy."

"I mean, you had only known her a couple of weeks," Logan pointed out. "But really? In bed? I'd expect that from me. Not from you. Keeping it classy."

Cole gave him a smug smile and shrugged. "Hey, she said yes, didn't she?"

"That she did. And she's had two of your kids since."

"Mhmm. So I must be doing something right."

"I think the actual phrase here would be: you must be doing *her* right. Now get the hell out of here, would you?

I don't want to make you feel bad when I show Tate the office you begrudgingly handed over to me today."

Cole turned and headed for the door, and once he was there, he looked back to Logan and smiled. "You're right about the office. Fuck you for that. But I'm very happy for you about Tate."

Logan couldn't have stopped the grin from crossing his mouth if his life depended on it, because he was pretty damn happy about that too.

Chapter Ten

WHEN THE ELEVATORS opened on Mitchell & Madison's floor, Tate moved to get off, but came to an abrupt stop when he spotted Logan standing there with a hand in his pocket waiting for him.

"Hello." The devilish glint in Logan's eyes had Tate remaining exactly where he was as Logan entered the elevator, pushed the button of the floor they needed, and then rounded back to grab hold of Tate's jacket and tug him in for a kiss.

Tate didn't bother greeting Logan with words as the doors slid shut; instead he took Logan's face between his hands, deepened the connection, and groaned as Logan slipped his hands down his front and inside his leather jacket to circle his waist.

So damn potent, was the only thought running through Tate's head as Logan walked him backward to the elevator wall. Tate knew there wasn't a long trip between here and their final destination, but if Logan wanted to take that time to greet him like this, he wasn't about to stop him.

Teeth nipped at his bottom lip, and when Tate grunted in response, Logan chuckled and raised his head.

"Have I mentioned I *love* how easy you are?"

Tate lowered a hand down to palm the erection he could feel pressing against his own, and when Logan ground his hips into his hand, Tate squeezed. "Like you ever play hard to get."

"Now that's an incorrect statement. I *always* play hard." Tate bit at Logan's lip, and when the elevator dinged, Logan took a step back. "So needy. I didn't bring you up here for that, Mr. Morrison."

"No?"

Logan took his hand and walked backward through the open doors. "No. I brought you up here so I could—"

"Show off?" Tate said, remembering Robbie's words. "And maybe, oh, I don't know, impress me with your big…office?"

Logan cocked his head as if contemplating Tate's words, and then smiled slowly. "That's right."

Tate let out a laugh and rolled his eyes. "Okay then, Mr. Fancy Lawyer. Impress me."

As he stepped off the elevator, the first thing Tate noticed was the huge spotlight set up directly to their left. It lit up the immediate area like a stadium, but with the thick structural pillars and night sky filtering in through the walls of windows, darkness and shadows danced over the rest of the concrete that made up this level of the building.

This was the first time Tate had been up to what would soon become the main floor of Mitchell & Madison. He'd seen the blueprints Logan had brought home, and he'd shown him the basics and explained what would go where. But when Tate surveyed the space, empty save for the obvious mess that came with renovation, he stopped and let go of Logan's hand to just, well, stare.

The area was enormous and open right now, and it was somewhat humbling to be standing in one of Chicago's downtown high-rises and know that your boyfriend had earned his way up here with all of his hard work and—

"You're impressed, aren't you?"

That big fucking brain of his. Tate looked over at the man who never failed to blow his mind in every way imaginable, and found himself thinking, as he often did, how he'd gotten so damn lucky. "I'm getting there."

Logan shoved his hands into his pockets and rocked back on his heels with a knowing look on his face. *That cocky as hell expression fits him just as well as his charcoal suit.* "You gonna show me around, or do I just get to see it from here?"

"Oh, hello," Logan said. "Look who's being all high-handed tonight."

Tate sauntered forward and looked Logan up and down, then reached out to run his fingertips down the lapel of his suit jacket. Then, out of nowhere, Robbie's words came back to him—*"You were ballsy and possessive. You may not have said it, but your attitude that day screamed, 'He's mine. Back the hell off'"*—and suddenly, everything Tate had been worried about the night before vanished as his fist curled into the material, and he yanked Logan forward.

Why should he ever worry about showing this man

off? Logan was fucking amazing, and if someone couldn't understand or see that, then they weren't people Tate needed in his life.

"Someone's got to keep your ego in check," Tate whispered against full lips. "Now, show me around. I need to know where to find you on the off chance I need a good lawyer."

With his hands now on Tate's chest to steady himself, Logan ran a finger down the zipper of his jacket. "I'm sorry. Did you just say a *good* lawyer? Were you or were you not the person who insisted on reading the write-up in *Businessweek* this past weekend while the, and I quote, '*Top* corporate lawyer in Chicago' rode your cock?"

Tate's dick stiffened at the reminder. "Hmm. Now that you mention it—"

"Yes?" Logan said, as he smoothed his hand down Tate's chest to his waist.

"I seem to recall the wording from that article being particularly inspiring, so you might be right."

Logan's gaze dropped to Tate's mouth. "I am right. But let me show you around just in case you ever *come* here...for a top lawyer."

"Always got to get the last word in, don't you?"

"You know it." Logan winked and then backed away, turning around to pull Tate up beside him. "But it's time to concentrate. There are some heavy-duty renovations going on here. We've got to be serious."

Tate bit back a laugh, because that was basically

Logan's version of *stop distracting me so I can focus.*

"Yes. Let's be serious," Tate deadpanned. "Because I'm the one who needs to concentrate in a construction zone."

Logan narrowed his eyes. "Are you trying to imply something?"

Tate shook his head. "Nope. I'm being *serious.*"

"You're making fun of me. I'm not that bad around this kind of stuff."

Tate opened his mouth to refute that and found himself grinning. "Umm, have you forgotten last Christmas when you and Cole put together Thomas's swing set?"

"*No.* But in our defense—"

"You have no defense." Tate started laughing. "Telling a child that Santa had to work really fast on Christmas Eve to excuse the bolts he missed, leaving the swing set lopsided, is *not* a defense. Now, if you two admitted you can't follow instructions or use a tool to save your lives, then maybe you'd have a leg to stand on."

"So what are you trying to say, Morrison?" The slight flush on Logan's cheeks could've been from annoyance or embarrassment; Tate wasn't sure which. But whatever had caused it was making Logan real hard to resist as he glared Tate down.

"Nothing. I'm not trying to say anything."

"Hmm, sure you aren't." Logan turned back to look out at the empty building. Scattered around were sawhorses and paint buckets, some of which had been emptied and turned over to serve as seats for the workmen during breaks. And on one side of the room was what looked like a large waste receptacle filled with all kinds of debris from knocked-down walls, to stripped siding, and even the old pulled carpet.

These were all things that Tate was familiar with after having helped with some of the bar renovation. Logan, on the other hand—not so familiar, or adept, when it came to anything *remotely* to do with tools or handiwork.

Tate ran his thumb over the inside of Logan's palm, and then leaned in to whisper in his ear, "Show me your office, Logan. I want to see how *big* it is."

Logan didn't look at him. "Fucking flirt." And then he launched into his rundown of the space.

* * *

LOGAN WAS ACUTELY aware of every move Tate made as he led him past the place reception would be, through the taped-off section of the conference room, down to where Cole and Priest's offices were located, and now, as he walked ahead of him, toward what would eventually be his office.

It wasn't that Tate was touching him—he wasn't even speaking all that much other than to say what he liked about the new setup. It was the undivided attention he had focused on Logan that was making the air vibrate. He was one hundred percent absorbed in what Logan was telling him, and there was nothing he enjoyed more than Tate's focus solely on him, whether it be sexual or, like now, genuine interest in what he was saying.

When they came to the spot where the tape on the floor had a break in it, marking where the double doors to his office were going to go, Logan halted Tate and then stepped inside and did an about face.

Tate's eyes drifted past his shoulder to the windows flanking the two sides of the building behind Logan, and then came back to his as he crossed his arms. "You going to invite me in, counselor?"

Yes, I fucking am, Logan thought, and then moved to the side as though the area already had walls and a door, and gestured for Tate to enter.

Tate strolled inside, casually shoving a hand into his jeans, and as he passed by, Logan couldn't stop his eyes from traveling down to where the denim was ripped across the back of Tate's left thigh. *God, that's hot.*

"By all means, come in, Mr. Morrison."

Tate stopped to look back at Logan over his shoulder, and the fiery glint in his eyes had Logan clearing his throat. An arrogant grin tugged at the corner of Tate's lips, and it was all Logan could do not to say screw the damn tour and demand that the guy get naked. But the spotlight on the floor lit up parts of the office space like an FBI raid, and there were windows literally everywhere. *So...maybe not.*

Tate had wandered over to the far corner of the

building now, so he was looking out at what Logan had been earlier in the day. When he let out a low whistle of appreciation, Logan said, "Well? Impressed now?"

Tate didn't turn or look back at him, merely nodded and continued to look out at the giant glass and steel structures surrounding them. "I told you, I'm getting there."

Logan walked over to stand beside him so their shoulders almost touched, but decided to keep the slight distance between them until they were somewhere private where they could finish what was brewing between them in a satisfying way. "You're a hard man to please if this view doesn't satisfy you."

Tate shrugged, and the cologne he wore floated across the short distance separating them and had Logan's dick stiffening behind his zipper.

"Maybe I've just been looking at things that are hard to beat."

Jesus. Okay. The sexual tension between them right now was fucking insane. And for the first time in, well, forever, that hadn't been Logan's intention. He'd really just wanted to show Tate the new floor. *But hell if that's what's on my mind now. Perhaps it was all that talk with Cole about marriage—*

"I mean," Tate said, interrupting Logan's thoughts, "you're pretty impressive to look at."

Or maybe it's just Tate.

Logan closed the space between them and ran a hand down Tate's arm over the supple and worn leather. "Are you purposely trying to drive me crazy right now?"

Tate chuckled, and it was low and sensual as it wrapped around him. "Maybe a little," he said as he backed away from Logan, and then turned to head over to the other side of the space where the balcony was located.

"Maybe a little, he says..." Logan muttered as he wandered back to the middle of the office, needing the distance more than ever if he was going to keep his damn hands to himself.

When Tate got to the glass door that was sealed shut for now, he continued walking a little ways down then stopped and cupped his hands on the window to get a better look outside. "That's going to be nice in the spring and summertime. Might be a little frosty in the winter, though," he said, straightening back up. "How'd you get Cole to give it up?"

When Logan didn't respond, Tate looked his way. "Logan?"

"Huh?"

The smug as fuck expression that flashed across Tate's face at Logan's response guaranteed no more office talk, rational thinking, *or* rational behavior.

Logan could barely remember his own name right then—he was so focused on the man stalking across to him that he was trying to recall the reason he'd been keeping distance between them in the first place.

Oh right... The spotlight and windows. Yeah... Suddenly they didn't seem to matter so much as Tate muscled him back to the pillar behind him and then placed a palm on either side of Logan's head, caging him in.

"I asked how you got Cole to give it up."

I told him I want to marry you, was the first thing that popped into Logan's mind. But he managed to swallow those words, thank fuck, because this wasn't where he wanted it to happen. Or when. "I, uhh…"

"Yes?" Tate asked as he brushed his lips across the top of Logan's.

"I can't fucking think while you're doing that. Jesus, Tate. This place is lit up like the Fourth of July. What are you doing?"

As Tate kissed and sucked his way up Logan's jaw, he snaked a hand down to palm the erection between Logan's thighs.

"You can't tell? I must be doing it wrong," Tate said, and then raised his head. "What's the matter? You worried someone's going to see us? Worried that they're in a building out there about to watch me strip one of the owners of this firm out of his suit, turn him around, and fuck him where he stands?"

Logan's chest rose and fell as he stared at Tate, any and all coherent thought gone after that little speech as he decided to hell with waiting until they got home.

"Logan?"

Logan's eyes flicked around the space and then came back to Tate's. *Fuck waiting.* Then he swallowed and said, "I'm more worried I'm going to come without you having done *any* of that."

Chapter Eleven

"GET OVER HERE." As Tate's order hit Logan's ears, the only thought running through his head was, *Try and stop me.* But Tate wasn't waiting for him to obey tonight. He grabbed hold of Logan's hand, tugged him to the other side of the column where the shadows were at play, and then spun him around so Logan was staring at the floor-to-ceiling pillar.

Tate's body was an immediate presence behind him, as his hands found Logan's waist and pulled him back into the wall of muscle that was going to, *please God*, hold him prisoner against the solid surface.

One of Tate's hands moved around to the buckle of his belt, and as it did his mouth came down to Logan's ear, and the feel of his breath against it made a shiver of anticipation race up his spine.

"I'm so fucking hard for you right now," Tate said, and Logan shut his eyes, sending up a quick prayer he wouldn't come before he at least had Tate's hands on his naked skin. "And I haven't even gotten your belt undone yet."

Jesus, you and me both, Logan thought, as he heard his buckle release and ground his ass back against the solid erection Tate was referring to.

Fuck, he wanted that in him. He wanted his pants around his ankles, Tate's fingers digging into his hips, and that thick cock tunneling in him hard, fast, and out of control.

He blindly reached for the hand Tate was now using to unbutton and unzip him, and when Logan found it, he guided it inside his open pants, behind the material of his briefs, and then—"*Ahh,* hell yes"—he curled his hand over the top of Tate's where he most wanted it—on his aching dick.

Tate's chuckle was arrogant as all hell, and the strong, solid strokes he began had Logan's hips punching forward to fuck the fist working him.

"That what you want?" Tate said by his ear, and Logan's hand left his briefs to come out and grab at Tate's thigh for something to hang on to.

"Fuck yes, it is," he said, as Tate twisted his hand around the tip of his cock and Logan thrust into the touch. He bit his lip as he continued to rock his hips, Tate's hand providing the perfect amount of friction to torment but not quite get him there.

"So needy." Tate's low rumble sent a thrill down Logan's spine as he remembered their earlier conversation in the elevator. "So *easy* when it comes to me. You're right, that is hot. And I love it. You have no idea how much. But you will soon."

Logan groaned, and Tate laughed again in his ear,

and that confidence, that attitude Tate was throwing off, was making this impossibly hotter.

"So...what's next, do you think?" Tate asked. "We can't just stand here like this all night." Tate stopped moving his hand, and Logan clenched his fingers in Tate's jeans.

"*Hell.* Don't stop."

"Then answer my question." Tate's demand had Logan's dick throbbing. *Bossy fuck is gonna make me come by just ordering me around.*

"Come on, Logan." Tate's teeth nipped at the shell of his ear, and Logan's jaw bunched. "I'll do anything. But I wanna hear you *ask* for it."

"Fuck."

Tate stroked down to the root of Logan's cock and squeezed. "Start talking and we will."

Logan shut his eyes and tried to calm his racing pulse. But that was no use when Tate's hand was wrapped around him and his breath was floating over his skin. *God, where to start...where to start?* "Take my goddamn pants off."

Tate's grunt of approval made any blood left in Logan's brain race directly south. Then Tate's fingers were in either side of his slacks, yanking them, and his briefs, over his ass to his thighs.

As the night air hit Logan's bare skin, Tate shoved him forward two steps and said in his ear, "Hands up. Legs spread. As wide as these pants of yours will let you get 'em."

Logan placed his palms against the cool concrete of

the pillar and widened his stance. Tate then crowded in
behind him, and the rough denim grazed Logan's naked ass
as he planted a hand by either side of the ones Logan had on
the column.

Breathe, Logan told himself. *Shut your eyes and breathe
or this is going to be over before it starts.* He was pretty close to
congratulating himself for getting it together under the
circumstances, but then, of course, Tate shattered it with one
filthy fucking comment.

"Mmm." Tate smoothed a palm over the rounded
curve of Logan's ass. "It's gonna be a real tight fit in here
tonight."

Holy. Shit. This was about to get out of hand real fast,
and Tate knew exactly what his dirty talk did to Logan's
peace of mind.

"So...what's next?" Tate asked, and Logan couldn't
stop himself from bucking back against him, needing some
kind of contact.

"Maybe I just want to rub against you." The teasing
taunt slipped past Logan's lips before he thought better of it,
and Tate, being in the mood he was in, wasn't about to let
him get away with it. With surprising strength, Tate put *all*
his muscle behind shoving him forward until his arms gave
way and his cheek, chest, and erect cock were pressed up
against the unyielding surface of the pillar.

"You mean like this?" Tate asked, as he began to roll
his hips, grinding his erection up and down Logan's crack
until he was desperate. He wanted to beg Tate to spread him

wide, unzip those jeans he still wore, and tunnel inside of him, *right fucking now.*

But he didn't, and Tate—*the teasing motherfucker*—continued to dry-hump him until Logan's eyes almost rolled to the back of his head and he gave in and demanded, "Get rid of your fucking jeans, Tate. Jesus Christ." Tate's lips grazed the back of his neck, and Logan growled, "*Now.*"

Tate's body left his in an instant, and Logan heard the rustling sound of clothes being removed echo off the walls, then, *hell yes,* the sound of a packet being ripped open followed, and Logan lowered a hand between his legs and began to pump his cock.

It didn't take but a few seconds or so, and then Tate was back, wedging his lubed dick right where Logan wanted it most. And when Tate's palms came up on either side of him, caging Logan in where he stood, Logan groaned.

Finally. Skin on fucking skin.

* * *

THE SOUND THAT left Logan's throat as Tate's cock left a slippery path along the dark crevice of his ass was nothing short of desperate. With one hand braced on the pillar, and his pants pulled down around his thighs, Logan made a sinful invitation as he worked his rigid shaft—one that Tate planned to take full advantage of.

The distorted glow of the spotlight caused shapes

and outlines to dance on the interior walls, but they were far enough away from the windows that Tate wasn't concerned in the slightest that anyone could see them.

His cock was leaving its mark all over Logan's backside as Tate moved as though he was already inside him. He was as hard as the pillar, and by the time he got through with Logan, Tate planned to have him begging for a good fucking.

"Damn, Logan," Tate said as he ran his fingers through the pre-cum he'd left all over Logan's skin, making him shudder.

"In me…" Logan said on a rush of air. "*God…* Put something the fuck in me."

Tate slipped his slick fingers down the heated skin of Logan's narrow cleft, and when the pads of his fingers found his hole and massaged over the top of it, Logan cursed.

"Oh hell yes," Tate said, and put his mouth by Logan's ear. "Gotta say, I'm loving the acoustics up here. My name's gonna sound real sweet bouncing off the walls of your new office, Mr. Mitchell. Don't you think?"

Tate then pushed a finger in nice and deep, the way Logan loved it, and when his head fell forward and his shoulders bunched, Tate's cock throbbed. There was something insanely hot about seeing Logan so strung out while still wearing his suit jacket and tie. "Yeah, Logan. Go crazy for me. I wanna watch," he said as he withdrew his index finger and then slid it back inside.

"Tate," Logan growled as Tate added a second to the mix, rubbing and pushing at the entrance he was stretching.

"Ask me for it." At his words, Logan turned his head, and Tate saw that his pupils were blown and his teeth clenched. *He's real close now.* "I want to hear you. Ask me, Logan."

Tate added a slight pressure to his hole, and Logan's breath rushed out.

"I'm going to kill you."

"No, you're not," Tate said as his fingertips entered Logan. "Now come on..." he said, and twisted his hand. "*Beg* me for it."

"You goddamn sadist. If you don't hurry up and fuck me with something, I—"

That was as far as Logan got, because as far as begging went, that demand was music to Tate's ears, and he was right there as promised, ready to grant Logan his wish.

* * *

LOGAN DIDN'T CARE what Tate planned to put in him first, his fingers or his cock. He. Didn't. Care.

All he knew in that moment was that he wanted his ass filled and he wanted to come. And as he demanded just that, Tate thrust two fingers into him and Logan arched back, pushing his cock through his fist as the intense pleasure of having something in him hit. Tate then pulled those fingers free, and when a third joined in to massage over Logan's prostate, he clamped a tight fist around the base of his cock. "Fuck."

Tate's mouth found his neck then, and as he dragged his tongue up the line of it and bit down, his cock bumped against Logan's ass cheek as he continued to slowly and methodically stretch him, bringing Logan to the brink time and time again.

"I'm gonna fuck you so hard," Tate said against his cheek as he pulled his fingers free, and Logan's hole clenched at the loss, wanting—*needing*—exactly that. Then he felt a hand on the back of his neck.

"You might want to brace yourself," Tate suggested, and then gave Logan a rough shove forward, and hell if that didn't turn Logan on even more as he quickly brought his left hand up to support himself against the pillar.

"That's it," Tate said as his other fingers dug into Logan's hip and then the head of his cock nudged against his pucker. "Now, Logan. Say it."

And nothing could've stopped the words from flying free of Logan's mouth then. "Fuck me, Tate. You—"

Tate was balls deep inside him before Logan even finished his demand, and the delicious burn that accompanied the force of his thrust had Tate's name ripping from Logan's lips and echoing around them, just as Tate had predicted.

The hand at the back of Logan's neck tightened, and shit, who knew that being forcefully held in place would be such a damn turn-on as Tate withdrew, and then jammed his hips forward, drilling into him.

Christ. The strength of that thrust had Logan stumbling slightly, but Tate was right there, his hand moving to Logan's shoulder to haul him back so that his spine was flush against Tate's chest and his hole was swallowing his dick.

"Ahh… God*damn*, that's…" Logan's voice cracked and then left him, as Tate's arm wound around his waist to take hold of his cock.

"Deep. I'm so fucking deep, and your ass is *so* tight." Tate stroked his fist up to the head of Logan's dick, and Logan groaned at then intense pleasure that racked his body as it clenched around the thick shaft.

"Any final requests?" Tate asked, and Logan's chest heaved at the ragged tone of his voice. Tate sounded like a man who was a hair away from losing his shit, and fuck, he wanted that.

As that thought hit his brain, Logan was reminded of Saturday in the bar and that possessive look in Tate's eyes when he'd seen the mark on his neck, *and yes*, he had a final request, all right. "Bite me."

Tate's eyes narrowed, and when he bent his head, clearly going for Logan's ear, Logan jerked his head to the side, locked eyes with him, and panted. "Not like that."

"No?" Tate said, and the molten heat in his eyes told Logan that Tate knew *exactly* what he wanted. He was just fucking with him. Pushing him. And finally, Logan reached back, grabbed a fistful of that taunting fucker's hair, and yanked his mouth to his.

"*No,*" Logan growled, his control and patience finally snapping. "I want to feel your teeth through my shirt, marking me while you fuck me until I can't walk."

The fist around Logan's cock close to strangled it, and Tate gave it a rough pull as his hips surged forward. Then Logan found himself plastered against the pillar with his arms drawn up over his head, Tate's hand holding them in place, as he tugged aside the collar of Logan's jacket and drove inside of him.

There was nothing gentle about what happened next, as Tate grabbed Logan's hip to hold him still and he began to fuck into him time and time again.

Next came the teeth on his shoulder, and they were sharp and stung in a way that made Logan's blood hum, and as he grunted and struggled against the hold Tate used on him, Logan reveled in the brute force Tate exerted to keep him where he wanted him as he took and took and fucking took.

"Ah *fuck*...fuck," Logan said, his voice failing him, as Tate's fingernails bit into his wrists.

"Give me your tongue," Tate said, and Logan's head turned in an instant so Tate's mouth could find his, and then Logan went wild.

His hands twisted and clawed above him, trying to get leverage on the column so he could shove back harder on Tate, wanting more—*always more*—until Tate's fingers laced with his and pinned them in place.

The hot throb of Tate's cock pulsed inside of him, and Logan shut his eyes, trying to rein in that greedy, dark side of himself that reveled in being so thoroughly fucked. But it was no use. The leash was gone. All his decorum shredded to shit. And all Logan could think about was how badly he wanted to come. And what he'd do to get it.

"*Move*," he said between clenched teeth, and when Tate held his stare but remained still, goading him to act, Logan did the only thing he could think of to get Tate to move: he whipped his head to the other side and sank his teeth into Tate's bicep—*hard*.

Tate cursed so loudly it made Logan's ears ring, but then he released Logan's hands, grabbed his hips, and said in his ear, "You fucking savage," and let him have it.

* * *

TATE'S ARM STUNG where Logan had just bit him, and as he held on to Logan's hips, he relished the feeling.

Logan had snapped right around the moment Tate had shoved him against the pillar by the back of his neck, and now? Now Logan was going out of his fucking mind.

With his hands on the column and his legs barely parted due to the confines of his pants, Logan's hot hole was a challenge Tate was enjoying getting his dick in and out of. He couldn't seem to temper his own fevered response to the way Logan was reacting to him, and hell if he wanted to.

"Yes. Jesus. Harder, Tate. Fucking *harder*." Logan's

words were clipped, his movements now methodical as his hand moved in time with his pistoning hips as he ruthlessly chased after the climax building in him.

The grunts that were echoing throughout the floor were accompanied by curses and threats that made Tate's lips curl and his balls tingle. He'd always loved a good argument with Logan, and enjoyed the fight for dominance between them during sex. And hell if he wasn't about to bask in the satisfaction he was about to take in filling Logan's ass in the most primal way he could.

With one hand on Logan's hip, Tate raised his other to grip the back of Logan's neck again, and the second he did, Logan started to beg. *Deeper, harder, more, now*—Logan wanted anything Tate was willing to give, and, luckily for him, tonight, that was everything.

He wasn't sure how long it took the two of them then. Minutes? Seconds? Tate had no clue. It was as though time stopped as every nerve ending in his body lit on fire. Then Logan shouted his name, and Tate detonated.

A harsh growl left his throat as Logan's entire body arched back into him. Tate heard his name leave Logan's lips as his ass clamped on to his dick, as though it would never let it leave, and then he came all the fuck over the concrete pillar.

Well, Tate thought, as he stood there with his arm wrapped around Logan's neck and his cock still lodged inside of him. Logan had definitely *claimed* his new office.

Chapter Twelve

"TATE? WHERE YOU at?" Logan kicked the condo's door shut as he balanced a pizza box in one hand and a plastic bag in the other. It was nearing three on Wednesday afternoon, and the two of them had been packing since eight that morning.

"I'm in the study," Tate called out as Logan navigated the half-filled boxes in the living room, accidentally stepped on a sheet of bubble wrap, and then finally made it to the door of the study.

Around an hour earlier they'd run out of the heavy-duty tape and realized it was way past lunchtime, and Logan had eagerly volunteered to head out and pick up supplies, leaving Tate to deal with the disassembling of the office furniture.

When Logan came to a stop in the doorway, he spotted Tate seated cross-legged on the floor in amongst piles of books, DVDs, and paperwork in various files and binders. There was stuff everywhere, and when Tate looked over his shoulder at Logan, he couldn't stop himself from smiling at the picture he made.

Tate was wearing grey sweats and a faded green t-shirt with some band he'd seen years ago printed on it. But that wasn't what had Logan crossing to him, wanting a kiss. No, that'd be all those damn curls. They were sticking out all over the place and framing his face as Tate aimed that charming grin of his up at Logan.

Logan bent down and pressed a kiss to those curved lips, and Tate hummed and gladly returned it. "Looks like you've made some progress," Logan said.

Tate looked around and nodded. "Yeah, a bit. God, that smells amazing."

"Here." Logan handed him the box. "No point in moving. I'll grab some paper towels and drinks. What do you want?"

Tate put the pizza box down in front of him. "A water."

Logan shook his head and then headed out to the kitchen, calling over his shoulder, "I'll never understand how you drink water with your pizza. That's just wrong."

"I've always had water with it. Habit, I guess. Oh, hey? Are you still okay with going to Jill's this weekend?"

Logan grabbed the paper towels, a Coke and water from the fridge, and then walked back into the study, tossing the bottled water. "Yeah, of course. I assume you decided it would be a good idea?"

"I don't know that I'd go that far. But I want to see my nephews, and I'd really like you to meet them and my friends."

Logan tried to keep his face neutral as Tate's words

went straight to his heart. But damn, not only was he proud of Tate, he felt incredibly loved by him in that moment. "Then we should go."

Tate flipped open the pizza box and scooted over to make room for him, and as Logan took up the vacated spot, he let his eyes wander around the disaster zone and cleared his throat. "This room is a mess."

Tate tore off a paper towel and then picked up a slice of the deep-dish pepperoni they'd decided on. "I'm thinking it'll probably take us the longest. Who knew we had so much junk in here?"

Logan reached for a DVD set sitting on the top of the pile and screwed his nose up. *"He-Man and the Masters of the Universe?* Really? I think we need a trash pile. Have you started one of those?"

"Hey," Tate said around a bite of his pizza. "Don't even think about it. I grew up watching that."

"The important part of that sentence is you *grew up."* Logan flipped the DVD over in his hand, read the back of the box, and then raised a questioning eyebrow. "This might actually explain a few things about you."

"Really?" Tate rolled his eyes. "Then it must also explain a few things about the majority of young boys in the eighties. That was a popular show. You aren't throwing it out; it's nostalgic. Plus, you never know, if you sat down and watched an episode with me, you just might like it."

"Highly doubtful." Logan put the box down and reached for a slice of pizza.

"Okay. Okay. I know you were more into books than TV," Tate said, as his eyes went to the mountains of literature stacked in piles against the far wall. "What was something you read as a boy? Is it in one of those piles?"

Logan swallowed his mouthful of food and looked over at the books while Tate kept on talking.

"I mean, there are some pretty old-looking ones mixed in there with the autobiographies, textbooks, and *National Geographics*."

Logan looked back to Tate and narrowed his eyes. "Pretty *old* ones? What am I, sixty?"

Tate unscrewed his water and took a long gulp, draining half of it, then put the lid back on and set it down. "Nope. About to turn thirty-eight, last time I checked."

"How about you *stop* checking?"

Tate chuckled and picked his pizza back up. "You didn't answer my question."

Relieved that Tate had switched subjects, Logan said, "The Hardy Boys."

"Oh, I've heard of those."

Logan finished his pizza slice and then leaned back against one of the packed boxes. "Have you?"

"I think so. They're detectives or something, right?"

"Right," Logan said as Tate got to his feet and stepped over the pizza. "What are you doing?"

Tate ran his fingers down the spines of books neatly piled up against the wall until he stopped on one. Then he took the books off the top of that stack and grabbed the book he'd obviously gone in search of. "The Hardy Boys. *The Tower Treasure*." Tate looked down at him, and Logan nodded. "This looks well read."

"It is. That was one of my favorites. I can't tell you how many times I read that series. It was about two brothers who solved all these crimes. I used to imagine I had one when I read them. I got *that* when I was seven."

Tate rested up against the solid mahogany computer desk, fighting back a smile. "So it *is* old, then?"

Logan picked up the half-empty water bottle and threw it at Tate, making him laugh and dodge to catch it. He accidentally bumped into a photo album Logan had found earlier that morning.

As it went toppling to the floor, Logan quickly reached over to grab it, but before he got there, Tate crouched down and picked it up, along with several loose photos that had fallen free.

"What are these?" Tate asked as he sat back on his heels and turned over the image, and what he saw there had a massive grin splitting his lips. "Is this…?" He raised his eyes to lock them with Logan's. "This is you and Evelyn."

Logan snatched the photo album off Tate's lap and held his hand out. "Okay, hand it over."

"No way." Tate raised his arm above his head as Logan made a grab for it. When it was clear Tate wasn't going to give it to him, Logan sighed and sat on his ass, crossing his legs. "Why'd you tell me you didn't have any photos of you as a boy?"

Because I'd rather forget any and all things that remind me of Evelyn... That was the truth, but instead of saying that, he opted for evasion. "I didn't even remember I had them until I cleaned out the bottom drawer of the shelf today."

Tate eyed him for a second, and Logan knew what he was thinking: *Bullshit.* But instead of calling him out, Tate flipped open the album. "Fair enough. But since we found it now, how about you tell me a little about the boy in these photos? 'Cause I got to say"—Tate looked down at the open page and grinned—"he's someone I've wanted to meet for a while now. I mean, look at this," he said, and picked up the album, turning it toward him. Logan arched an eyebrow at Tate. *Fucker is having way too much fun with this.* "You're even wearing a polo shirt."

* * *

THE BOY IN the photograph was adorable. From his thick-rimmed glasses that were almost as big as his face, to the slicked-down coal-colored hair. Logan's rosy red cheeks and pouty mouth made for one seriously adorable package.

Adorable. Geeky. And so preppy that the polo shirt was buttoned all the way up to the very top.

Tate couldn't wipe the grin off his face. He still couldn't get over the fact he was finally seeing what Logan had looked like as a boy. He'd always told Tate he'd been a nerdy kid, but... "How old are you here?"

"Nine," Logan said in a put-out tone, which had Tate

laughing all over again. "Okay. That's it. Give it to me."

As Logan reached for the album again, Tate pulled it up and held it to his chest. "Oh, come on. Let me look. You've seen pictures of me, and I've always wanted to see what Logan Mitchell was like as a kid."

When Logan just continued to stare him down, Tate lowered his gaze to Logan's mouth. "Are there any of you in college?"

At the question, Logan's lips twitched and he finally relented. He moved until he was over sitting beside Tate with their backs against the side of the desk and their legs stretched out in front of them. Him in his sweats and Logan in his jeans.

"No, there are not. And fine. Let's get this over with," Logan said, and reached for the album, opening it on their laps. "*Try* and hide your enjoyment over my humiliation a little better, though, would you?"

Tate bumped Logan's shoulder with his and then kissed his temple. "I'm not making any promises."

When Logan turned his head to pin him with a *you'll pay for this* look, Tate winked and then looked back at the photos beneath the protective sleeve. There were four per page, and the first spread had several of Logan ranging from maybe seven to ten, Tate would guess. They had been taken in the same place year after year, in front of a fireplace, and in each of them Logan was all put together with a very smart backpack and a big, bright smile for the camera.

"First days of school?" Tate asked, and Logan

nodded then started chuckling.

"It was always my favorite day."

"The *first* day was?"

"Mhmm," Logan said, and turned the page. "Nerd, remember?"

"You did look awfully happy for a kid heading off to school." Tate pointed to a photo on the top of the next page. It had been taken out in front of a single-story white house, and in it was mother and son. "Ah, Evelyn's in this one."

Logan nodded. "Yeah. That's when we lived in Naperville with Ken the dentist. He was boyfriend number six." Logan picked the album up and took a closer look. "God, look at her hair. Talk about a tight perm. Ha, she'd hate that photo. Maybe I should send it to her for Mother's Day." Logan put the book back on their laps. "But that was another reason I was happy for the first day of school each year. It meant Evelyn-free days in a row. That was exciting in and of itself."

Tate looked over at Logan, but he was busy staring at the woman and boy in the photo. "What was she like back then?"

"Slightly less selfish than she is today." Logan ran a finger down the photo and tapped it lightly. "But still selfish enough to have no idea whose house that was if we were to ask her today."

"Really?"

"Really. Sad, huh? Ken was one of the good ones, too. I think he actually loved her."

Tate narrowed his eyes on Logan and then took his hand. "And what about you?"

Logan looked over at him. "What about me?"

"Did he love you too?"

Logan frowned and then shrugged. "I don't know. We weren't there for very long—"

"But you said that you think he loved Evelyn."

"Right."

"So why not you too?"

"Shit, Tate. I told you. I don't know. Drop it, would you?" Logan said, and pulled his hand free to shut the photo album.

As they sat there in silence, Tate waited, knowing he had a hell of a lot more patience than the man currently doing his best to ignore the fact that he was staring a hole in the side of his head.

The truth of the matter was that Logan had just as many family issues as Tate did. But where his were all up in their faces constantly, it felt like Logan's were conveniently out of sight and therefore out of mind.

A selfish mother. A father who'd never acknowledged him. And a brother he hadn't known existed until he was practically an adult.

Yeah, if two people were ever more suited… He's just as messed up by his relatives as I am.

"I can feel you staring, Tate."

"I sure hope so. I'm doing it real hard."

Logan angled his head toward him and sighed. "I'm

sorry. I shouldn't have snapped at you."

"It's okay."

"No, it's not." Logan reached up to the desk behind them, and then he brought the Hardy Boys book down and gave it to him. Tate frowned as he looked at the worn cover that had two boys on the front of it staring up at an old tower. *They were about brothers solving crimes,* Logan had told him. *I used to imagine I had one whenever I read them.*

And look at that, Tate thought. *One has black hair, just like Logan, and the other is blond, like—*

"Open it," Logan said, as Tate sat there with the book in hand. He ran a palm down the front of it and then very carefully Tate opened the book. The pages were old and had that yellow tinge to it that old paper sometimes got. And there was a watermark in the corner at the top of the first page. But that didn't stop him from treating the book as though it were a priceless artifact. This book of Logan's obviously meant a lot to him if he'd hung on to it since he was seven, and there was no way Tate was going to do anything to jeopardize its condition.

Logan pointed to the inside of the cover, and that was when Tate saw it. A handwritten message.

To L.,

While I know you're big enough and smart enough to hunt down the buried treasure your mom hid for you today, should you need a partner to assist, I would be glad to do so.

Happy birthday!

*And just like Frank and Joe Hardy, may you have many
great adventures in your future.*

From K.

"You asked me if he loved me. I think he could have.
But the afternoon of my seventh birthday, Evelyn decided to
tell him she'd 'loved' our next-door neighbor. Ken left later
that night."

So that explains his aversion to birthdays. "Fucking
Evelyn."

"Yes," Logan said, and laughed derisively. "That was
the problem. *Everyone* fucking Evelyn."

Tate shut the book and the album, and put them
down on the floor beside him. As his eyes travelled around
the study, he thought how appropriate it was that the two of
them were sitting in the only clear space of what otherwise
resembled a disaster zone. Then he shifted his body and
reached for Logan's face.

"You do know that Ken, he *already* loved you."
Logan remained silent, but blinked behind the lenses of his
glasses, and Tate flashed a crooked smile at him. "You and I,
we're a bit of a mess lately, aren't we?"

"A little bit." Logan brought his hand up to cover the
one on his cheek. "But there's no one I'd rather get messy
with."

The truth in those words cut straight to the heart,
and there it was—that expression he'd caught in Logan's
eyes time and time again lately. *Love. Trust. And a kind of*

wonderment. But at what?

He lightly skimmed his lips over the top of Logan's, and when he sighed and opened for him, Tate slid his tongue inside and shut his eyes.

A hand came down to rest on his chest, and when Logan's fingers curled into the material of his shirt and he pulled him closer, Tate obeyed. He shifted until Logan was slowly reclining to his back on the floor with him on top, and *damn,* it was sweet.

The moment. The man. The taste of Logan had Tate's brain shutting down to everything other than the lips under his as the two of them fell into something familiar and peaceful in amongst the chaos surrounding them.

Chapter Thirteen

"SHERRY!" IT WAS Friday afternoon and Logan had been pacing his office for the past forty minutes. He glanced at the clock on the wall for the hundredth time, and was just about to call out his PA's name again when the door opened and Sherry stepped inside.

"You rang?"

Logan stopped where he was behind his desk and placed his hands on the back of his leather chair. His morning had been insane. With three hearings on the schedule, he'd gone from one courtroom to the next until he'd finally finished up and been set free. And now...*now* he was left with nothing to do other than sit around and wait for Cole so he could finally tell someone about the absolutely brilliant idea he'd had last night. "Is he back yet?"

Sherry let out a put-upon sigh. "No. Mr. Madison has not arrived since you last asked me"—she paused for a second, checked her dainty wrist watch, and then looked back at Logan—"*seven* minutes ago."

"Well, when he is—"

"I'll be sure to jump out from behind my desk, block his path, and crash-tackle him if necessary."

"Are you mocking me, Sherry?"

Sherry placed her hand on the door handle. "I wouldn't dream of it, Mr. Mitchell."

At the use of his last name, Logan narrowed his eyes. "Okay, that's enough out of you. Get out of my office." As she went to shut the door, Logan called out, "But if you see Cole—"

"I'll personally drag him in here by the collar. If for no other reason than to have you stop interrupting me every seven minutes. Use that," she said, pointing to the small red stress ball on the corner of his desk. "I have a job to do."

As she shut the door behind her, Logan grabbed the ball she'd given him the *second* time he'd called her in there, and started to pace again, tossing the damn thing in the air and squeezing the shit out of it when it came back down.

Where the hell was Cole, anyway? Logan had been counting down the hours to see his brother since he'd come up with his plan, *and now, of course, he's nowhere to be found. Typical.*

Last night when he'd been eating dinner with Tate and they'd been talking about the movers this Saturday, he'd been struck with the perfect idea. It was fucking genius. And the more he'd thought it over, the more it made sense. This was it. This was how he was going to ask Tate to—

Knock. Knock. Knock.

Logan froze as the door pushed open, and when Cole stuck his head inside, Logan's palms started to sweat.

"I have been told I am not to leave your office until I

have done whatever is required to 'calm you the hell down.'"

Cole came inside and shut the door, then put his briefcase on the couch and took a seat. As he unbuttoned his jacket, he looked up expectantly to where Logan stood frozen and unspeaking. "Well? What's going on?"

And finally, Logan said what he'd been dying to say since he'd woken up this morning: "I'm going to ask Tate to marry me tomorrow."

* * *

LAST NIGHT TATE had suggested that he and Logan stay at the loft, since the condo resembled a storage unit for now. They'd pretty much finished with packing their stuff up, and all that was left now was moving it out and disassembling some of the bigger furniture pieces for tomorrow's move.

He'd just finished getting showered and changed for work, and was coming down the stairs to head into the bar when he spotted Rachel through the narrow glass of the window by the private entrance, with Lila on her hip.

Tate headed over to the door and opened it, and when he came into view, they looked up at him and smiled. "Hey there," he said, stepping aside so Rachel could get inside out of the cool wind that was whipping around.

"Hey," Rachel said as he kissed her cheek and then straightened.

"'Ello, Unca Tate." Lila waved at him as Tate locked

the door, and then he tickled under her chin, making her giggle.

"Hello, little miss." And before she had to demand it, Tate gave her a kiss on the cheek, just like he had her mother. "What can I do for you lovely ladies today?"

Rachel hitched Lila up her waist and shook her head. "No, silly. It's not what you can do for us. But what *we* can do for you."

Tate walked over to the door that led into The Popped Cherry, unlocked it, and pushed it open. There was something peaceful about being in a place that was usually so crowded and loud when it was empty.

"Do you want a drink or anything?" Tate asked as Rachel headed straight to his favored booth. "Juice? Soda? Coffee?"

"I'd kill for a cup of coffee."

"No murder necessary. Just give me a minute." Tate winked at her and then turned his attention to Lila, who was standing on the seat of the booth while Rachel unbuttoned her puffy coat. "What about Lila?"

"Oh, she doesn't drink coffee." When Tate laughed, Rachel smiled over her shoulder at him and then unzipped the huge bag she'd put on the table. "I have hers in here. She's set."

"Okay. I'll be right back."

A few minutes later, Tate headed back with two coffee mugs and the half-empty carafe. As he slid into the seat, Lila looked up from the paper Rachel had put down in front of her and pointed at the scribble across the page.

"Dog," she said, and when Tate tilted his head to try and get a better look, Rachel chuckled.

"Trust me. This is one of those occasions where you have to use your imagination."

Tate looked back to where Lila was busy coloring again. "And what noise does a dog make, Miss Lila?"

The crayon stopped on the paper and Lila quickly glanced at Rachel before turning back to Tate. "Woof!"

"That's right," he said, and when Lila clapped her hands together, Rachel said, "We're learning all about animals and the different sounds they make right now, aren't we, missy?"

When Lila nodded, Rachel ran her hand down the back of her hair. "Last week Cole brought this book home about a little girl who can't fall asleep and all the animals she goes to for advice. It's become the new favorite." She leaned across the table and said in a mock whisper, "But don't ask to meet the bear—it's too scary."

Tate grinned and turned his attention back to Lila, who was ever so carefully coloring in her...dog. Then he sat back in his seat and crossed his arms. "I'm not scared of bears."

Lila's little head whipped up, and she dropped the crayon, forgotten on the table, and pinned him with a fierce look that was so out of place for her that Tate had to bite his lip to keep from laughing.

A soft little *grrr* started, as Lila slowly brought her

hands up with her fingers curled into tiny claws, and when they were by either side of her face, she let out a very cute—but ferocious—growl.

She snarled at him with her nose scrunched up, as she scratched her hands through the air, and Tate couldn't help it then—he totally lost it. Rachel did also as she reached over and tugged Lila onto her lap in a huge bear hug, kissing her temple. "Ooh, you're so scary." Lila wriggled on Rachel's lap and growled again. "*Soooo* scary. Look, you even scared Uncle Tate."

Tate covered his mouth to hide the smile, but nodded. "Mom's right. That was very scary. I think you need to show Uncle Logan next time you see him."

As Lila settled down, Rachel looked over her head at Tate and grinned. "I'm pretty sure Logan's seen his fair share of bears over the years."

"No doubt," Tate said around a broad grin. "But not for some time. She *might* be able to scare him."

As Lila rested her head back, she put a thumb in her mouth and looked sleepy. Rachel kissed her on the cheek, and as mother and daughter snuggled with each other, Rachel said, "Speaking of scaring Logan, I'm here about his birthday."

Shit. With everything that had happened over the weekend, and then getting the condo packed up, he'd totally forgotten to call Cole and Rachel back about what he wanted to do next month for Logan.

"What day does his birthday fall this year?"

"A Thursday, I think," Tate said. "November ninth. But we'll just do the weekend anyway."

"I figured. So what'd you have in mind? You need some ideas where to have it?"

"Yeah, about that. Sorry. I meant to call but I got kind of caught up with everything that happened last weekend with Jill and then packing… But I have a few ideas I'm trying to decide between. Can I get back to you?" Rachel gave him a skeptical look, and Tate rolled his eyes. "This time I promise I actually will."

"Okay. But since I'm here, how about you tell me what you had in mind for him?" She paused and waggled her eyebrows. "I'm good at keeping secrets."

Tate studied her mischievous expression. "Got a lot of them, huh?"

She shrugged and made a show of zipping her lips before pointing to Lila, who was now sleeping. "I better keep quiet now. You know, to let her sleep."

"Sure…" Tate said, but narrowed his eyes on her, and when Rachel winked, he couldn't help but feel like there was something he was missing—but she was right. Lila needed her sleep, and *he* had a bar to get ready to open.

* * *

COLE SAT UP as though someone had pinched his ass, then scooted so far forward on the chair that Logan thought he just might fall off. His mouth was hanging open in what

Logan could only assume was shock, and if any other conversation was about to be had, he would've found the entire situation hilarious.

"Cole?" Logan said, and snapped his fingers in the air between them. "Did you hear me?"

Finally, Cole shut his mouth, and as Logan stood there waiting for some kind of response, a smile hit his brother's lips. "You're serious."

Logan tossed the stress ball at Cole, and when he caught it and held it up to inspect its mangled sides, Logan said, "What do you think?"

Cole squeezed the ball and looked at him. "I think you're fucking serious."

That was what finally had Logan's grin threatening to break his face.

"Holy shit," Cole said, and sat back in his seat. "You said tomorrow."

Logan nodded and came around the desk to sit in the chair beside Cole.

"You're going to ask Tate to marry you? Tomorrow?"

Logan started to chuckle. "Yes. I feel like you used to be smarter than this."

"So do I."

That really made Logan laugh.

Cole shook his head and put the ball on Logan's desk. "You're really going to do it?"

"I am." And as those two words left his mouth,

Logan realized how happy the prospect made him.

"Well... Shit."

"You already said that."

Cole's smile dropped and he shot Logan the finger. "Shut up. I'm in shock over here. I figured you'd take months, hell, maybe years to talk yourself into actually doing this."

You and me both, Logan thought, but then he remembered the past weekend and how connected he'd felt to Tate after it. And the other night, when they'd made out in the study like a couple of teenagers... *I'm not waiting any longer to make him officially mine.* "What can I say? I love him. I fell in love with him four years ago. That's not going to change."

Cole sat back in his chair, and the two of them stared out the windows. There was a reflective moment of silence, and then Cole turned his head to look at Logan. "You're going to tell me how, right? That's why you asked me in here. You want to run your plan by me and make sure you don't screw it up?"

That was exactly what Logan wanted, but before he poured his heart out, he needed something. "It depends."

"On?"

"Did you replace your Macallan yet?"

Chapter Fourteen

"ONE MORE TRIP and I think we'll be done." Tate put a box marked *study* in the new office off the kitchen and turned to see Logan lounging against the counter drinking from a bottle of water.

It was late Saturday afternoon, and they'd been up and at the whole moving business since six that morning—and, of course, it was raining. The movers had arrived at seven thirty, packed up the furniture within a couple of hours, and the two of them had been unpacking boxes, rearranging the furniture, and making a few final trips for the remaining items. Their plan was to finally be out of the condo tonight so the place could be repainted this week and they could hand the keys off to Priest.

Logan screwed the lid on his empty bottle and put it on the counter as he looked over to the table and chairs they'd put in the breakfast nook by the back door. "I think you're right. We just have a couple more things to grab and then we'll officially be out of there and moved in here."

"Yeah," Tate said as he crossed over to Logan and laid a hand on his waist. "So how about we head over there now, get them, and then pick up some dinner on the way back and eat in our new place?"

Logan pursed his lips as he took hold of Tate's hips and tugged him between his feet. "*Or* we could skip all of that and I could just eat you out *in* our new place."

Tate laughed and shoved him in the chest. "Be serious."

"I'm being dead serious."

"We need to be out of the condo by tonight. You know that."

"Hmm...I also know there are plenty of hours left until the clock strikes twelve," Logan said. "Plus, I think you need to be out of these clothes more than we need to be out of the condo—"

"Logan..." Tate kissed him quickly but then took a step back when Logan's hands started to slide around to his ass. When he was out of reach, Logan pushed off the counter and let out a long-suffering sigh.

"Okay. Fine," Logan said as Tate started walking backward to the living room. "Let's go and get the last of it. But Tate?"

"Yeah?"

Logan started in his direction, his eyes burning a hot trail in their wake as they roamed all over him.

"Just know that when we come back here tonight, your ass, and the rest of your sexy self, is going to belong to me."

Tate's feet faltered at the fierce look of possession in Logan's eyes—*Jesus, he's all kinds of intense right now*—then he stumbled as his calf hit one of the boxes in the living room and his back hit the front door.

A sensual smirk crossed Logan's mouth and then he kissed Tate and switched on the porch light for later. "Let's go. Sooner we leave, the sooner I can get you back here."

* * *

IT WAS AROUND the moment that Tate parked in his spot at the condo's parking garage, for what would likely be the final time, that Logan's nerves kicked in.

Oh, he'd been trying to play it cool all day. Actually, he'd been trying not to think about tonight so he wouldn't slip up in any way. But as the day had moved along, he'd started to run over his plans in his head to make sure he hadn't missed anything, and now that it was here... *I'm nervous as hell.*

"I'm surprised you're not jumping out of the car." Tate's voice pulled Logan from his thoughts and had him turning his head to face him. He looked damn near perfect sitting behind the wheel of his chromed-up and polished muscle car.

In a pair of faded ripped jeans, a simple white V-neck Henley, and his leather jacket—the one with the patch on the sleeve—Tate was sexy as hell. All Logan could think as he looked at those windblown waves of his was, *James Dean, eat your fucking heart out.*

"Logan?"

"Huh? What'd you say?"

Tate started laughing. "I said I'm surprised you're not jumping out of the car. You were in such a hurry to get here so we could leave."

That was half true. Logan *had* been in a hurry to get to the condo, but not for the reason Tate thought—though *that* idea in his head now was a difficult one to push aside.

He'd actually been in a hurry because he'd texted Cole as they'd been leaving so his brother could get inside and put the final things in order, and when he'd text Logan back to say it was done, well, they couldn't dawdle after that.

"It's been a long day, that's all." Logan added a wink, and when Tate leaned across the car as though he were going to kiss him, Logan reached for the door handle. *If he puts his mouth on me here, we are* not *going to leave the damn car.* He pushed open his door. "Don't try to distract me. Out. Now."

Tate chuckled. "Fine. Have it your way. If you don't want me to kiss you, I'll just save it for someone who does."

Like hell. Logan moved so fast then that Tate barely had time to blink. He grabbed a fistful of that white Henley and one side of Tate's leather jacket and yanked him across the console. As Logan crushed his mouth over the top of Tate's, a growl left him and went straight to Logan's balls. *Christ, this is not part of the plan, Mitchell.* But when Tate's hands came up and cupped either side of his face, any and all plans flew the fuck out of his brain.

Tate's tongue in his mouth had Logan's temperature spiking in an instant, and Tate's hand reaching between them was almost enough for Logan to shove Tate's seat back so he could unzip him and suck the cock he knew would be hard as a rock in those jeans but…it was the vibrating in his pocket that finally had Logan putting a palm to Tate's chest and gently pushing him back.

When Tate's eyes found his, they were dark with desire and wild with a need Logan wanted to fulfill. But before he did any of that, he said, "I want you upstairs." And he really meant it.

More than he wanted his next breath, Logan wanted Tate upstairs and in the place they had lived for the past four years so he could finally make him his in all possible ways.

* * *

TATE BLINDLY REACHED behind him for the handle of his door, not willing to take his eyes from Logan's until he absolutely had to. That kiss had been something else. And the way Logan was looking at him right now was… *Damn*, it was making his heart trip as much as it was making his cock throb.

"You need to get out of the car," Logan said.

"I am."

"No, you're not."

Tate nodded but didn't move, and when a small

smile played on Logan's lips, Tate's heart did that funny skip-a-beat thing again.

"Get out of the car, Tate."

Tate bit his lower lip but then pushed down on the handle and tore his eyes from Logan. This was the last time they were ever going to be at the condo alone, and if Logan wanted him upstairs one final time? Then he sure as hell was going to get his ass out of the car and into that elevator.

He shoved open the door and was out and shutting it behind him as Logan walked around the hood of the Mustang and waited. As Tate got closer, he noticed Logan's jeans weren't doing shit to hide the erection he was sporting, but they looked *good* on him with the black tee he'd worn today. Right now, he also had on a Northwestern University full zip hoodie that he'd left undone, and for some reason this particular outfit was hands down one of the sexiest things Tate had ever seen him wear.

"You've *got* to stop looking at me like that," Logan said when Tate stopped opposite him.

"Why?" Tate took hold of either side of Logan's hoodie. "Don't you like how I'm looking at you?"

Logan put his hands on top of his. "I like it too damn much."

"Then what's the problem?"

"No problem." Logan chuckled, as Tate brushed their lips together. "You are so impatient tonight."

Tate bit Logan's bottom lip, and when he groaned, Tate smiled against his mouth. "Yeah, I am." He saw Logan swallow, and then took a step back and held his hand out.

"Then let's go upstairs."

Tate narrowed his eyes slightly. He'd fully expected to have to fight to keep his clothes on as they made their way upstairs after that blistering kiss in the car. But as he slipped his hand into Logan's and they headed to the elevator, Logan remained quiet.

What's going on with him? Tate thought, as Logan punched the up button and then swept his thumb over the pulse point of Tate's wrist, making a shiver race up his spine.

When they stepped into the elevator and the doors shut, Tate leaned up against the back wall and Logan moved to stand beside him, and they each watched the numbers above the doors light up.

As they went from the parking levels to the lobby, Tate grinned. "I remember the first time I ever got into this elevator." Logan's eyes found his, and Tate winked. "I was so damn nervous."

Logan scoffed, and knowing what he was likely thinking, Tate rolled his eyes at himself. "I know. I know. It's crazy to think about now. But I swear, it took hours for this elevator to reach your floor that night."

"*Our* floor. And I think it still does," Logan said, frowning, and Tate looked back at the numbers.

"You called me that night. Do you remember?"

"Yes," Logan said. "I thought you got lost."

"Liar. You were just impatient."

The elevator reached their floor and dinged, and when the doors slid open, Logan said, "I still am."

And as Logan led him out into the hallway, Tate decided he had absolutely no problem with that.

* * *

LOGAN REMINDED HIMSELF to breathe as he stopped at their front door and pulled his keys from his pocket. Tate was standing so close behind him that Logan could feel his breath on the back of his neck, and he knew Tate had no idea what was planned.

It appeared Tate thought exactly what Logan wanted him to. That he was bringing him up here for one final "goodbye" to the place—and in a way, he was. Just not the goodbye the gorgeous man behind him expected.

Tate's hands on his waist had Logan's shaking a little as he inserted the key and unlocked the door. He could feel the rigid length of Tate's arousal against his behind, and it was taking all of Logan's control not to take care of that first and then maybe ask this next question when Tate was in a state of euphoria. But when he'd gotten out of the car, Logan had quickly checked his phone to see the text that had come through from Cole: **We just left. Everything is set. Good luck. Call us when it's official.** And Logan knew there was no turning back.

As he pushed open the door, he stepped aside, and Tate walked around him and gave a deliciously salacious grin before running his fingers down Logan's chest, then he turned and headed inside. Logan shut the door and followed, and as he got down the hall and into the living space, he took in a seriously unsteady breath.

Cole and Rachel had done good. They'd followed his request to a tee, and as Logan's eyes adjusted to the lit candles placed all around the living room floor, across the kitchen island, and by the door that led out to the balcony, he finally noticed that Tate had stopped dead center and was silent.

Okay, this is it, Logan thought, as he slipped his hand into the pocket of his hoodie and felt around for the box. Once his fingers were wrapped around it, he took the final steps so he could reach out and get Tate's attention.

Finally, he turned around. Tate's mouth was tipped up on one side in a crooked kind of smile, and he had a look of confusion on his face as Logan took a step toward him.

Logan swallowed, knowing it was now or never, and lowered to one knee, determined to do this right. Determined to make it perfect. As soon as his knee touched the hardwood and his eyes found Tate's, Logan saw his feet falter. Tate's crooked grin turned to a slack jaw, and then he blinked a couple of times.

Logan turned the box over in his pocket before he cleared his throat and said, "Tate."

When Tate said nothing in response, letting his eyes scan around the room again before coming back to Logan wide and even more confused, Logan started again.

"Tate..." When his voice trembled, Logan cleared his throat. He'd never had so much trouble getting words out of his mouth in his life. "Tonight when we were coming up here, it was funny you brought up the first time you came to this place, because over the past few months, that's all I've been able to think about."

"Logan, I—"

"Please," Logan said. "Let me get this out or I just might forget something important, and when it comes to you, everything's important. Four years ago, when I met you, I never could have imagined that this is where it would lead me." As Tate stared down, Logan saw his Adam's apple bob, so he took the hand by Tate's side and laced his fingers through Tate's. "I had a plan for my life. Rules and a motto I lived by, because that's the way I am. I like to research things. I like facts. And I liked knowing where I was going. But after one conversation with you, those rules and motto, they changed. And after a *month* of knowing you, they no longer existed. Instead, you became my plan."

Tate shook his head a little and then looked around again. But when Logan gently squeezed his fingers, Tate brought his focus back to him, and Logan continued.

"We both know I'm a little slow on the uptake when it comes to relationships and settling down. But I'd like to think that's changed. Actually, I *know* it's changed." Logan drew Tate's hand up to his lips and shut his eyes as he kissed it. "I love you, Tate. You changed my life's plan in the best way possible and made me want things I've never wanted before—with you."

Logan took the small box out of his pocket, flipped it open, and looked up to lock eyes with Tate. "William Tate Morrison, will you marry me?"

Logan's heart was thumping so loudly he wished he could stop it for a second so he wouldn't miss Tate's reply as he came down to his knees opposite him. Now, face to face, it was easier to see Tate's features in the flickering light of the candles, and they looked...strained. And when a tear slipped free of those blurry brown eyes that Logan loved so much, Tate whispered, "No."

Logan got his wish then.

His heart stopped.

And then it shattered.

Part Two

Us:

You & Me

Chapter Fifteen

ONE HEARTBEAT.

  TWO *heartbeats.*

  Three...

  Tate counted the pounding of his heart as he watched the man kneeling opposite him. It was the only way he was convinced he was still alive as he waited there in the dead silence that had now engulfed the room.

  You need to say something, he told himself as he blinked, trying to clear his eyes. Jesus, he was crying again. But one look at Logan's collapsed shoulders and bent head as he twisted the small box in his hands had them blurring all over again.

  He couldn't believe what had just happened. Was still trying to wrap his brain around it even as he saw a wall being laid brick by brick between Logan and himself with every second he didn't open his mouth and speak.

  You need to fucking say something. "Logan—"

  Logan flinched, and it was like Tate had fired a gun. Reaching out, thinking if he could maybe touch Logan it would be easier to somehow explain what was going through his head, Tate went for his hands. But before his fingers touched skin, Logan shot up to his feet.

The action was so sudden that it jolted Tate and had his head snapping up to follow Logan's movement. But there wasn't much after that. Logan may have been on his feet, but he went no further. He had his left hand over his mouth and was staring out at the balcony behind Tate in complete silence.

Get up. Get. Up, Tate thought. *If you don't get up, he's going to leave before you have a chance to*— But before he could move, Logan had turned on his heels and was, *fuck,* heading for the door.

Tate scrambled to his feet and went after him, and just as Logan hit the foyer, he managed to get a hand around his arm. "Logan, wait. I—"

Logan spun on him, and what Tate saw had his words coming to an abrupt halt. Logan's blue eyes were full of tears, glistening in the candlelight, but his jaw was bunched and he was fighting them. Fighting them with every fiber of his being.

Tate swallowed, trying to think of what he'd been about to say, but nothing came until Logan jerked his arm away from him. "Logan—"

"Don't." The word was so quiet that Tate almost missed it. Quiet and final.

"But I—"

"I said *don't.*" Logan's focus was off over Tate's shoulder now, anywhere but at him. "Don't speak. Don't explain. I asked you a question," he said, and when his eyes came back to Tate's, they were far away, distant. "And you gave me an answer."

Tate shook his head and reached for him again, but Logan took a step back. "It's just... Jesus, Logan. Give me a second to process. This is...was—"

"A mistake."

Tate's mouth parted at the frigid tone of Logan's voice, and he hated that he'd been the one to put it there. Because no matter what Logan was saying now, this was no mistake. Logan had carefully planned this out, and then Tate had come along and stomped all over it.

The candles...

The speech...

The ring...

Logan, the man who'd always claimed he would never settle down, *never* get married, had completely and utterly blindsided him.

Tate was desperately trying to think of the words to relay all that he was thinking, but it was difficult when *this* hadn't even been on his radar. Not even close. On the list of things he thought would happen in his life, this ranked about *never*. Coupled with everything from the past week still weighing heavily on his mind, the magnitude of what had just happened here... What was *still* happening, as Logan seemed to be disconnecting from him with every second that passed... *God*, it was all too much.

"Logan. You've got to let me—"

"What, Tate?" Logan asked. "I've got to let you

what? Explain? No, thanks. I don't need you to explain to
me the fundamentals of the word *no*. I'm a pretty smart
guy." He paused and then added, "Most of the time."

As Logan turned away again, Tate lunged for him
and yanked him back around so they were toe to toe, not
willing to let him leave like this. Not yet.

"Let me go, Tate."

Tate's fingers clenched in the material of Logan's
hoodie, and he shook his head. He couldn't let him leave like
this. Not without explaining. But Logan was done listening;
Tate could tell by the cool detachment of his expression.

"Let. Me. Go." Logan brought a hand up to the fistful
of material Tate had and pulled it free, then he immediately
released him as though Tate's skin had burned him—and
really, he had, hadn't he?

Without another word, Logan turned on his heel and
headed for the door. With every step he took, the distance
yawned wide between them, until Tate felt as though he'd
never be able to reach him again.

When the door opened, he called out Logan's name a
final time, but wasn't shocked by the lack of response,
because who could hear the shout of someone you'd left a
million miles behind?

* * *

LOGAN WASN'T SURE how he'd ended up down at
Belmont Harbor, but as the wind howled around him and he

stared out into the vast darkness where the boats were
moored, the miserable October night matched his mood.

Numb. He was completely and utterly numb on the
inside and out.

Tate had said no.

Logan shut his eyes as he replayed the scene in his
head, unable to comprehend what he knew to be true. But
each time the rerun ended, the outcome was the same. Him,
eagerly awaiting the one word that would make his world
perfect, only to be given one that had instantly devastated it.

Tate said no.

He studied the hands he had braced on the railing,
and figured the chill of the night should actually *hurt* as he
stood there. But not even the sting of the night's
precipitation was penetrating the pain that had radiated
from his heart to every fiber of his body until it had decided
to just switch off and not feel at all.

How had this gone so horribly wrong? How had he
totally misread where Tate was at? How he felt about him?
Them… *Us.*

As he thought about what that meant for them,
Logan's chest tightened and he tried to swallow in a gulp of
air. As the frigid temperature hit his throat, he coughed
violently, and thought he was perilously close to drowning
right there on dry land.

Bringing his hands up to his face, he pressed his
fingertips to his mouth and squeezed his eyes shut, and he
couldn't decide if he was trying to hold back a cry or shout

as his body started to shake and the tears he'd been keeping inside finally fell free.

As the anguish, heartbreak, and total fucking disappointment of the night hit him, Logan's stomach twisted until he thought he was going to be sick. *Fuck.*

He grabbed the railing and bent over it as his stomach convulsed, but when nothing happened, he just stayed there staring at his reflection in the water.

Tate said no.

And as Logan stood there looking at a man who no longer had a clue where his life was going, he heard himself ask, "Why?"

* * *

IT HAD BEEN nearly an hour since Logan had left the condo, and as Tate sat on the floor in the foyer where he'd kind of fallen earlier, he noticed some of the candles closest to him had started to drip wax onto the floor.

He'd been staring at his phone ever since the door had shut behind Logan and he'd pulled it out to call him. But there'd been no return call and no text. Not that he'd expected one.

He still couldn't believe what had happened tonight. One minute they'd been fooling around in the car and heading upstairs, and the next—*Logan asked me to marry him.* He still couldn't fully comprehend it. *Logan* wanted to get married. *Since when?*

Marriage was a notion Tate had never entertained when it came to the two of them, because he knew how against the idea Logan had always been. And it wasn't only him—Tate had his own issues when it came to that particular institution, so he'd never really minded Logan's aversion to it.

But tonight, when he'd walked inside the condo and seen all the candles and then turned to find Logan down on one knee, all of the *issues* he had chosen not to deal with had come charging to the forefront and left his mouth with one word—*no*.

Goddamn it. How was he ever going to explain this to Logan? Would he even get a chance to? The look on his face when he'd left didn't give Tate much hope. It had been full of anger, hurt, and something that had wrenched at Tate— betrayal. Logan had looked at Tate as though he didn't know who he was. As though he'd never seen him before.

Tate looked at his phone again, and when he saw the blank screen, he shook his head and finally got to his feet. *He's not going to call you, you fucking idiot. He doesn't even want to look at you right now.*

Shoving off the wall, he flicked the light switch and winced as his eyes adjusted to the bright glare. Then he took in the empty living room, the bare kitchen, and the doors that led into the study and their bedroom, and Tate found himself thinking back to earlier in the night, when they'd been reminiscing about the first time he'd ever come up to this place.

"Where are you, Tate?"

Tate bumped the helmet against his thigh. "Standing at your door."

He could hear shuffling through the phone and presumed Logan was moving closer to open it.

"And how does it look from out there? I always thought it was pretty boring—cream paint, doorknob, standard black peephole to look at strange men lurking in front of my place."

Tate felt the corner of his mouth tilt up. "I'm not lurking."

"But you've been standing there for the last—"

"Five minutes," Tate said.

"Ah. And?"

Closing his eyes, Tate tried to think of a response.

"You sure you're ready for me to open the door, Tate?"

That night he hadn't been sure of anything other than his need to see the man on the other side of that door, and from the moment he'd walked inside, his entire life had changed course. And tonight, Logan had opened yet another one.

Tate blew the candles out one at a time, and once they were all extinguished, he headed to the balcony door and slid it open to let the smoke escape. As it spiraled and swirled out into the night, ghosts from their past continued to haunt him.

He could still see the two of them out there that first night, or over on Logan's couch, and ever since then, all of the days and nights in between. Tate shoved a hand through his hair as he slid the door shut and turned his back on those thoughts.

God, the place felt empty all of a sudden. And it wasn't just the lack of furniture or their belongings. It was the essence that Logan brought there. His fire, his spirit—it felt as though it had been snuffed out, and it was as though he'd packed up all of the good memories they'd shared there and taken them right out the door—and Tate hated himself for that.

Unable to stand the screaming silence any longer, Tate pulled his phone out and called the only person he figured would understand where he was coming from, and when the phone connected, he let out a shaky sigh of relief. "Dad? Can I come over?"

* * *

LOGAN SAT ON one of the benches down at the harbor and focused on, well, nothing in particular. At some point he'd staggered over to the seat under one of the lampposts and made himself zip up his hoodie so he wouldn't catch pneumonia, and as he watched the boats bob with the ebb and flow of tonight's swell, he felt his phone vibrate for what seemed like the millionth time.

He'd thought about turning it off the first few times Tate had called, but then he'd shoved it into his pocket and forgotten it was even there. The problem was, whoever was calling him this time wasn't letting up, and because it was annoying the shit out of him, Logan pulled the damn thing out of his pocket, determined to turn it off, but then he saw a name he hadn't expected—Will Morrison.

Tate's dad? What the— And then, of course, his brain went straight *there*. Straight to the horror that had unfolded in his life, and Will's, four years ago. And not even caring what had happened earlier, Logan answered the phone and brought it to his ear, needing to know Tate was safe.

"Wi…Will…" When his voice cracked around Tate's father's name, Logan cleared his throat and tried again. "Will? Hey."

"Logan. Oh, good, you answered."

Logan's mind was racing with possibilities as to why Will had been calling him so insistently, until finally he had to ask the only thing he really cared about at that point. "Is everything okay? Tate isn't hurt—"

"Oh no, no. Nothing like that, son."

Son… Where that word had made his heart ache with a sense of happiness and fulfillment just last weekend, hearing it now made it ache from the pain of knowing he'd never really be this man's son in any legal way. *Because Tate said no.*

"Logan?"

Logan blinked and rubbed at his chin. "Sorry, what did you say?"

"I… Are you all right?" Will paused, and when Logan didn't immediately answer, he continued, "Did I catch you at a bad time?"

Yes. Your son just tore my heart out and I'm trying to work out how to function without it. "No, I...I was just out for a walk. That's all. Was there something you needed?"

"Oh, uhh." Will procrastinated then, and when he spoke again, Logan knew why. Tate's father had finally clued in that something was up between Logan and his boy. "I just got off the phone with Tate. He's on his way over here, but he sounded, I don't know, strange, uhh...upset. He wouldn't say why, but I thought maybe it was his sister."

Until you spoke to me, Logan thought. *Well, at least I know where Tate's going to be tonight.* He shut his eyes and tipped his face up to the night sky, and as he did, a fat drop of rain hit him in the center of the forehead. *Shit.* He needed to answer Will. "I... I think you need to talk to Tate."

There was silence at the other end for a second, and then Will said, "Logan?"

Logan bit down on the inside of his cheek, not wanting this man to be nice to him. Not while he was feeling so open, so...vulnerable. "Yeah?"

"Are you okay?"

The tears Logan thought he'd cried out started up again, and as he swiped at them, he said, "No. I don't think I am."

There was a scraping sound, and Logan could imagine Will taking a seat at his kitchen island. "Where are you?"

As several more drops hit him, Logan said, "Belmont Harbor."

"Look…" Will stopped whatever he'd been about to say and let out a sigh. "I don't know what's going on here with you or Tate. But I want you to go home, Logan. Whatever it is, you two will deal with it, but it's miserable out tonight, and with Tate on his way here, I won't feel comfortable ending this call until I know you're going to be safe too."

Logan tried not to let Will's concern gut him, but it was no use. He was too raw right then to protect himself. He ran a hand over his face and made himself stand. "Okay. I'm going."

"Good. Oh, and Logan?"

"Hmm?"

"Whatever's going on, you'll work it out. You two always do."

Yeah, he wasn't sure how you worked something like *this* out. How did he ever stop seeing Tate's confusion, and how did he ever stop hearing no? "I'm going to go, Will."

"Logan?"

Logan had started walking back along the trail with his hand shoved in his pocket as the rain fell a little harder, and all he could think was, *Let me go… Please let me go before I hear Tate walk through your door. Before I hear his voice again.*

"Text me when you get home. I won't tell him it's you. I just want to know you're safe."

Logan bit his tongue and nodded, and when he realized he actually had to give a verbal answer, he said, "Okay," and then ended the call.

Chapter Sixteen

BY THE TIME Tate pulled into his father's driveway, the sky had opened up and the rain was beating down on top of the Mustang—*because what better way to end this night.*

As he cut the engine, he was surprised to see the porch light switched on and his father pushing open the front door to step out onto the porch. Tate hadn't said much on the phone when they'd spoken, just that he wanted to come over. But before he had ended the call, his father had asked if he was okay, obviously sensing something was wrong. *He's probably been waiting for me to show up in one piece ever since.*

Tate ran a hand through his hair, and when he lowered it and saw that it was shaking, he clenched a fist. He looked through the rain pelting his windshield and saw his father had moved to the railing and put his hands there as he stared down at the car, and Tate took in a deep breath.

Grabbing his phone from the center console, he checked it again on the off chance Logan might've called, and when nothing was there, he slipped it in his jacket pocket and shoved open the car door. He tugged the side of the leather over his head and jogged to the stairs and out of the rain, and when his feet hit the landing and he lowered the coat, his father turned to face him.

"Rough night?" he asked, and Tate got the feeling he was talking about more than the weather.

"Yeah." Tate looked out at the rain, now falling so hard it was difficult to see his car. "It went to shit pretty fast."

His dad reached out and patted his arm before he headed to the front door and held it open. "Why don't you come in and get out of those boots and jacket and tell me about it?"

Tate stopped before heading inside. And with a directness he'd learned from this very man, Tate looked into his father's eyes and finally said out loud the one thing he knew to be true right then: "I fucked up tonight."

His dad nodded, and his eyes were grave. "Come on. Let's get you inside and a drink in hand. Then we'll talk."

Tate hoped it would be that easy. But somehow, he didn't think it would be to find the words he needed to say.

* * *

WHEN THE UBER pulled up at nineteen sixty-six Evergreen Avenue, Logan looked out the window and grimaced at the rain, which was now coming down in sheets. He'd hoped it would let up a little on the way over there, but if anything, it had just gotten harder.

Knowing he had no other choice than to make a run

for it, he got out his keys and found the shiny new brass one that Tate had added to his keychain earlier that morning. Logan took his glasses off and slipped them into the pocket of his hoodie.

"Glad it's you and not me," his driver said, and when Logan met his eyes in the rearview mirror, he shrugged.

"Just kind of how my night's been going."

"If that's the case, probably best you're home."

Logan looked out at the two-story home behind the iron fence, and his eyes went straight to the porch light that shone like a lighthouse through a storm. But instead of feeling as though it were guiding him safely home, he remembered kissing Tate earlier that afternoon when he'd switched it on, and felt as though his heart was being pounded against the sharpest of rocks.

"Right," Logan murmured, then opened the car door and made a run for it. Within seconds, he was inside and shutting the door behind him, and as he turned the lock, Logan stood frozen in place, not wanting to turn around, not wanting to see the large, empty house that had his and Tate's belongings scattered about it.

There goes the stomach again, he thought, as he rested his forehead against the door and shut his eyes, his hand still fastened to the doorknob. *Damn it.* Shoving away from the door, he refused to look at the living room, instead choosing to go up to the rooms they hadn't started unpacking yet.

He took the stairs two at a time, and as he walked

down the quiet hallway, he allowed himself to think about what Tate might be telling his father right then. But he didn't have a clue. Not really. He still didn't understand everything that had happened tonight, so how could he begin to guess what Tate was sharing with dear old dad?

When Logan got to their new bedroom, he stopped by the door and took in the unmade bed and frame that had been brought upstairs first thing this morning, and the boxes stacked one of top of the other in the corner marked *main bedroom, Tate's clothes,* and *Logan's clothing department*—and it was shit like that, the jokes, the hints of *them,* that cut the deepest.

He tore his eyes away, figuring he'd find something dry to wear in one of the boxes by the oversized chair they'd also had brought upstairs. And as Logan headed over there, he stripped out of his wet hoodie and then toed off his soaked Nikes. His eyes flicked to the naked mattress and then the headboard of their bed, and he shook his head. There was no way he was going to lie down on that bed tonight, *no fucking way.*

This was not how he'd expected to spend their— *his*—first night in their house, and as he pulled open one of the boxes and rifled through the contents, he saw it was one of Tate's, and he seriously contemplated going down to the kitchen and searching for a bottle of something to drink.

Deciding alcohol wasn't the answer, he fingered a pair of grey sweats and red t-shirt and pulled them up to his nose to take a deep inhale before shutting his eyes.

"Damn you," he whispered into the fabric that smelled exactly like the man he was cursing. "Damn you, William Tate Morrison."

* * *

"SO..." TATE'S DAD said from where he sat in his recliner. "It's been a little over thirty minutes and you haven't said a word."

Tate stared into the tumbler of whiskey his father had given him when he'd first gotten there. But as soon as Tate had sat down on the far end of one of the loveseats, he'd forgotten all about it, too busy remembering the last time he'd sat in that very spot and Logan had been beside him, supporting him as he dealt with—

"Tate?"

"Huh?" he said, and finally looked over at his dad.

"What the hell is going on? Why isn't Logan with you?"

Tate swallowed and finally made himself move, putting the tumbler on the side table beside the couch— untouched. He bent forward, rested his forearms on his knees, and put his face in his hands. "Honestly," he said, and then turned to his dad, "I don't know where he is."

Tate thought he saw his father's eyes narrow a fraction, but he'd already looked away, not sure he could say what he was about to while looking at his dad.

"I don't understand. Did something happen between

you two?"

Yes, Tate thought, staring down at the hands he couldn't stop twisting together. *Yes, it fucking did.*

"Tate?" his dad said, more forcefully this time. "What happ—"

"Logan asked me to marry him."

When silence was all that followed, Tate turned his head back in his dad's direction to see him shuffling forward to the edge of his seat. He looked completely and utterly dumbfounded, and as his mouth opened and then shut again, Tate shook his head. *Well, that shut him up.*

Several minutes passed, and when his father had apparently processed what Tate had just told him, he said, "Did you just say that Logan asked you to marry him? *Logan?* The same guy who—"

"Used to break out in a cold sweat whenever the word *marriage* was mentioned? Yes, that's what I said."

"Wow," his dad said, and then slumped back in his chair.

Wow is right, Tate thought, and then pictured Logan as he'd been when he'd asked him. There'd been no cold sweats tonight—not from Logan, anyway. He'd been so sure of himself.

So open.

So vulnerable.

And so damn beautiful as he'd knelt at Tate's feet and completely shaken the ground he stood on.

"I was not expecting that." His dad rubbed a hand

over his lips then sat up and pinned Tate with the same look that had always made him tell the truth as a child. "And you said no."

Tate dropped his head into his hands and shut his eyes, hating that word now more than ever before. He gripped his hair in his hands as hard as he could, thinking that maybe if he caused himself pain, it would somehow stop the heartache that came from his father's words—*no, from my own words*—but it didn't help. It still felt as though it was being torn from his chest.

With his head down, Tate didn't see his father walk over to him until the cushion beside him dipped, and a large palm settled on his back. Then Tate looked up at him and nodded slowly. "I said no."

* * *

LOGAN SETTLED INTO the chair he'd turned to face the window, and propped his feet up on the box he'd taken Tate's clothes out of. Now dry in the sweats and t-shirt, he watched the rain hitting the glass and running in rivulets down the pane.

It was kind of ironic, Logan thought, that this would be the perfect weather for a romantic night. But considering he was now sitting alone trying not to think about how much his eyes stung from tears and his stomach ached from anxiety, it just seemed like a cruel twist of fate.

He'd turned his phone off around five minutes ago

after texting Will to let him know he was home, because he didn't want to wait around to see if he would answer. Didn't want to risk Tate calling or texting him, either. He needed some time to think about what all this meant. But Logan also knew he wouldn't really be able to understand or deal with it fully until he talked to Tate, and he just wasn't ready yet.

He scooted down into the chair and rested his head against the soft cushion. How was it that something that had never overly mattered to him before was now making him so fucking miserable because he was being denied it?

He wasn't sure. But as he drifted off, Logan wondered if the hollow feeling inside his chest would ever go away...

"LOGAN? LOGAN, WAIT up, would you," his asshole half-brother, Cole, called out as Logan booked it down the hallway of Christopher Walker's dorm and headed for the double doors that would lead him out to the campus grounds. He needed to get the fuck out of there, and fast, after that very public—not to mention humiliating—rejection from Chris.

The last thing Logan wanted was a post-smackdown convo with Cole, who for some reason had chosen today to give a shit that he even existed. Not exactly the brotherly bonding moment I had in mind, *Logan thought, as he tried to imagine telling the straight ass still calling out his name that he liked dick.*

When he finally reached the double doors, Logan shoved them open and didn't bother looking back as they shut and locked behind him. He practically ran down the stairs, deciding to head to the library, since it was only one building over, when again, he heard his name being shouted. Jesus, why won't Cole just fuck off?

Logan put his head down, determined to ignore him, and then made a turn to take the path up to the library stairs. He was about halfway up them when he felt a hand on his arm jerking him around, and when he came to a stop on the stair above Cole, Logan glared down at him.

"Hey, I've been calling out to you," Cole said. "Didn't you hear me?"

"I heard. I was just choosing to ignore you."

"That's real mature, Logan."

Logan pulled his arm free of Cole's grasp. "Hmm, ask me how much I care."

As Logan whirled around to continue up to the library, Cole was right there beside him. But before he got the door open, Cole grabbed one of the straps of his backpack and tugged him off to the side.

"Look, dipshit," Cole said, and Logan tilted his head to glare up at him. "I just saved your ass back there."

Logan regarded Cole closely and decided, right then, Might as well get this out in the open, since he pretty much already despises me. *"Trust me, my ass was the one thing back there that would've been happy* not *to be saved. But thanks for finally stepping up, and, you know, being a decent human being for a change."*

Cole's eyes narrowed, and Logan waited for the light bulb moment.

One...

Two...

Thre—

"Wait up. You and Chris were...are..."

"Fucking?" Logan said, and Cole blinked at him like a deer caught in headlights. "If that's what you're trying to say—and failing at spectacularly, I might add—then yes." Logan leaned in close to Cole. "We were. Are you scandalized?"

Cole shoved him in the arm, and as Logan took a step back, he smirked, masking his nerves with bravado as he stood there waiting to see if Cole would make a move to punch him, just like that asshole Chris had.

But Cole didn't raise his arm, didn't ball his fist. "I don't give a shit who you're fucking."

Logan opened his mouth with an automatic go to hell at the ready. But as Cole's words sank in, he found himself wide-eyed and shocked. "Really?"

Cole crossed his arms. "You know, I was coming to find you today because after months of you being a pain in the ass, I thought it could be cool to hang out. Then I see you getting beat up by Christopher Walker, who you now tell me you're fucking like it's some kind of accomplishment." Cole leaned in and pointed in Logan's face. "But listen to me, brother. Your boyfriend is bad fucking news. He has a reputation, and I don't want anything to do with him."

"Neither do I anymore. And he's not my boyfriend," Logan said quickly, even though for a while there he'd hoped that Chris could become just that.

Cole raised one of his blond eyebrows, studying Logan in a way that made him fidgety. "Really?"

"Really," Logan said, thinking about the hateful words that had come out of Chris's mouth, not to mention the fact he'd been going to hit him to save face. "I don't do boyfriends. Or girlfriends, since we're on the topic."

Cole looked unconvinced, but the more Logan talked, the more he liked this new resolve of his.

Yeah, fuck Christopher Walker. *He didn't need some declaration of undying love to make him happy. He just wanted to enjoy his life. Be able to do what he wanted* when *he wanted, and that included people. Boyfriends, girlfriends — they just made shit messy, and from here on out, he was done with that.*

"If you don't do relationships, then what do *you do?" Cole said, looking genuinely curious.*

Logan thought about that and shrugged, liking this new idea more and more. "Whatever, and whoever, I want. Try a little, take a lot if I like them, and make sure I'm the one who comes out on top in the end. Each and every time."

Yeah, that sounds like a good motto to live by. And never *ever* let someone have the power to break my heart again...

LOGAN WOKE WITH such a start that his feet fell off the box they'd been propped up on and landed on the hardwood with a thud.

Shit. He hadn't thought about Chris and, well, *any* of that stuff for years. It made sense that it was on his mind tonight, though. Chris had been the catalyst when it came to him and relationships, and it wasn't until Tate that Logan had really let his walls down, and now...

And now what? Logan thought with a mocking laugh. *There's no way I'm going anywhere without Tate, so that stupid motto can just fuck the hell off.* And that was it, wasn't it? That was what the dream had really meant. Logan put his feet back up and settled into the chair again.

That day with Chris had been a turning point for him. A moment that had led him down a path until Tate, and then that gorgeous, stubborn man had stopped Logan in his tracks and made him choose a different road.

As Logan sat there thinking about the one who owned not only the clothes he was currently wearing, but also half of the house he was sitting in, Logan knew he needed to talk to Tate. He needed to understand what was going on, because he had no idea, and until he did, the two of them were going nowhere, and that just wouldn't work for him.

* * *

"TATE."

TATE HEARD his father say his name but didn't respond, too busy hearing his own confession over and over in his head. But then his dad shifted closer to him and said, "It's okay, son. You were allowed to say no."

And it was *that* comment that snapped Tate back to

reality. He got to his feet and looked down at where his father was staring up at him with a troubled look on his face.

Tate began to shake his head. "It's not okay. You don't understand— Oh God. I feel like I'm going to be sick," he said, and put a hand to his stomach.

His father got to his feet and reached out to touch his shoulder. "Breathe. Deep breath in, then let it out."

As Tate did just that, he placed a hand on his father's arm and bent at the waist as the room began to spin. Jesus, this house was starting to really mess with his damn head whenever he set foot in it.

When he finally got his stomach to calm a little, he looked to his father, who had a tight-lipped expression and that glint in his eye that told Tate he wasn't going to get away with the silent routine much longer.

"Right," his dad said. "You need to start talking. Help me understand what is going on."

Tate swallowed and nodded, then brought a hand to his mouth and rubbed it across his lips, as though it would erase what they'd said earlier that night. But it was too late for that. What was done was done. So finally, he spoke. "I didn't mean to say no."

When his dad frowned, Tate ran a hand through his hair and tried to organize his thoughts.

"I don't understand."

"I *know*," Tate said as he spun away and then blurted out, "Neither do I. It was like one minute we were fooling around in the car, and the next we walked into some kind of alternate universe where Logan—*Logan*—was down on one knee with a ring in his hand. There were candles and…and…it was perfect. *He* was perfect, and I…" Tate turned back to face his dad. "I freaked out."

His dad came over, put a hand on either arm, and looked him dead in the eye. "Why?"

Tate shrugged, but his dad shook his head.

"No. That's not good enough. Not for this. *Why*, Tate? Why would you tell Logan no, when I know how much you love that man and want to marry him?"

Tate blinked, trying to keep focus, and then finally he said the one thing that had him so scared. "Because I can't fail again at this, Dad. Not with him. I wouldn't survive it."

Chapter Seventeen

LOGAN WOKE THE following morning when he went to shift in the chair and something in his back twisted. *Motherfucker*, he thought, and opened his eyes to see that the darkness that had surrounded him all night had now been replaced by an overeager sun.

With a hand to his lower back, he winced as he pushed himself up to sitting. *I feel like an old damn man. But in hindsight, sleeping in a chair probably wasn't the best idea.* As he cracked his stiff neck, Logan turned it from side to side to try and loosen it up, but when his eyes landed on the man seated at the edge of their unmade bed, he came to an abrupt halt.

Tate.

The pain in his back was forgotten in an instant as Logan stared across the several feet that separated them and wondered how long Tate had been sitting there. He looked like death warmed over, and even though it hurt worse than anything else then to see him there, to Logan he was the best fucking sight he'd ever seen.

Reaching for the glasses he'd put on one of the boxes beside him, Logan slipped them on and took in a fortifying breath, then turned so he was facing Tate head-on.

With more patience than he knew he possessed, Logan waited for Tate to look in his direction, and when he finally did and Logan saw the bloodshot eyes, the weary features, and the fear all over Tate's face, he wasn't sure he was ready for whatever was about to come next.

He swallowed, trying to unglue his tongue from the roof of his mouth so he could actually speak. "I, uhh, didn't hear you come in."

Tate chewed on his bottom lip. "Got here about an hour ago."

Fucking hell, this was painful to sit through. Logan had never felt so far away from Tate in his life, and just as he was about to say so, Tate stood. Logan looked up at him, and as Tate walked over and went down to his knees, Logan caught and held his breath.

He wasn't sure what to do with his hands as he sat there staring at the man only inches from him, and he hated that he was suddenly afraid to touch him. *And that's what I am, totally fucking terrified.* Because right then, Logan wasn't sure he could keep his shit together if he actually touched that silky brown hair.

"Tell me you don't hate me." Tate's words were so soft that Logan thought he'd imagined them, until he raised his face and pinned him with that bold and honest stare. "Tell me I didn't break this. Break us."

Always so brave, even when it hurts, Logan thought for the second time in a matter of weeks, and decided it was time for him to be too. He brought one of his hands forward and slid his palm along the dark stubble that Tate hadn't trimmed for a couple of days now. As soon as his fingers touched Tate's skin, he shut his eyes, and Logan bit his lip to stop himself from making a sound, allowing the reconnection to begin without words, since those were what had caused the disconnect in the first place.

Tate leaned into his hand as though Logan's touch was giving him life, and when his eyes reopened, Logan said, "I could *never* hate you. Not ever. But Tate…" He paused, gathering his nerve and some backbone to get out his next words. "I need some kind of explanation here. A reason. I always thought I was the one who didn't want this, not you—"

"It's Diana."

Logan froze, and when Tate didn't continue, he said, "I'm going to need more than that."

Tate nodded and reached up to where Logan's hand still rested, and when he brought it down and held it, Logan waited, not sure of what he was about to hear next.

* * *

TATE HADN'T BEEN sure what kind of reception he'd get from Logan when he showed up this morning. After the way things had been left the night before and the fact that Logan's phone had been sending him straight to voicemail, it could've gone one of two ways. But after spending the night at his father's and talking everything out, Tate had woken up this morning determined to go and find Logan.

Now here he was. Kneeling at Logan's feet and hoping that after he was done talking, Logan would somehow be able to forgive him. Tate looked up to find Logan's blue eyes trained on him like a laser, and he felt choked up, unable to speak.

Shit, why is this so fucking hard to say? But he knew he had to, so, gathering his nerve, he did. "I failed when it came to Diana."

He watched for some kind of reaction to his words, but Logan didn't move a muscle. The only telltale sign that he was still breathing was the ticking of his jaw, and Tate knew he needed to keep going. He needed to get this out so the man staring down at him wasn't wondering where his heart was at when it came to them, because it had never been more apparent to Tate that it was right there between them—in Logan's hands.

"I failed with our relationship," Tate said, and cleared his throat when it cracked. "And...I failed with our marriage. From the beginning to the end, I failed in ways I never thought myself capable of when it came to her."

When Logan made a move to pull his hand away, Tate tightened his grip. "Logan... You asked me for an explanation. And trust me, this isn't something I like talking about any more than you do, but—"

"*She's* the reason you're saying no to me now."

As Logan's eyes left his and he turned to look out the

window, Tate could see the confusion and disbelief etched
into his expression and knew that he was reliving
everything from last night.

Getting up on his knees, Tate reached for Logan's
chin and turned his face back to him. "What I said last night
was a knee-jerk reaction from panic. From...*fear.*"

Logan said nothing, just looked at him, clearly
waiting for more, and Tate knew he wasn't doing the best
job. It was hard to confess to someone as confident as Logan
that he was terrified of screwing up the thing in his life that
mattered the most.

He sat back on his heels and ran a hand through his
hair, frustrated for feeling the way he was, but at the same
time knowing he couldn't change it. And the only way
they'd be able to move past this was to get it out in the open
and deal with it.

"I was—*am*—scared, Logan. The entire time we've
been together, you've never talked about wanting to get
married. You've always been the one who refused to even
acknowledge the word. And I was okay with that. I'd never
try and change you or ask you to do something you didn't
want to, and my first go around was such a fucking disaster
that I certainly wasn't thinking about doing it again. But
then..."

"Then I changed the rules of the game." Logan held
his stare with such determination that Tate felt it in his
bones. Logan was still unsure of where he stood, and Tate
needed to make this clear as a bell so it didn't get

misconstrued in any way.

"This is not a game. *You* are not a game for me, Logan. I failed Diana from the beginning because I didn't love her. Not the way I'm supposed to." Tate licked his lips, worrying them as he carefully thought over his words. "With Diana, I never felt like half of me walked out the door when we would fight and she would leave. And I never missed her like it had been a year instead of one night if for some reason I had to be away from her."

He scooted forward until he was between Logan's legs, and when Logan went to move back in the chair, Tate took his hands and brought them to his lips. "I also never felt as though my heart would stop because I may have broken hers. But last night, knowing what I had done to you just about fucking killed me. I failed Diana because I didn't love her in half of the ways that I love you. And *that* is what made me panic." Tate kissed Logan's knuckles, apologizing without words for hurting him in ways he knew he would never be able to take back. And then he raised his eyes to Logan's and said, "What if I fail with you?"

* * *

LOGAN DIDN'T KNOW what to say as Tate knelt there staring up at him, but as he began to pull his hands free, Logan knew he had to move. Before he thought better of it, he slid forward on the chair and ran his hands through Tate's hair, allowing himself to savor the pleasure of finally having Tate back in front of him.

As Tate's words swirled around them, Logan let them drift off in the periphery as he trailed his fingers down one of Tate's cheeks and across his familiar lips, reminding himself that this face, this man, was everything to him, and that fact would never change, even though he was hurting.

He didn't want to think about Diana. Didn't want to think about a time where he wasn't the one that Tate was with. But even as he tried to ignore what he knew to be true, Logan was more than aware that he was trying to erase something he couldn't.

Diana was a reality that would never go away. She wasn't a fling. She wasn't merely a girlfriend. She had been Tate's wife. *His fucking wife.* And somewhere in there, Logan had allowed himself to conveniently forget she even existed.

With his hands still threaded through Tate's hair, Logan bent his head and rested his forehead on Tate's. "What if you don't fail?"

Tate wrapped his hands around Logan's wrists and gently tugged them down. "What if I do? What if it all goes to shit? Then what? You walk out the door? You divorce me?"

Logan was stunned and totally taken off guard by the very real and obvious fear in Tate's eyes—not to mention his words. Last night, Logan had been so consumed by his own hurt at Tate's rejection that he hadn't stuck around to listen, or hear, what had been behind it. And now as he looked into a face full of anxiety, full of apprehension, Logan felt guilty over his desertion.

Divorce? God, did Tate really think Logan would let him go anyfuckingwhere if he had a say in it? *Oh no, there'd be no divorce between us. There'd be no leaving of any kind, married or not.*

"Tate—"

"Logan. Don't tell me I'm being stupid. Up until last night, I didn't even know you *wanted* to get married," he said, and got to his feet. As Tate turned, Logan also stood. "You've always been the one who refused to even say the word, and now you're suddenly ready?"

Logan stared at Tate's broad shoulders and frowned. "People can change. I can. It isn't unheard of. I thought this is what you wanted?"

Tate whirled around and shook his head. "No. Don't do that. I would *never* want you to change for me. I would never ask you to."

"I know that."

"Do you?" Tate asked, and took a step forward that ate up the distance between them in an instant. "You've always told me that we didn't need a piece of paper, that we didn't need to be 'normal,' to be complete."

"I still think that." Logan could feel his irritation at last night, this conversation—and his own words being thrown back at him—rising. "But that doesn't mean I can't change my mind."

"And what's to say in a year you won't change it again?"

Logan's eyes narrowed to slits as he glared at the
man waiting for an answer, and he wondered if Tate was
really worried about that or if he was just running scared.
"Do you really see me changing my mind about you? About
us?"

"No," Tate said, jaw clenched, and then turned away.
"But I never saw you changing your mind to *this*, either.
And if you did? I can't even go there, Logan. You were in
that conference room. It was a fucking nightmare the first
time around. And I don't ever want to sit across some table
from you while we divide up our assets."

Logan grabbed his arm and spun him back to face
him. "Would you stop for a minute? You have us divorced
already and you haven't even said yes to marrying me in the
first place."

"Yeah, well, if you divorced me, I'd be fucked,
wouldn't I, since you own a law firm?"

Logan's emotions from last night and this morning
were roiling through him, and he told himself to keep a lid
on them, but with everything so close to the surface, he
failed. "I don't need to divorce you for that. But just so we're
clear, there's no way on God's green earth I'd let you leave
me for any reason other than one that's beyond my reach.
And even *then*, I'd put up a good fucking fight."

Annoyance flashed across Tate's eyes. "Christ, you're
arrogant."

"And you're stubborn. So do you really see either
one of us giving up on the other? *Ever?* I love you. Married

or not. But don't act like you aren't the one who's always told me it's not a bad thing to be like normal people."

The incredulity on Tate's face at that comment would've been laughable, had it not been directed at Logan.

"*Normal* people? This is what I mean. Since when has Logan Mitchell ever done anything normal?"

"Since yesterday, apparently. And look how well that turned out."

Tate let out a long sigh. "This is getting us nowhere."

"Agreed. So that's it, then. Topic is done and over with."

"No," Tate said. "The topic is not done."

"Have you changed your mind?" When Tate frowned, Logan shook his head. "Then it's done. I asked. You said no. And now I know why. We'll just chalk it up to a momentary lapse of insanity on my behalf."

God, he needed some space. He needed a minute or thirty on his own so he could process this without Tate's eyes on him. Two no's within twenty-four hours was about all his ego could take, and if he didn't get out of there, and fast, there was no telling where this heated argument would go.

He turned around, about to head into their new en suite, when he realized he didn't have clothes, there were no towels in there, and no damn soap. But before he could go and look for the box marked *bathroom*, Tate took his hand and pulled him back around.

"This topic is *not* done," Tate told him. "I want to

talk to you about it."

"And yet suddenly I no longer want to discuss it."

"Now who's being stubborn?"

"I call it self-preservation. There's only so many times I can hear you say no, Tate."

"That's not fair. Until yesterday, I didn't even know this was on your radar, and with everything else that's been going on this past week, you caught me off guard." Tate tugged him in close and fingered the hem of his shirt, and it was only then that Logan remembered he'd pulled these clothes out of Tate's box. "You don't get to take this off the table," Tate said. "You put it on there—"

"And you said no."

"And I told you why. I need time with this, Logan. I want to talk to you about it. Do you understand?"

He did, but at the same time, he didn't relish the idea of discussing something that might not ever happen. If he buried it now, and the conversation was over, he could forget how much he'd liked the idea and go back to his usual way of thinking. That way, this stabbing pain he felt every time he thought about last night would eventually dissipate—*right*?

"Well, do you mind if we talk about it later? I'm about tapped out right now."

Tate reluctantly let him go, but before Logan got far, Tate pointed to the clothes Logan was wearing. "Only thing you could find last night, huh?"

"No," Logan said as he headed to the boxes with his

name marked on them. "It was the closest thing to having you here. They smell like you."

"Logan?"

Logan stopped what he was doing and looked over his shoulder to where Tate still stood by the window with the sun making his curls shine. "Yeah?"

"Are we going to be okay?"

The worry on Tate's face hurt almost as much as the question, but no matter what had happened between them last night, there was no way Logan would ever let him think this, what they had, was broken. Maybe a little bent, but certainly not broken. "Yeah, Tate, we'll be okay."

Tate slipped his hands into his jeans and gestured to the door with his head. "I guess I'll go down and start unpacking."

And though it would've been so easy to invite Tate to join him in their new shower, Logan let him walk out the door, finding he needed a few minutes by himself to work out how to be *okay*.

Chapter Eighteen

TATE HEARD THE shower turn on upstairs and headed through the living room and into the kitchen. There were boxes all over the place. Some empty, some still taped shut, and some that had been left halfway unpacked when they'd left the house yesterday.

He stepped over some bubble wrap and headed toward the office that would soon be set up for Logan. As he pushed open the double French doors and saw the heavy oak desk that had been used as a storage shelf in their previous study, Tate made his way over to it and ran his fingers over the shiny surface. He looked over to the opposite wall and the inbuilt bookshelves and thought about the man upstairs and how perfect this space was for him. He could imagine Logan in here, surrounded by his books, with the walls decorated by his many degrees and accomplishments. Maybe a lamp in the corner, over by the window there.

Tate liked the space. It was perfect for his lawyer. *Yes, my ever-surprising lawyer*, Tate thought, as he headed over to a box sitting in front of the shelves.

Office was scrawled across the side of it, and Tate

figured it was as good a place to start as any. He grabbed a Stanley knife from the kitchen counter and then headed back in to slice through the tape holding the box shut. After he'd safely put the knife on one of the shelves, Tate opened it to see some of the contents from the desk.

He carried it over and placed it on the floor by the sturdy wood piece, and started unpacking pens, Post-its, a stapler, files, and notebooks. He stacked them one by one on the desk and then pulled out a drawer organizer and put all the pens inside. Once they were neatly in order, Tate slid open the top drawer and found a yellow notepad sitting inside. He pulled it out so he could put the organizer in place, and when he did, the top page fell open and some writing caught his eye.

He shut the drawer and then flipped the first page of the notepad over again, and when he realized what he was staring at, he turned around and rested his ass up against the desk because, *fucking hell*, he suddenly needed the support.

There at the top of the page, in Logan's perfectly precise handwriting, was the date. It was a memo from at least a month and a half ago, right after their New Buffalo trip, and under that were the names of several real estate agents and areas around Chicago. But that wasn't what had Tate bracing a hand on the desk beside himself. He'd known Logan had been researching neighborhoods in the area. It was what was under that.

There, in the same handwriting as above, was his full

name—William Tate Morrison—and under *that*:

William Tate Morrison-Mitchell
William Tate Mitchell-Morrison

....

William Tate Mitchell

Tate stared at the page and tried to remember if Logan had
ever hinted anything about this, but no—*hang on, wait.*
Logan had been sleeping like shit for the last few weeks
now. He'd been restless, preoccupied, but he'd told Tate it
was just work and the move that had him a little off.

Then there was the way he'd been looking at him
lately, Tate thought, remembering that day the realtor had
given them the keys, and in the bar with Priest, and last
weekend after dinner with Jill... *Shit. He's been thinking about
this for weeks. Almost two months? Why didn't he say anything—*

"Starting in the smallest room in the house, huh?"
Logan's voice behind him had Tate quickly turning. Logan
walked into the office in a grey Killers t-shirt and jeans that
outlined his long legs, as he headed over to the boxes in
front of the bookshelf. Tate dropped the legal pad into the
drawer guiltily and shoved it shut with his thigh just as
Logan faced him with an expectant look on his face.

"Oh, uhh, yeah. Seemed less overwhelming that
way."

"That's smart," Logan said, and grabbed the knife
Tate had put down on the shelf. "I guess I'll start with the

books, then. When I came downstairs and saw the disaster in the living room, I was reminded of why I hate moving."

Tate had tuned out somewhere around *living room* and zeroed in on Logan's face instead. He'd swept his damp hair back from it and must've put his contacts in, because he'd left his glasses off. He hadn't bothered with a razor this morning, whether it be because he couldn't find it or just couldn't be bothered, and even as he continued to talk about anything that *wasn't* last night, Tate was crossing over to where Logan stood.

As he got within a couple of feet, Logan must've seen something in his eyes, or sensed it, because he stopped talking and backed up until he was boxed in against the wall.

When they were toe to toe, Tate tilted his head to the side and let his eyes roam over the familiar, but suddenly different, face in front of him, and when he got to Logan's lips and he licked them, Tate realized he was making Logan…nervous.

"You know that I love you, right?" Tate said, his eyes locked with the insanely blue ones he'd been mesmerized by from the first time he'd met Logan. When Logan slowly nodded, but said nothing, Tate desperately wanted to ask if he felt the same. But he didn't. He just worked on reassuring the cautious man staring back at him. "That hasn't changed for me at all."

"It hasn't for me either," Logan said, unknowingly answering him.

Logan sucked in an unsteady breath, and Tate let his hand fall away, not wanting to push his luck. He was more than aware of the tension that still thrummed in the air between them, and knew he'd been the one to cause it. But before his hand was out of reach, Logan took his fingers and brought it up to his mouth. Tate held his breath as Logan's eyes fluttered shut, and as he pressed his lips to the center of Tate's palm, more was said in that one gesture than any words ever could. *I love you. We'll get through this.*

When Logan opened his eyes and let his hand go, Tate didn't lower it immediately. Instead, he gently traced his fingers down Logan's sculpted jaw to his chin and held it steady, then he leaned in, allowing Logan a chance to stop him if he wanted, and brushed a kiss across his lips.

At the intimate contact, Logan shuddered and brought his hands up to clutch at Tate's waist as he teased his tongue along Logan's lip, seeking permission to enter.

A soft groan left Logan as he opened to him for the first time in what had to be the longest twenty-four hours of his life, and Tate slid his tongue inside. The hands on his waist moved around to his back, and as Logan drew him in closer, Tate cradled the sides of his face and was reminded of a moment very similar to this, yet so far removed it had a smile curving his lips.

As he raised his head slightly, Logan's eyes opened, and Tate could see they were full of questions.

"Do you remember the first time that I kissed you?"

Logan blinked at him, and when Tate ran a thumb

along his bottom lip, he groaned.

"It was in your conference room…"

"Yes," Logan sighed.

"I had you backed up against the wall just like this, and I remember thinking: what is this guy doing to me? You'd just kissed my brains out, and as I stood there I thought over and over, *You need to leave.* I told myself to pick my shit up and go."

When Logan swallowed but said nothing, Tate traced the lines of his lips, chin, and cheeks with the pads of his fingers, making sure Logan was real. Making sure he wasn't still trapped in the nightmare from last night, where Logan was nowhere that he couldn't reach him. And once he was satisfied Logan was there, that he was in front of him, Tate said, "And do you remember happened next?"

"Yes. I do."

"I didn't pick up my things, and I didn't go anywhere other than right back to you. Back to where I belong. And with you there against that wall, I got so lost in you that I never wanted to leave. Now here we are, years later, and I feel exactly the same."

Before Logan could respond, Tate crushed their lips together, and a deep rumble came from Logan as his fingers dug into Tate's waist. It was always like this with Logan. Always had been ever since he'd walked into Tate's life, and the thought of anything he'd done coming between them made Tate desperate to prove what they had hadn't changed.

"Don't shut me out," he whispered against Logan's lips as he gently ran his fingers down the sides of Logan's face.

Logan's body trembled as his eyes found his, and he ghosted a kiss across Tate's lips that just about had his knees buckling. "I wouldn't even know how."

Tate shut his eyes as Logan's lips found his cheek, and as they kissed their way up to his ear, he felt his heart thud harder with each touch.

"Put your hands on me, Tate." The request was husky, and sounded slightly broken. But Tate slipped a hand under Logan's t-shirt to run his fingers over the warm skin of his abs.

"I don't ever want to be away from you again. Not like last night. Logan, I'm—"

"No. We're not doing this right now, remember? I need... Shit, Tate. I just need some time before we examine this all over again, okay? Can we just, I don't know, have the morning to unpack and forget it happened for a while?"

Tate nodded, but once again felt as though they'd taken two steps back. He lowered his hand and moved away, granting Logan his wish for time. It was the least he could do.

Last night still lingered in every move they made and every word they said, and Tate hated that instead of focusing on the new house they'd bought together, all they could seem to think about was how to move around while dodging the land mines they'd discovered upon closer inspection. "Yeah, we can do that."

"Okay, good." Logan pushed off the wall and pointed to the bookshelves. "I'll start on the books."

Tate watched as Logan turned back to the box he'd opened minutes earlier, and tried to squash the hurt he felt from the dismissal, but he knew Logan wasn't blocking him out. This was Logan's way of protecting...Logan. And for right now, Tate would let him do whatever he needed to heal.

* * *

LOGAN COULD FEEL Tate's eyes on him as though he was still touching him, but told himself to stay where he was. There was nothing he wanted more right now than to turn around, strip Tate down, and lose himself in how good he knew he would make him feel.

But that would just be putting a Band-Aid over a wound that required much more. And Logan wasn't quite sure he could handle Tate's body inside of his right then— even though it was the exact thing it craved.

There were some serious points of contention between them right now, differences he never could've imagined, and Logan couldn't help but wonder how the hell the tables had turned so drastically. It was like the world had shifted off its axis and he was still trying to get his footing. But every time he was close to being steady, Tate opened his mouth and Logan once again found himself struggling to stay upright.

He just needed an hour of normalcy between them, a day where things felt as they always had, and then maybe he'd be able to move on from there.

"So," Tate said, as he pulled several binders out of the box he was digging through, "I thought I'd call up Jill and cancel this afternoon."

Oh shit, Logan had completely forgotten about that. But there was no way he was letting Tate skip out on something so important. He turned around with a couple of books in hand and shook his head. "No, no. Don't do that. What time is it again?"

"Logan, come on. I doubt you really want to—"

"Tate," Logan interrupted, making it clear he wasn't interested in getting out of anything. "What time?"

Tate stared at him from behind the desk. "She texted that it starts at three."

"Okay." Actually, that was the perfect excuse to get out of talking. If they were around others, Logan could have a little more time to...process. "Let's get as much done here as we can and then we can head over."

Tate scrunched his nose up and ran a hand through his hair. "I, uhh... I'm not sure I really want—"

"Tate." Logan put the books on the shelf and then walked over to Tate. Logan could see the nerves riding him, and suddenly wished he had the ability to make everything between them easier right then, but he couldn't. The truth was, he couldn't even make them easier for himself. "This is important. Just a couple of days ago, you told me you were ready for this, remember? That you *wanted* to see your nephews again. I refuse to be the reason you don't go."

"You're not. I'm not worried about them meeting you. I want them to."

The instant way Tate came to his defense made Logan want to kiss him. But he'd missed Logan's meaning. "I wasn't talking about that."

"Oh."

"Right." Logan backed away then, knowing he only had so much self-control. "So let's do what we can in here, and then we can deal with *that* this afternoon."

As he walked away, Logan heard Tate call his name and stopped to look back at him. The frown had gone but had been replaced with a serious expression that bordered on grim as Tate said, "You're everything I want. Promise me you know that."

Fuck, he hated this. Hated that they were in a place where they had to reassure each other. "I do."

Tate nodded but didn't look overly convinced as he lowered his eyes to the box he was rifling through, and Logan knew that no matter how hard last night and right now were, the two of them loved one another and would work their way back to where they were meant to be.

Chapter Nineteen

"DO YOU KNOW how many people are going today?" Logan's question found Tate over the steady beat of the song playing on the radio as he drove down the interstate.

The two of them had spent the rest of the day unpacking Logan's office and the kitchen, and then it had been time to get ready. They'd fallen into a relatively comfortable groove where they spoke about house stuff and work stuff and very neatly avoided anything about, well, marriage stuff.

"Uhh, she didn't say. But I doubt too many. Their house isn't that big, and even though the sun's out, it's kind of cold today. She'll likely have us all inside." Tate glanced over to Logan in his casual pair of navy-blue pants and a light blue sweater, and chuckled when his eyes fell to the white collar of the shirt he wore under it—it was perfectly pressed from the pointed tips of that collar to the tails.

"What are you laughing at?" Logan asked as he looked down at himself, no doubt checking to make sure nothing was out of order.

"Nothing. I was just remembering your frantic search

for the iron earlier."

"We really need to unpack all the clothes, shoes, and hangers next. I hate not being able to find what I'm looking for. And my *frantic* search, as you call it, will save me grief tomorrow when getting ready for work. It's one of the most important appliances we own I'll have you know."

"The iron?"

"Yes. How else do you get the wrinkles out?"

Tate shrugged. "I throw my stuff in the dryer." Logan looked him over, and when a deep crease formed between his eyebrows, Tate laughed again. "Something you obviously think worked very well from that response."

"Well, no," Logan said. "It totally works for you. You look—"

"Careful..." Tate warned, tongue in cheek, enjoying the teasing nature that had slipped back between them for the first time in hours.

"You look sexy and, uhh, rumpled."

"*Rumpled?*"

Logan rolled his eyes. "You know what I mean. You're the kind of person who can roll out of bed, pull a shirt on with some jeans, and you look great. Me, I need—"

"Not a goddamn thing, and you look hot as hell."

Logan's mouth was open midway with whatever retort he'd been about to give, when he stopped and cocked his head. "Are you flirting with me?"

Tate peered at him over his sunglasses. "Yes. Got a problem with that?"

The two of them had been so careful around each
other for most of the day that he wondered if Logan *would*
take issue with him saying something that usually would be
so normal between them.

But Logan shook his head. "No."

Tate returned his eyes to the road, happy for the shift
to familiar territory for five minutes. "Good. Because your
frantic search paid off. You look very handsome this
afternoon."

"I'm glad you think so."

"I do," Tate said—*and I want to kiss you so bad, I ache
from it.*

As they exited the interstate and Tate drew the car to
a stop at a red light, he looked over and wished he didn't
feel so uneasy with the man next to him. He hated this
feeling, and even though Logan said things would be okay
between them, the discomfort still lingered.

"I'm looking forward to meeting your nephews."
Tate sighed, and when Logan looked his way, he asked, "I
shouldn't be looking forward to meeting them?"

Stop being so polite, Tate wanted to tell him. But again,
he had no place telling Logan how to act right now, so he
kept his mouth shut. "No, you should. I am too. It's just
going to be a little strange to see them after all this time, but
good, you know?" Logan nodded, and Tate offered him a
hesitant smile. "I think they're going to really like you.
Especially Cooper."

"Oh? Why's that?"

"Coop's always been the bookish type. Interested in learning everything he could, and *reading* everything he could. Well, he did when he was seven, at least. I can't imagine much has changed."

"Imagine that. A young mind eager for knowledge through books instead of the Internet."

"Yes...imagine."

"Well, I think Cooper and I will get along just fine."

Tate couldn't help himself then, and hoped that Logan wouldn't pull away from him as he reached across the car and placed a hand on his thigh. "Who wouldn't get along with you?"

Their gazes held in the silence until the light changed and Logan gestured to it with a tilt of his head. "Time to go."

Tate nodded but was reluctant to leave the moment. "Yes. It's time to go." And before the cars behind him started to blast their horn, he put his foot to the gas and took off down the road.

* * *

SNAP OUT OF it, Mitchell, Logan thought for what had to be the millionth time. But as Logan was finding out, it was much easier to tell yourself to be fine and okay than to actually feel it.

All day they'd been politely circling one another. There'd been conversation about paint colors, discussion on the weather over the past month, and something or fucking other involving them deciding where to hang the clock in the kitchen.

It was all so calm. So damn civilized. And it made Logan want to rip his hair out. But, for some reason, he couldn't snap out of it long enough to fall back into their normal groove. *Time. I just need time.*

Around twenty minutes later, Tate was pulling up alongside the curb of a quaint little house that had a perfectly manicured lawn. Actually, all the houses were quaint and had perfectly manicured lawns.

"This is it." Tate was unbuckling his seatbelt as Logan continued to stare out at the American dream in front of him, and if he thought Cole had up and moved to suburbia, then this house confirmed that his brother and Rachel still had some of their rebellious tendencies lurking under the family unit facade. At least their home was unique to them. This house was scarily similar to the one on either side of it, minus the blue door.

"Looks like we're the first here," Logan said as he scanned the empty drive.

"Yeah, I'd say so. Maybe if we're lucky we can get in and out before anyone else arrives."

"Maybe." Logan pushed open his door just as Tate did, and as they climbed out, a blast of cold air hit them. "Damn. It's going to be a brutal winter this year if it's already this cold in October."

"I know," Tate said as he flipped up the collar on his leather jacket. "You really should've brought a coat."

"I figured we'd be inside and my sweater would be enough." Logan crossed his arms and rubbed his hands up and down the outside of the wool. "But you might be right."

Tate came around and slowly held a hand out, as though he wasn't sure if the gesture would be well received. But Logan slipped his palm against Tate's and was grateful when he pulled him to his side.

"Better?" Tate asked.

In so many ways, Logan thought, but merely nodded.

"Good. Now let's get you inside so you don't catch a cold."

Logan didn't say anything as Tate led them toward the blue door that beckoned them, and once they were on the porch, Tate just stared at it.

"Hey," Logan said. "You've got this."

Tate glanced at him, and when a frown creased his forehead, Logan wondered if it was his phrasing or the thought of what was about to happen that was troubling Tate. But no matter what it was, and even with all that was going on with them, Logan wasn't about to let Tate go in there believing he was doing this on his own.

He squeezed Tate's fingers and gave him the most supportive smile he could muster. *"We've* got this, okay? I'm right here if you need me. For anything."

And with that, Tate turned and knocked on the blue door.

* * *

TATE TRIED TO push aside the stab of hurt he'd gotten
from Logan's initial slip, knowing he hadn't likely meant it
the way he was taking it. But it still cut to hear him phrase
his support in the way he had.

You've got this. *Not we, you. Shit,* he'd really messed
things up between them, he thought as he concentrated on
Logan's hand in his, and he wished right then he could say
fuck it to this get-together, drag Logan back to his car, and
then take him somewhere so they could work this out—
now.

He didn't even care how long it would take. *One
night? Three? A week?* He just wanted to get Logan
somewhere private so he could beg him to say what it was
he needed so they would be okay. The problem was, Tate
didn't even think Logan knew the answer to that...yet.

Tate knocked on the door, totally preoccupied with
everything but the fact he was about to come face to face
with his nephews after four years, and waited for it to open.

The sound of footsteps was what he heard first,
followed by someone laughing, and then the door opened to
reveal a gangly boy with a mop of brown curls. He had
glasses pushed up his nose, and when he saw who stood in
front of him, a huge grin split across his mouth.

"Uncle Tate," Cooper said, and then burst forward
with all the enthusiasm of an eleven-year-old to wrap his
arms around Tate. He returned the gesture automatically
and told himself to keep it together.

When Cooper stepped back and looked up at him, he was practically bouncing on his toes with excitement. "Mom said you were coming, but I didn't believe her. Ahh, this is the best day ever."

Tate laughed, Cooper's joy one hundred percent contagious, and reached out to ruffle his hair. "It is pretty cool, isn't it?"

"Yeah. So cool."

Cooper's eyes shifted to Logan, and Tate turned to see him looking down at the boy with a grin on his lips, and he wondered what Logan was thinking just then.

"Hi, I'm Cooper." Cooper then shocked the hell out of Tate by holding his hand out in Logan's direction.

Logan stepped forward and took Cooper's hand, giving it a firm shake. "Hello to you. I'm—"

"Logan, right?"

When Logan looked at Tate, he shrugged. He hadn't spoken to Cooper until right now, so this had to be Jill's doing.

"That's right," Logan said, and returned his attention back to the boy. "I'm Logan."

"Uncle Tate's boyfriend."

Tate was glad no one was addressing *him* right then, because Cooper, in no more than three words, had put all the cards on the table and rendered him mute. Logan, on the other hand, relaxed before his very eyes. And Tate was surprised to hear laughter bubble up out of him.

"That's right. That's exactly who I am."

"That's cool. I have a friend with two dads," Cooper went on, and Tate, having not even made it two steps in the front door, was completely floored by the acceptance coming from one as young as Cooper, when his own mother couldn't even wrap her brain around it.

"That is very cool," Logan agreed.

Cooper beamed at the both of them. "Mom's in the kitchen and Dad's out back with Jon getting the grill fired up. Man, he's gonna freak when he sees you're really here. Come on."

Cooper headed off down the hall, clearly expecting them to follow, and as Tate started off in the same direction, he heard Logan say from behind him, "Your father's genes run strong. That kid looks just like you and your dad."

Tate looked over his shoulder at Logan, who was staring down the hall after Cooper. "It's the hair."

"And the eyes. You and Jill got both those things from him. It's crazy to see. A little shocking, too. But he's great."

Tate nodded, still a little surprised from the brief conversation at the front door. But then he turned around and headed off down the hall in search of the rest of the family.

SEVERAL HOURS LATER, Tate had to admit that he couldn't remember what he'd been so worried about. Jill had been right. Not only was his family cool with him and Logan, the friends she'd invited over didn't so much as flinch at the two of them together.

Okay, so that wasn't entirely true. Jeff Peterson, whom Tate had music lessons with in high school, had looked all kinds of confused when Tate introduced Logan as his boyfriend. So naturally, Logan, being Logan, decided to clear things up in the clearest way he was able. "Boyfriend as in we live together and sleep together."

But Tate should've known that Jeff, whose mouth had always been a source of either embarrassment or troublemaking shit, would give it right back to Logan once his brain computed the shock.

Leaning in to Logan, Jeff said, "If that's *all* he's doing while he's in your bed, then Morrison here ain't really your boyfriend, now is he?"

The rest of the night had gone along without so much as a hitch.

It was nearing seven thirty, and Cooper and Jon had disappeared into their bedroom to play video games. Tate found himself cornered on one side of Jill's living room with Jeff and Matt, who were reminiscing about the good old days, while Logan was across the room with Jill, Sam, and a few other couples, who were asking him all about his job and that recent win with Berivax.

Unfortunately, it had been like that for most of the night. Tate didn't think it was intentional, but he found himself pulled in one direction while Logan was pulled in the other. And where they'd usually make sure they were standing as close as possible any other night, tonight they'd let themselves head off to opposite sides of the room.

As Matt continued to talk about the teachers they used to loathe and the pranks they used to pull, Tate's eyes found the charismatic man across the room. As if Logan felt Tate's gaze, he glanced over in Tate's direction, and their eyes locked and held. The connection there was instantaneous, and for the first time in what felt like forever, it was familiar, electric, and hot as hell—then it vanished, and Logan inclined his head in acknowledgment before going back to the conversation he was having.

Tate had totally zoned out on what was being said beside him until Jeff nudged him and Tate realized he was asking him a question.

"So Logan, huh? A guy," Jeff said as he looked across the room to Logan. "Who knew *you'd* turn out to be the adventurous one in the bunch."

Tate dragged his eyes off Logan and turned back to Jeff. "Not me. But if anyone was going to make me try it his way, it was going to be Logan."

"Well, he is a lawyer—you'd hope he could make a convincing argument," Matt joked, and Tate had to laugh, because no one was more convincing than Logan when he put his mind to something. "Unlike us schmucks whose ammo was to take a girl to the drive-in, hardly talk at all, and hope like hell we could convince her to let us make out for five minutes. Actually, come to think of it, you held the record for the most action out there, didn't you, Tate?"

"Now this sounds like a conversation I should be a

part of."

Logan's voice had Tate looking over his shoulder to see him standing there with an arched eyebrow.

"You held the record for the most action *where*? And just so I'm not misunderstanding, we aren't talking action as in fighting, are we?"

"Hell no." Jeff laughed. "Morrison was a lover, not a fighter."

"Is that right?" Logan said in a tone that made Tate very aware that something in the last few minutes had shifted between them. Ever since that look they shared.

"Yeah," Jeff said. "Always was one of the nicest guys around. Everyone loved him."

Tate shook his head. *Jesus, they make me sound like a fucking choirboy.* But when he saw Matt open his mouth, clearly about to fill Logan in on what they'd been talking about, Tate had an idea, one that he hoped would be a bit of fun for the two of them after everything that had happened.

"I think that's enough of a walk down memory lane tonight, okay, Matt?" Tate said, and luckily for Matt, he got the message.

Logan, of course, didn't miss the fact he was changing topics. "Well, that's not fair."

"Too bad," Tate said, and took Logan's elbow in hand, giving a quick wave to his friends. "Let's go and find our hosts. I think I'm ready to leave."

"Really? It's not even eight," Logan said, and then frowned. "Are you okay? Did I say something to upset you?

I was only joking back there."

Tate stopped them where they were, and turned on Logan then. The last thing he wanted was for Logan to think he was upset. So he bent in close enough that he'd be heard even as he whispered, "No. You did the exact opposite."

Logan's eyes darkened as the words sank in, and that look, that expression in his eyes, was one Tate had been missing.

"Okay. Then let's find Jill."

"Yes. Let's," Tate agreed, and then straightened. "Because there's somewhere I want to take you."

Chapter Twenty

LOGAN LOOKED OUT the window as Tate drove them through the backstreets of Jill's neighborhood. They'd just come to an intersection and pulled up at a red light, and the road was deserted. Not another car in sight on this chilly Sunday night.

There's somewhere I want to take you… Tate's words were still echoing in his head as the Mustang growled to life and Tate drove them straight across the four-way intersection.

As they left the subdivision with the perfectly manicured lawns and eerily similar houses, Tate navigated a winding road that took them away from suburbia and through several miles of nothing but dark road and wooded fields, and Logan *still* had no idea where they were going.

The night had gone well, all things considered. Tate's nephews were a trip, and they'd sure shocked their uncle when they hadn't cared in the least that he had a boyfriend.

Jill and Sam had been extremely welcoming, and Jill had even taken them on a quick tour before others got there, showing them the tub they'd been talking about with that nightmare renovation. Then, when their friends had arrived, each and every one of them had been nothing but lovely. Some had given Tate shit for just up and vanishing, but everyone was genuinely interested in getting to know more about the boy they'd known in high school and the man he was now living with.

The afternoon had been so busy and full of questions about how they'd met, what they did, and Tate's new bar that neither of them had had a chance to think about things beyond the twenty questions they'd been subjected to, which was just fine by Logan.

"You cold?" Tate looked over at him, and Logan took the opportunity to appreciate the way the lights from the dash played over Tate's strong features. That masculine jaw, the bow lips surrounded by the scruff, which was the same color as his broody eyebrows and those curls dusting his forehead, and Logan wasn't cold in the slightest.

"No. I'm good. You?"

Tate's eyes flicked down to Logan's lips and then back up to his eyes. "No. I was just checking, since you're not wearing a coat. The temperature dropped quick tonight."

"It did. But the heater in here works good," Logan said, putting his palms up in front of the vent.

Tate's attention was alternating between Logan and the road as he nodded. "Hmm, yeah, it does."

"Tate?"

"Yeah."

"Where you taking me?"

When an artless grin curved Tate's lips, Logan felt his cock react instantly. *Jesus, it's been a little while since* that *happened*. But in that jacket with those black jeans and plain V-neck, Tate looked like the high school senior they'd all been remembering tonight, and he was irresistible. And considering Logan had been resisting his impulses *all* day, he was close to being done. He needed to touch Tate. Needed some kind of contact with the man he was used to being able to take without restrictions.

"I'm not telling you."

Oh, looks like I'm not the only one feeling things. So he wants to play a little tonight. Okay. "Why not?"

"Because it's a surprise," Tate said as though it should be more than obvious. "Be patient."

"Yes, because we both know that's my strong suit." Logan sat back in his seat. "Okay, well, since you started this little game, can you at least give me a clue?"

As Tate watched the road ahead of them, he chuckled. He was obviously happy Logan had decided to play along. "It's somewhere we have to go to in a car."

"Really? Like I couldn't guess that, since we are currently *in* a car."

"Hey, you asked for a clue, and I gave you one."

Logan sighed and looked out at his surroundings again. He had absolutely no idea where they were. He didn't venture out of the city unless it involved going to the airport or heading to New Buffalo, and clearly they were not going to either of those places. "Give me another one."

"Hmm…" Tate tapped his fingers on the steering wheel. "Let's see. I'm pretty sure I'm going to make you do something tonight that you've never done before."

That piqued Logan's curiosity instantly. "Really?"

"Mhmm. In fact, I'll be shocked if I'm not your first."

Okay, fuck. Tate had to know what he was doing to him after twenty-four hours of not touching. *Right?* Logan shifted in his seat, and when Tate turned to look at him, Logan said, "You better be taking me to a place where I can touch you. Because I'm just about done with keeping my hands to myself."

"And if I'm not?"

"I'm not sure that I care." Logan ran his gaze down Tate's body to his thick thighs. "I need to put my hands on you. And wherever you stop this car next, I plan to do so."

Tate slowed the car to a stop at a stop sign and flicked his indicator on. "We're stopped."

The smirk playing on his mouth made Logan want to kiss it right off, but instead he reached between his legs and palmed his stiffening cock. "You enjoying my misery?"

Tate's eyebrow rose. "You don't look too miserable to me."

"Where are we going?"

But Tate merely shook his head and turned back to face the road.

* * *

JESUS, LOGAN WAS making it hard to concentrate. *Making it* hard *in general, for that matter,* Tate thought, as he made the final turn and drove down the deserted road.

When he'd started this little tease, hoping Logan would bite, Tate had been close to pumping a fist in the air when Logan responded. And since the moment they'd left Jill's subdivision, it had been game on.

It took everything Tate had not to take another look over to Logan watching him with a hand between his legs. But damn it, nothing would happen if he ended up driving them off the road.

He'd gotten this brilliant idea of his after talking with Matt about places they used to go as kids. And while *they'd* been reminiscing over the girls they'd scored with, this particular location had popped into his head as somewhere he'd like to take Logan.

"The Harvest Moon Drive-In?"

Tate looked over to Logan, now leaning forward and staring out the windshield at the dilapidated sign that no longer lit up and was half hidden behind overgrown trees. "Uh huh."

"You brought me to a *drive-in?*"

"No." Tate slung an arm across the back of the car seats and put his hand on Logan's headrest. "I brought you to an *abandoned* drive-in."

As the words sank in, Logan tongued his top lip. "Did you now?"

Tate nodded and tightened the hand he had on the

steering wheel, because the look Logan was now aiming his way was the same one they'd shared back at Jill's, and it was making him seriously want to just park there and to hell with the rest of his idea... *But no. Not yet.* "Ever been to a drive-in movie theater, Mr. Mitchell?"

Logan shook his head. "I have not. But apparently I'm not going to one *tonight*, either."

Tate went to run his fingers through the back of Logan's hair, and hesitated for a second, but then he decided, *Fuck that shit.* Logan had said he wanted to touch, so he should have no objections over the fact that Tate wanted to. So Tate ran his hands through the silky black strands and then aimed a smile at Logan before letting go. "Oh, you're going to one..." he said as he took the car out of park and drove off the side of the main road and onto the old dirt one. "You're just not going to see a movie."

* * *

AS TATE STEERED the Mustang past the sign that had seen better days, Logan said, "So if I'm not going to see a movie, then *what* exactly are we doing here? I'm not sure my mother would approve of me driving around this late at night in some boy's car."

Tate took his eyes off the road long enough to pin Logan with a devilish glint in his eye. "Really? I don't know, your mother isn't like most...plus, she thinks I'm rather charming. Remember?"

Logan scoffed but didn't dispute Tate's words, because Evelyn *did* think Tate was charming. That was saying something, considering the second time they met, Tate told her in no uncertain terms that if she ever fucked with Logan again like she had that night at The Peninsula, then she would have him to answer to.

And hell, Logan was close to positive he would've tattooed Tate's name on his ass that night if he'd asked him to.

"Yeah, yeah, so you won Evelyn over. She's not the one sitting in this car, though." Logan looked out the window as Tate maneuvered the car around a bend and through some thick foliage. "A forest on the way to some secluded place."

"Aww, don't tell me you're scared," Tate said, and flashed a wolfish smile. "Actually, that might work in my favor. Want me to hold your hand?"

Logan started laughing, and it felt amazing. God, it felt good to be comfortable again in his skin with the man now leering at him. "And how many girls did you use *that* line on?"

"A few." Tate winked as the car bumped its way along the road slowly.

"Uh huh. Let me see if I can paint an accurate picture here. You at sixteen—"

"No, seventeen."

"You didn't get your license until you were seventeen?"

"No, I had it—Dad just didn't let me use the Camaro until I was seventeen."

"*Ohh*, my mistake," Logan said. "So you at seventeen in your father's Camaro. Long hair or short?"

Tate shrugged. "Longish."

"Okay. So basically, curls all over the place, like now." Logan ran his eyes over Tate. "Hormones racing. A dark, secluded spot at the back of a drive-in and…little Mary Sue sitting beside you in her prettiest summer dress."

Tate let out a booming laugh, and then cursed when the Mustang hit a pothole. "That's your fault. You distracted me."

"I don't know. I think it was the thought of the summer dress and the easy access. It's much harder to get into a pair of pants. Do you even know how to?"

Tate lowered his eyes to the zipper of Logan's pants and nodded. *Fuck me, I'm now hard as a rock.*

"I know how to get into yours."

"You think so, huh?"

"I do."

"So cocky…"

"Just the way you like it. Right?" Tate said, their familiar banter right back in place.

"I definitely like *cock*-y." As Logan smirked, the headlights slipped through the narrow opening of the road and finally lit up a wide-open field in front of them.

There were rows and rows of small concrete bumps with grass grown over where the cars used to park, and stands beside each spot for trays and speaker jacks. Off at the far end on each side of the grounds were two huge screens. There were floodlights bordering the outskirts of the area, and in the middle of the field was a small building with a giant arrow that obviously lit up once upon a time. It had the word *Mel's* across it.

The Mustang idled on the outskirts of the old drive-in, and Logan's pulse began to pound in time with his throbbing dick at the thought of "parking" in this secluded place with Tate.

"Was I right?" Tate's gravelly voice caught Logan's attention and had him dragging his eyes away from the possibilities he knew lay ahead of them out there in the field.

"About...?"

Tate's tongue licked over his lips as though he were having the most delicious thought. "Me being your first?"

The sexual tension in the car sizzled, and Logan couldn't help it. He reached down and applied heavy pressure to his aching erection, which was responding eagerly to Tate's very blatant invitation that it come out and play. "My first *what*, exactly?"

"The first boy to take you to a drive-in, park, turn off all the lights, and hopefully get in your pants."

Logan bit the inside of his cheek to hold back the groan he wanted to let free, because the idea of Tate doing what he had just said was making it really difficult to not unzip and start without him. "This will be my first drive-in experience, yes. As for getting into my pants, that's still up for debate."

"Oh, it's definitely *up*."

"You know, a nice boy wouldn't point that out."

That filthy smile Logan so loved curled the sides of Tate's lips. He lowered a hand down between his own legs and began to massage the discernible bulge behind the zipper of his jeans.

"Whoever said I was nice?"

Logan narrowed his eyes and had to admit that there were definitely times when Tate was *not* so nice. And damn if Logan didn't love it when *that* boy came out to play. But in the spirit of the game, Logan shrugged and said, "You know, all the girls."

Tate chuckled, and the sound was so lighthearted, so relaxed, Logan loved hearing it. This familiar ease that was back between them was welcome, and it was unbelievable how long twenty-four hours could feel when you were at odds with the other half of yourself.

"*All* the girls? There weren't that many. And just because I was nice to them doesn't mean you'll share the same fate."

Logan zeroed in on the hard dick Tate was rubbing as he said, "There must be something wrong with me, because I *really* hope that's the fucking truth."

As Tate leaned over the console, Logan caught and held his breath, because hell if he wasn't two seconds away from demanding Tate shut the car off where they were and get his hands on him.

"There's not a single thing wrong with you. Though I thought you'd be a little more nervous, considering this *is* your first time."

Logan turned his head on the headrest, and when their eyes locked, the match was lit. "I'm nervous."

"Doesn't seem that way to me…" Tate closed the gap between them and bit down on Logan's lower lip, *and shit,* it took everything Logan had not to grab hold of him. "But why don't you loosen up a little while I find a place to park." Tate pushed down on the seatbelt release, and as it came free and retracted across Logan's chest, he added, "Unbutton and unzip your pants, Logan."

This close, Logan could see how dark Tate's eyes were from the reflection of the dash, and without looking away from him, Logan reached down and undid his pants. "You know, boys have become a lot more forward since I was in high school." His voice sounded strained even to his own ears. This little field trip Tate had taken them on was fast becoming a fantasy Logan never knew he had.

"Really?" Tate said, and pressed a quick kiss to Logan's lips. And that tiny taste just wasn't enough. "Then maybe you were dating the wrong people."

"I *didn't* date in high school."

"Never?"

"Nope. Too busy studying."

"Well… That's a shame," Tate said, but his tone told Logan otherwise, and he had a feeling that Tate liked that little fact.

As he moved back to his side of the car, Tate aimed his eyes down at Logan's lap and said, "I guess I'll just have to make up for lost time, then, won't I?"

Logan raised an eyebrow. *Perhaps…we shall see.* Then Tate put the car into gear and drove them toward the left end of the field to find a place to park.

Chapter Twenty-One

TATE PARKED THE Mustang in the far back corner of the field, as far away from the entrance as possible. Not that he was worried about anyone coming out there—the Harvest Moon Drive-In had shut down two years after he'd graduated high school due to poor attendance, and the place had been abandoned ever since.

Tate switched off the engine, pulled the keys from the ignition, tossed them in the center console, and turned to face Logan, who was sitting with his pants open and his thick erection visible under the material.

Without taking his gaze off Logan, Tate rolled down the window, knowing things were about to get hot and humid inside the car, no matter how cool it might be outside. His cock was impossibly hard behind the now tight denim of his jeans, and when he reached down to unbutton and unzip, Tate heard Logan groan.

He glanced across the car to see Logan's eyes on his hands, and he had one more ace up his sleeve he hoped would work in his favor. Tate slowly pulled his zipper down and spread open his jeans, and when Logan saw he'd gone commando, those wicked blue eyes flew up to Tate's.

"Fucking hell, Tate. Can I—"

"Are you really asking permission?" Tate said as he shoved his hands inside his jeans. When he freed his shaft, Logan's lips drew into a tight line. "If you are, I think you should just sit over there and watch me for a little bit. You know, until you decide you really want it again."

Tate wrapped his hand around the root of his dick and slowly dragged his fist up his length, and then slid it back down to the base as Logan watched him.

He'd always loved Logan's eyes on him from the very beginning, and Tate knew whenever he did this, put on a show for the man currently devouring him with his hot and hungry stare, that Logan's desire, his arousal, would eventually take over, and *that* was what he wanted tonight. He wanted Logan to take anything he wanted.

"Give me something to look at," Tate said, and Logan's breath left him on a rush. "Show me your cock, Logan."

Like a man under a spell, Logan slipped his fingers into his pants and inched them down his hips so he could wrap his fingers around his engorged length, and as soon as he had himself in hand, a low groan left his lips, and he aimed a hot as fuck look Tate's way.

There he is, Tate thought. *That's right, come back to me...*

"Now, stroke it." Tate's voice was low, but it was obviously clear enough to reach Logan, because without any hesitation, Logan began to masturbate. Up and down, the sexy man licked and bit at his lips until Tate couldn't stop himself from moving his own fist in time with Logan's, each of them eye-fucking the other as they worked their stiff dicks to the point where the only sounds in the car were their heavy breathing.

"Fucking hell, Logan."

"*Mmm.*" Logan brought his hand up so he could spit in it, dropped his eyes to where Tate was working himself like he hadn't been touched in months, and then Logan was back to fisting and stroking his length faster and harder than before.

Tate gnashed his teeth together as Logan pumped his hips up off the seat, and he fisted the base of his cock tight, trying to keep his climax at bay. *And Jesus H. Christ,* Logan was something else to watch right now with his eyes ablaze, his cock in hand, and that strait-laced shirt and sweater set all still in perfect order. He looked like some preppy college kid that Tate had taken on a date to the drive-in. But the deviant glint in his eye spoke of a knowledge and maturity that went years beyond that of a clumsy college kid. Those eyes promised depravity.

"Come over here," Tate said before he knew he was going to. He needed Logan closer, wanted those full lips on his, and before he could blink, Logan was leaning across the console and taking hold of his jacket.

Tate ghosted his mouth over Logan's, teasing him with a kiss of his lips here and a bite of his teeth there. And with every single move, he drove the two of them closer to that point where they would eventually snap.

"What do you want tonight?" Tate whispered against Logan's mouth.

"You. Always you."

Tate sucked Logan's lower lip, and when a growl escaped his throat, Tate let go of his own cock and reached across to fist Logan's. As soon as his hand took over, Logan brought his up and took hold of the other side of Tate's jacket, then he thrust his hips up, tunneling his hard length through the large palm surrounding him.

"Ahh fuck, Tate."

"Hmm. You can have that. But not here. We're too big for the *tight* confines."

"Shit," Logan said as he continued to fuck Tate's hand, leaving a mess all over it. Then Tate swept his tongue over Logan's bottom lip, and when he tried to suck on it, Tate pulled away, making him groan.

"Come *on*, Tate. This has gone on long enough. I need you...you're driving me fucking crazy."

Tate tightened his fist around the sensitive head of Logan's shaft, and when his eyes locked on to his and fucking flared, Tate asked, "What do you want tonight?"

* * *

WHAT DID HE want? He wanted to pull Tate out of the car, force him to his knees, and make the man who had his emotions all over the place kneel at his feet while he reclaimed him in the most basic way he could think of. *My cum, all the hell over him.*

That was what he wanted.

"Logan?"

Logan's chest heaved as he stared into Tate's fiery eyes. God, he loved him, so fucking much. And though he hated what had happened the night before, Logan understood why. He knew Tate's reasons weren't make believe, but still, that didn't erase all the hurt and disappointment of the last twenty-four hours.

"Tell me," Tate said. "I can see it in your eyes. You want something. What is it?"

Logan's hand whipped out then, and he speared his fingers into Tate's curls and twisted them hard. Tate winced, but Logan didn't let up, the sweet and innocent game of two boys at a drive-in well and truly over. "I don't want the nice boy. I'll tell you that right fucking now."

"No?"

Logan tugged on the hair in his hand and tilted Tate's head back a little. "No. *Nice* has no place here between us. Not tonight."

Tate shuddered, and Logan could tell he was right there with him even before he said, "Then tell me what you want."

Logan licked a path over Tate's Adam's apple. "I want you to get out of this car and wait for me." Tate swallowed, and Logan knew he thought that was it. But that wasn't even the half of it. "Down on your knees, Tate."

Tate's eyes found his, and Logan was stunned that even in the shadows of the car, he could tell Tate's had just darkened.

"I can do that."

"Good," Logan said, and released him. "And leave your jeans undone. Like you said earlier, I want something to look at. Now get out of the car."

Tate didn't say a fucking thing then, merely moved back to his side of the Mustang, opened his door, and got the hell out.

Logan thought about trying to squash whatever this clawing need was he was suddenly experiencing, but then decided that maybe this was exactly what he needed. He'd felt somewhat detached from Tate ever since he'd left the condo last night, and tonight Logan wanted to regain his confidence in their relationship.

With his mind firmly made up, Logan opened the door and climbed out, making sure to pull his pants up so they didn't fall off his hips. With a rough slam of the door, he glanced across the roof of the car and was pleased to note he couldn't see Tate anywhere, which meant he'd followed Logan's instructions.

The cold air didn't even faze him now as he walked around the hood of the car, and when he came up alongside the driver's side and saw Tate, Logan was more concerned with overheating than anything else.

There, under the night sky with his jeans pulled down to mid-thigh and his cock in hand, Tate knelt by the

car door, aiming a wild-eyed look up at Logan, who almost
skidded to a stop at the decadent picture Tate made. The
denim of Tate's jeans were wedged in the dirt and his hair
shifted in the breeze, but none of that seemed to bother Tate.
No. Tate had an expression on his face that was part
supplicant and part seducer, and had Logan taking the
necessary strides to get within touching distance of him.

When he was close enough to Tate that he had to
crane his head back to look up at him, Logan took hold of
his chin then bent over and said against Tate's lips, "You're
mine. Now, tomorrow, fifty fucking years from this very
moment. And by the time we leave here, there will be no
room for doubt. Do you understand?"

As Tate's eyes roved all over his face, Logan raised
his head and replaced his lips with his thumb, dragging it
along Tate's bottom lip. "I'm going to make a mess of this
gorgeous face tonight."

The tortured groan that escaped Tate got caught
somewhere in his throat, and after he swallowed it down, he
licked his lips, grazing Logan's thumb with the tip of his
tongue. *That's right,* Logan thought, *you know exactly where
this is going.* And by the look on Tate's face, it was obvious
the filthy fucker couldn't wait.

Logan straightened to his full height, and when he
reached inside his pants to pull his cock free, Tate muttered,
"Fuck yes."

Logan watched Tate reach for his own dick, and
when Tate's fingers wrapped around his thick erection,

Logan's lids lowered and he began to stroke himself in time with the man kneeling at his feet.

Things were about to get down and dirty.

As in Tate would be going down, and Logan would be making him real fucking dirty before this was all said and done.

* * *

TATE COULDN'T TAKE his eyes off the picture Logan made as he stood over him, cock in hand, masturbating only inches from his face, and he knew what was about to happen. Knew it, and wanted it, more than he could put into words.

His dick was throbbing like a motherfucker as he ran his eyes over the respectable picture Logan made—except for the hand he was using to milk the thick length Tate wanted in his mouth.

God, he was fucking sexy. Logan had barely pulled his pants and black briefs down, so they cradled his balls and pushed them up like a goddamn prize, and Tate wanted to be the lucky winner.

I'm going to make a mess of this gorgeous face tonight. Logan's words were on a loop in Tate's head, and *sweet Jesus*, he had to close his eyes for a second as the thought of Logan doing what he was suggesting, outside in the middle of nowhere, slammed into him all over again. It was so fucking hot.

"Eyes on me, Tate." Logan's voice had Tate opening his eyes and focusing, as Logan took a step forward and directed his cock toward Tate's mouth. "Open."

Tate's lips parted immediately, and Logan rubbed the plump head of his shaft along his bottom lip.

"Mhmm," Logan said, as he kept his eyes locked on Tate's and did it again, painting a slick trail of pre-cum along that same lip. "Such a sexy mouth. Bow-shaped, fuckable lips that are so good at sucking me it's a wonder I ever let a day pass where I don't demand it from you. Just like now."

Tate blinked, Logan's words casting a sensual spell as he continued to tease and torment Tate by sliding himself across his lips.

"Would you like that, do you think? Me making you suck my cock each morning before work? I think you might. You look pretty fucking good down there on your knees, Tate."

Tate couldn't stop himself from jerking his erection at the thought as the taste of Logan hit his tongue and his words sent all the blood to his aching dick. The cold air was a slight relief against his blazing skin, but when Logan fisted his hair and yanked his head back roughly, any relief Tate may have felt vanished.

He was on fucking fire, and the one whose cock was teasing his lips was the one stoking the flame. Tate flicked his tongue out, wanting to get a stronger taste of Logan, knowing that tonight he wouldn't be swallowing him down his throat, and the growl that left Logan from the touch was close to feral.

"*Fuck.*" Logan pulled his head away a fraction, and Tate bit his top lip. "I didn't tell you to do that."

Tate, not sorry in the least, said, "No, you didn't," knowing it would get the strongest reaction, and the rough jerk of his head forward, and Logan directing his cock across the closed seam of his lips, proved his point.

"I'm going to fuck your mouth until it's too tired to talk back, and then..." Logan said as he let the wet slit of his dick leave a glistening trail along the side of Tate's cheek. "Then I'm going to come all over you."

Tate pinched the head of his dick, making sure it hurt, because what Logan had just said to him had his climax so close that it took some kind of pain to squash it.

"Now how about you put that tongue and those lips to good use and suck me until I tell you to stop."

Tate's mouth fell open, and as Logan shoved inside to the back of his throat, he knew he was in for a hell of a ride.

Logan was all about reclaiming him tonight. Marking and putting his stamp of ownership back on him in the most elemental way possible—and as Tate kneeled there at his feet with his mouth full and his dick in hand, he couldn't fucking wait.

* * *

TATE'S EYES WERE pinned on him as Logan began to thrust in and out of his hot mouth. He had one hand clamped around his cock, getting himself off, as his other held on to Logan's thigh—and hell if that sexy fucker wasn't making it difficult to hold back.

Logan reached out to shove his hand through Tate's hair and grab on to the riot of curls, and when he had a good, firm grip, he really started to fuck Tate's delectable mouth.

He wanted Tate's lips swollen, his jaw aching, and his skin smelling like him by the time he was done, and as Logan watched himself glide past those lips time and time again, he completely got off on seeing his cock glistening from the wet heat of Tate's mouth.

Logan pulled free, and when Tate slowly stuck his tongue out, Logan growled and was right there rubbing the head of his dick all over the flat surface.

Tate groaned and Logan kept his eyes locked on his hungry mouth as Tate began to suck and kiss his way down to his balls. Tate took one into his mouth to torment Logan further, and when he finally let him slip free and raised his head to drag his tongue back up to the slit of his cock and tongue it, Logan just about lost it.

"Oh *fuck*, Tate. Yes." Tate swallowed him down, and this time when he pulled back out, a ropey string of cum connected cock to lips. "Jesus, that's hot."

Logan shut his eyes for a second as Tate circled him with his tongue, licking and tasting him as though he'd never get enough, and when Logan couldn't bear missing another second, he opened his eyes and, with a hand on his dick, directed his swollen head over the stubble of Tate's cheek. The abrasion of the short hairs against his sensitive, taut skin had Logan's head falling back and a curse leaving his mouth, and then he was tapping himself against Tate's lips and tongue, demanding entrance once more.

Tate gave it to him without hesitation, and it didn't take long then. Logan took a tight hold of Tate's hair and started to really fuck that mouth, those lips, and that tongue of his, and Tate wasn't idle during any of it. He was madly jacking himself off as Logan pushed in and out and the sounds...*oh fuck*, the sounds coming from them both were enough to make Logan come without anything else.

Tate was groaning, grunting, and sucking away, and Logan couldn't stop the dirty shit flying from his mouth until finally it was all too much, and he knew it was about to be over.

With a hard yank of Tate's hair, Logan craned his head back, pulled his cock free, and stared down at him as he came all over Tate's neck, chin, and face, and fuck him, by the time Logan was through, Tate had called his name out and come right along with him, and the final image that greeted Logan left no doubt as to who Tate belonged to— *fucking me.*

Without a word, Tate brought a hand up and swiped his thumb over his lips, and then he licked it clean. He shrugged out of his jacket and brought the hem of his shirt up to wipe off his face before whipping it over his head.

Logan watched him climb to his feet, and once Tate was standing opposite him with dirt all over his knees, his jeans still open, showing off his spent cock, and his torso completely naked, Logan's dick stirred at the picture he made.

Fuck yes, Tate looked well and truly claimed, and the fire that had been in his eyes from moments ago was still there as he walked forward, grabbed the back of Logan's neck, and shoved his tongue between his lips.

Logan groaned at the taste of himself on Tate's tongue, and reveled in the way his scent lingered over Tate's skin, and when Tate pulled away, turned, and picked his jacket up off the ground to shrug into it—*minus the shirt*—he'd never looked hotter.

"Just so we're clear," Tate said as he sauntered back to the driver's side of the car and opened it. Logan was busy zipping and buttoning his pants, but once he was done, he looked over. "I'm not going anywhere. There was never any doubt in my mind over who I belonged to. There hasn't been since the first time you sat down opposite me. But..." He paused and let his eyes wander over Logan, and it was all Logan could do not to go over to him and demand round two. "Feel free to make that point whenever you feel I need a reminder. *That* was fucking hot."

Logan smirked and then headed off around the hood of the car, finally happy to be back on familiar ground and in full agreement with everything Tate had just said.

Chapter Twenty-Two

"EVELYN, TO WHAT do I owe this pleasure?" Logan held the phone to his ear Monday morning and reminded himself it was rude to hang up on one's mother—if Evelyn could really be called that.

"Have you forgotten what next week is? I'm calling to find out what you want for your birthday, of course."

Logan tossed the pen he was holding down onto the desk and spun his chair around so he was facing the windows. *Thank God they don't open,* he thought, *or I just might be tempted to jump out of one.*

"Logan?"

"Yes, I'm here. But sorry, you broke up for a second there. Why did you say you were calling, again?"

"Your birthday, son. I'm calling to see what you want for it."

Logan's lip curled up at the side as he told her in a tone dripping with sarcasm, "Trust me, you don't want to know."

"Don't you be like that with me, young man."

Logan pressed his fingers against his temple. It was

unbelievable how a two-minute conversation with Evelyn could bring on an instant headache. "I'm not being like anything. But there's nothing I want." *That you can give me.*

"Fine, I'll just have to call Tate, then."

"No, you won't. I don't do birthdays. You know that, Evelyn."

There was a pause and then, as if he hadn't spoken at all, Evelyn said, "What about something for your new home?"

"I'm going to hang up now."

"Logan, I'll just call Tate…"

"And I'll text him and tell him not to pick up."

Evelyn gasped. "You wouldn't."

Okay, he probably wouldn't. But shit, he didn't want or need anything. Especially from her. As Logan shut his eyes, he thought back to last week and the photos he'd been looking at with Tate.

"Do you remember Ken?" He wasn't sure why he asked, and wasn't even sure he really wanted the answer now that he had. But as he sat there looking out at the buildings in front of him, Logan waited to see what Evelyn would say.

"Ken? The dentist?"

Yes, Evelyn. Also known as the man we lived with for two years. "Yes. Ken the dentist."

"Of course I do. Why do you ask?"

Good question. But with the past week of emotional ups and downs, he'd apparently decided he wanted to delve into every damn memory he had, whether it be painful or not, just to examine it.

What the hell is the matter with me? Midlife crisis? Oh, hell no...I'm not that old.

"No reason. I was just thinking about him the other day. I found an old book he gave me."

"The Hardy Boys. *The Tower Treasure*," Evelyn said, surprising the hell out of him.

"Yes. That's the one."

Evelyn laughed softly, and Logan almost forgot the reasons why he avoided calling her. "I remember he spent days agonizing over which book to buy you. He knew how much you loved to read and wanted to get you something special."

Logan's heart tightened at the thought. "Really?"

"Really."

"I loved that book." *And him. Then you drove him away.*

"I know. You took it to school with you. Read it at night before bed. In the morning before you left. You must have read that book a hundred times."

"Probably more." And as he thought about the inscription on the inside cover, Logan heard himself asking, "Hey, whatever happened to Ken the dentist?"

Evelyn sighed. "Last I heard, he got married and had a couple of kids. A boy and a girl."

Oh wow. Logan wasn't sure why that piece of information hurt, but it really did. They were lucky kids. "I liked him."

There was silence at the other end, and just when he thought Evelyn might say something comforting or motherly, she took in a breath and then asked, in a voice full of over-the-top cheer, "So, what did you want for your birthday, then?"

And just like Ken had been back then, he was dismissed from her mind and *their* lives with no more thought than a change in her mood.

* * *

TATE HELD THE phone to his ear Monday morning as he stood at the bay window in their new living room. There was stuff everywhere, but they were slowly making their way through the house room by room—and he was about to tackle this one. Well, after he finished with his call.

He figured he was about to hit Rachel's voicemail when, at the fifth ring, the phone connected.

"Ahh, I'm so glad you didn't hang up," Rachel said by way of greeting.

Tate chuckled but turned to plant his ass on the windowsill, letting the sun warm his back. "Nah, I thought I was going to get your voicemail and was about to leave a message."

"No. No. Thank God you didn't. I would've died if you'd left a message. I wanted to congratulate you in person, but Cole told me to at least wait until I was invited over."

Tate frowned. *Congratulate me in person? What is she —
Oh shit. She's talking about the proposal. Wait, she knew Logan
was going to ask me?*

"So..." Rachel drawled. "Congratulations! Aren't
you just *wow* that Logan asked? How are you this morning?
Over the moon, right?"

As she continued to rapid-fire the questions at him,
Tate rubbed a hand over his forehead and remained silent.

God, how was he going to tell her? Did Logan even
want him to? And why hadn't Logan told him that Rachel
and Cole knew?

This was going to be awkward.

"Tate? You still there?"

"Yeah, I'm here, but that's not why I called."

There was a long pause. "It's, uh, not?"

Yeah, now she's staring to clue in. If his non-answer
wasn't obvious enough, Tate figured the tone of his voice
was. "No. I was actually calling about Logan's birthday."

"Tate...?"

Tate sighed. He really didn't want to get into this.
And he wasn't sure Logan would want him to. But he knew
there was no way Rachel would let this go. "It's
complicated, Rach."

"Complicated?"

Tate thought about Logan's face Saturday night, the
fear that plagued him and his ability to say yes, and Sunday,
when they'd practically existed around each other like
strangers—until last night, when Logan had let him know in

no uncertain terms that he didn't care if there was a piece of paper, a ring, or a damn ceremony between them. He was his in the most basic way that one mate could be to another—so yeah, what they had, it was complicated.

"Uhh...okay," she said when Tate offered nothing more on the subject, and he had a feeling that Logan would soon be getting a call or visit from his brother at work, if he hadn't already. "You two are still togeth—"

"Of course. That hasn't changed, Rachel."

"Okay. So, umm, Logan's birthday, then."

"Yeah, I finally decided what I want to do for him. You still on board to help?" Tate rolled his eyes at the hesitant way he asked, but he was unsure she'd want to help after knowing he'd likely hurt her brother-in-law. But he should've known better.

"You know I am," Rachel told him, and the smile in her voice had Tate breathing out a sigh of relief. "Just tell me what you need."

* * *

IT HAD JUST turned eleven when Sherry called through his door, "Tate's on line one."

Logan put his pen down and picked up the phone, pressing the flashing light and connecting the call. "Hey there. I already told Sherry I was leaving early, so don't worry, I'm not leaving you with all the heavy lifting."

Tate didn't say anything in response, and Logan said,

"Tate? You there?"

"Yeah, I'm here," he said. "I'm not calling about that. I, uhh, well, I just got off the phone with Rachel."

Oh shit. Logan didn't even have to ask to know what had been discussed during that conversation. *Fucking hell,* how had he forgotten to tell Tate that Cole and Rachel knew?

"Tate, I—"

"No, it's okay. I just wanted to give you a heads-up because I figure it'll take less than the time it took me to call you for her to text Cole."

Logan sighed. After he'd ignored a text from Cole on Sunday asking how everything had gone, he'd totally forgotten to deal with him after that. But the minute his brother got back from court today, he would be in Logan's office wanting to know what had happened this weekend.

"Logan?"

"Yeah?"

"I didn't tell her much of anything. Just that it was complicated. I'm sorry. I wasn't sure what to say, and I didn't want to lie."

"No. No. Of course you shouldn't lie." As silence fell between them, Logan pinched the bridge of his nose.

"They're probably going to hate me now, aren't they?"

"What? No. Why would they hate you?"

Tate didn't answer, but Logan wasn't about to let him go back down that rabbit hole again. There was no more room for guilt here. Not between them and not between their families. He was done with that emotion.

"Listen to me," Logan said. "You did nothing wrong. You were honest, and yeah, it hurt at the time, but I'd rather you tell me the truth than lie to me. What happened between us this weekend is nobody's business but ours. And if and when we're ready to talk about it again, we will. Okay?"

"Okay."

"And you and me, we're good. Tell me you know that." Logan's heart thumped hard. "Tate?"

"Yes, I know we're good."

"Good. Then I'm going to go and finish up some paperwork I have here so I can leave on time and come home to you."

"That's the best thing I've heard all day."

"Really?" Logan said, and he dropped his voice down to be sure nothing he said drifted out his cracked door. "What about this morning when you made me shout your name?"

Tate laughed, and Logan grinned in response. "Yeah, you're right. That was the best thing. But hurry home, okay? This house is too big and empty when you're not in it."

Tell me about it, Logan thought. And it was comments like that that let him know they were more than okay. "I'll be there as soon as I can get there."

"Logan?"

"Yeah?"

"Be here sooner." And with that, Tate hung up.

"YOU'VE BEEN AVOIDING my calls."

Logan didn't have to look up from his computer to know that Cole had just walked through his office door. Instead, he continued working and didn't bother stopping until Cole put his briefcase down in one of the chairs facing Logan's desk, and then planted himself in the chair beside it.

Logan rocked back in his seat, twirled his pen through his fingers, and stared at Cole. Then, because he knew it would distract Cole from what he was no doubt there to talk about, he said, "I had a dream about you the other night."

Cole cocked his head. "You did? Was I annoyed at you? Because that seems highly likely."

"Actually, yes, you were. It was that day on the university library stairs—you know, after you beat the shit out of Chris?"

"Oh yes," Cole said with a smile, as though he was remembering it fondly. "What made you think of that?"

Logan sat up and tapped his pen on his legal pad. "Ahh, just everything going on this week with Jill, I think. Brothers, sisters, that kind of thing."

"Really?" Cole's eyes narrowed, as though he didn't believe that, and Logan knew if he didn't keep talking that Cole would start asking questions. Questions he didn't want to answer. So the best way to deal with that was to be evasive as hell. *A.k.a. talk about what I want to talk about.*

"Yeah. You know that Tate and I went to Jill's last

night. I finally got to meet his nephews. They're great, by the way. And Copper, the oldest one, is the spitting image of Tate, only with glasses."

"As fascinating as that is, and it really is, I want to know more about it. How about you go back to the beginning of your weekend? To the part where you had Rachel and me go over to your condo and set the place up so you could ask Tate to—"

"Why? I already know Rachel told you how that ended. So why do we need to go over it all again?"

Cole uncrossed his legs and sat forward. "So he really said no?"

"Well, I'm not engaged, so…"

"Logan, stop fucking around for one second in your life, would you, and answer me."

Logan glared at Cole. "He *really* said no."

Cole looked as though someone had socked him in the stomach. *Probably the same way I looked the first time I heard Tate's answer.* "But…that makes no sense."

"It makes a whole lot of sense, actually."

"But Tate loves you. Like, crazy, ridiculous loves you. Everyone knows that."

"I know," Logan said, and smiled, because he did know that.

"Then why would he say no? And how are you smiling about it?"

"Oh, trust me. I wasn't smiling at the time. I almost called you guys to come get me Saturday night, but instead took a walk down at the harbor."

Cole frowned. "It was pouring on Saturday night."

"Yes, it was."

"Logan… What the hell happened?"

Logan took in a breath and got out of his chair. He slid his hands into his pockets and then wandered over to the window, knowing it would be easier to say this if he *wasn't* looking at Cole. "There were things I hadn't…considered, I suppose you could say."

"What kind of things?"

Logan closed his eyes and thought of Tate in their bedroom Sunday morning, confessing his deepest fears. "The past. Things I should've probably thought to talk to him about and didn't."

Logan turned around to face Cole and leaned back against the window. "The romantic gesture would've been amazing if we'd been on the same page. But for once in our relationship, I was several chapters ahead of him, and didn't bother to warn him about the giant twist that was about to take place."

Cole frowned, and Logan pushed off the window and walked over to his chair, putting his hands on the back of it.

"So where does that leave the two of you?"

"At first? In a really awkward spot. *God.* Sunday was painful. It was like we were walking on eggshells around each other, not knowing what to say. Not knowing how to act. It was the worst fucking feeling in the world."

"But now…?"

Logan smiled. "Now we're good. I never thought I'd say this, but I think going to Jill's was probably the best thing that we could've done last night. We both agreed to push the issue aside for the evening and just get through the night. Lord knows dealing with Tate's family and all of that was more than enough to distract us." Logan pulled his chair out, sat down, then placed his arms on the desk and grinned. "But then something amazing happened. We had a wonderful night. His friends and family were awesome. His nephews missed him and didn't even care that their uncle had a boyfriend, and after that, Tate took me to the drive-in."

Cole arched an eyebrow. "The drive-in? I thought the only one that was still functional around here was the Cascades. And you weren't that far out of town, were you?"

"Nope. He took me to the Harvest Moon Drive-In. It's *abandoned*." As Logan aimed a *get my drift* expression Cole's way, his brother sat back and steepled his hands over his stomach.

"Ahh, so that accounts for the smile?"

"Part of it. But yes, Tate and I are good. We've shelved the discussion for now, and honestly, I don't know that we'll ever go back to it."

"And you're okay with that?" Cole asked, and Logan took a second to really think about that, then nodded.

"Yes, I am. Do I want to marry Tate? Apparently I do. But he's not ready and might never be. That doesn't diminish or lessen the fact that before all of this I was one hundred percent happy and I still am. And as long as it's stated that I'm his emergency contact and that our wills are clear and up to date, then I will go on being happy. He isn't going anywhere. I know that."

Cole relaxed into his chair and put his palms on the arms. "Well, okay then. Is Tate all right?"

Logan slowly nodded. "I think so. He seemed okay this morning, and I'm knocking off in about an hour to go home and help him unpack. He took the night off from work so we could get some more done."

"I don't envy you that job. Rach and I don't plan to move house again for a very long time, if ever. What a nightmare." Cole got to his feet and picked up his briefcase. "Okay, I'm going to head to my office if you don't need anything else from me."

"I didn't need anything in the first place. You tracked me down to gossip, remember?"

"Oh, right." As Cole got to the door, he tapped his hand on it and aimed one last look in Logan's direction. "You sure you're okay? I can go hunt Tate down and kick his ass if you're not. I'm good at that—just ask Chris Walker."

"If it's all the same to you, I'd rather pry my eyes out and eat them for dinner than have to speak to him for any reason. As for kicking Tate's ass, don't you dare. The only person with permission to ever touch that part of his body is me, and kicking it is not what I plan to do with it. Him and I, we're just fine."

"Fair enough. I'll talk to you later, brother."

"Talk to you later."

Chapter Twenty-Three

"LOGAN," TATE CALLED out as he came downstairs Saturday morning. It had just turned ten, and Logan had let him sleep in a little after they'd spent last night finishing up with the final boxes.

They were almost done with getting everything in order, and all that was really left now was putting together some of the bigger furniture items and buying a few pieces they needed, now that they had more space and a couple of extra rooms to fill.

As Tate's bare feet hit the main floor, he thought he'd regret that he'd forgotten his socks, but when only warmth greeted him, he noticed that Logan had the fireplace going. Tate smiled to himself as he looked at the sun sneaking through the partially drawn curtains of the window, and was thankful Logan had gone with the gas, regardless of how hard the sun was trying.

This room had fast become one of Tate's favorites in the house. They'd purchased a three-seater couch that fit perfectly under the window, and yesterday, after it had been delivered along with a new coffee table, the two of them had finally hung the TV above the fireplace. And with Logan's original loveseat and recliner in place, the living room was complete.

"Logan," Tate called out again.

"I'm in the office."

Tate walked through to the kitchen, and the rich aroma of coffee filled his nose. He headed over to the pot and poured himself a mug, and then he made his way into the office to find Logan seated at his desk with his computer on and coffee in hand.

As Logan looked over to the double French doors that Tate had just stepped through, a lazy smile spread across his lips. "Hello. I was wondering when you'd make your way downstairs today."

Tate walked around the desk and bent to kiss Logan good morning. "Hmm, I was tired. Long week."

"Long few weeks, really."

Tate rested his backside up against the desk. "This month has been—"

"Full on?" Logan said. "I feel like we need a vacation from moving."

Tate took a slow sip of his coffee and nodded. "You know what, that's not such a bad idea."

"What? A vacation?"

"Uhh, I was thinking more a weekend away."

Logan shoved his chair away from the desk a little and kicked a leg out to urge Tate to slide down the desk and stand in front of him. "I could get on board with that idea."

Tate put his mug down on the desk and then leaned

over to put an arm on either side of Logan's chair. "Good. Because I need you to go upstairs and pack."

Logan sat back a little and narrowed his eyes. "Umm…don't you think we should maybe decide where we're going and book a place?"

Tate kissed him quickly and grinned. "Already taken care of." As he went to pick up his coffee, Logan reached out and took hold of his shirt. Tate stilled and chuckled at the deep frown now etched between Logan's brows.

"What do you mean it's already taken care of?"

"Well, I wanted to do something special for—"

"Do *not* say my birthday, Tate. Because I have to say, I was more than a little happy you acted as though it didn't exist. I've been trying to make you forget that date ever since we got together."

Tate rolled his eyes. "Do you really think I'd ever forget your birthday? November ninth. Don't think I didn't notice you conveniently worked late Thursday night."

Logan's mouth fell open. "I was busy."

"*You* are full of shit. But it doesn't matter because you're not getting out of this. Now go upstairs and pack a bag, Mr. Mitchell."

"And if I don't?"

"Well, I wouldn't care if you walked around naked for two days," Tate said as he removed Logan's hand from his shirt, "but everyone else might."

As the words sank in, Logan sat up and made a play to grab Tate. "Wait. Everyone *else*?" Tate dodged Logan's hand and made a beeline for the door, his coffee forgotten. "Get back here, Morrison," Logan called, but Tate just laughed and headed upstairs to pack his bag—and Logan's.

* * *

AN HOUR AND a half later, when the doorbell rang, Logan trudged down the stairs as though he was headed toward a firing squad, and the *only* reason Tate was still alive was because he'd invited himself into Logan's shower thirty minutes earlier.

Somewhere between getting him into the shower, lathering him up, and then helping him dry off, the sneaky fucker had informed Logan they were headed out of town with some friends of theirs and that they were going to be picked up at noon. *And he hasn't told me shit since.*

As Logan reached the bottom of the stairs, where Tate was waiting for him, he aimed a scowl in his direction, but it was hard to stay annoyed at someone who looked so fucking good—and Tate looked unbelievable.

In boots, blue jeans, and a burgundy sweater, Tate had a black scarf slung around his neck and a matching slouchy beanie sitting a little ways back on his head. He had his sunglasses hanging in the V-neck and a jacket in his hand.

"You ready?" Tate asked, as Logan came to a stop in front of him.

"I *suppose.* But for what I don't know, since you

won't tell."

Tate grinned and handed Logan his navy-blue peacoat. "That's right. It's called a surprise."

As Tate opened the front door, a bald man in a suit greeted them.

"Hello. Mr. Morrison?"

"Yeah, that's me. But you can call me Tate. This here is Logan."

The man looked at Logan and aimed a knowing smile in his direction. "Ahh yes, the birthday boy."

Logan aimed an *I'm going to kill you* look in Tate's direction, but Tate merely shrugged and slipped his sunglasses on. *Jesus*, it was going to be a long two days if this was what he had to look forward to.

* * *

ALTHOUGH LOGAN LOOKED as though he wanted to murder him, Tate couldn't help but admire the man as he hefted up his overnight bag over his shoulder.

Larry, their driver for the weekend, was walking up the path ahead of them as Tate waited at the bottom of the stairs for Logan to lock the front door. He took a moment to run his eyes over the back of his lawyer as he pocketed the keys and turned around to face him. In his hip-length peacoat, Logan looked sexy and stylish. He'd flipped up the collar and had now put on his black sunglasses as he started down the stairs. With the rest of his getup as dark as his coal-colored hair, the black designer jeans and pullover gave Logan a dark and dangerous vibe, and the scowl on his handsome face helped, too.

When he got to the bottom of the stairs, he finally glanced over Tate's shoulder, and the scowl turned to shock. "You hired a fucking limo? Are you out of your mind?"

Tate grabbed either side of Logan's coat and tugged him forward to kiss his mouth. "*Please* try and contain your excitement. If you don't calm down, I might have to subdue you."

"Very funny. But really, a limo? You know how I feel about my—"

"Logan?"

"What?"

Tate leaned forward and nipped at his lower lip. "Shut. Your. Mouth."

When Tate let him go, Logan reached for his sunglasses and lowered them slightly to peer at him.

"I'm replacing a bad memory with a good one."

Logan sighed and shook his head. "Well, I guess I can't argue with that."

Tate held his hand out. "No, you can't. Now come on. We don't want to be late."

"Where are we going again?"

"Ha. Nice try. But you're just going to have to wait and see."

"Fine. Fine. And who's in the car?"

"Again. You're going to have to—"

"Yeah, yeah, yeah. Has anyone every told you you're a pain in the ass? You could give me some kind of hint."

"I could," Tate said as he held open the small gate for Logan. "But where would be the fun in that?"

Logan continued to grumble as Tate shut the gate behind him, and when they got to the curb beside the back door of the white Hummer limousine, Larry opened the door and gestured for them to hop in.

As soon as Logan stuck his head inside the vehicle, Tate heard him groan and then try to back right on out. But Tate was there, shoving Logan inside whether he wanted to go or not.

Tate wasn't shocked by the faces staring at the two of them once they were inside. Nor was he surprised that when the door shut behind them, locking him and Logan in the vehicle, the tinted windows made it appear as though it were nighttime and allowed the neon to light up the interior.

"Gotta say, Tate, I wasn't sure you'd get him out the front door and into the car if he knew what was going on. I'm impressed," Cole said, then aimed a shit-eating grin in Logan's direction.

"Oh, stop it, Cole," Rachel said, bumping her shoulder against her husband's. "Of course Logan was going to show up. The entire weekend is about him."

"You know, there's still time for me to leave," Logan said, but Tate pointed to two empty spots and said, "Sit, counselor."

As Logan glared over his shoulder, Tate took his

glasses off and winked before he nudged Logan down into a seat, and the two of them looked around at the rest of the familiar faces.

Beside Cole and Rachel sat Shelly, who was holding a glass of champagne, and Tate thought a drink for himself and the man beside him didn't sound like a bad idea. And beside *her* was her husband, Josh, who raised a beer in their direction and then gestured over his shoulder to what looked like a minibar built into the side of the limo with an ice bucket, champagne flutes, tumblers, wine, beer, and—

"They got any hard liquor in there?" Logan asked, and this time it was the newest face in the crowd who spoke up.

"There's scotch or vodka," Priest said as he raised a tumbler filled with ice, and what Tate assumed was vodka, judging by the clear liquid inside, to his lips.

"I'll take a scotch—neat," Logan said to Josh, and Tate opted for a Corona.

Tate hadn't been sure that Priest would accept this weekend's invitation. But he'd surprised the hell out of him by saying yes, and Tate had to admit it was going to make things that much more interesting, considering he'd also invited the quietest passenger thus far, who sat directly beside him—Robbie.

"Did you already get a drink?" Tate asked, and Robbie shook his head.

"Oh, that's okay. I don't drink much."

Logan peered around Tate's shoulder and scoffed at

Robbie. "Since when? If I've got to put up with this and try to enjoy it, then you can at least have a drink. Plus, have you forgotten, I've seen you plastered, young man. Don't try and play the sweet and innocent card around here."

Robbie arched an eyebrow at Logan. "Fine." He aimed a look at Josh. "I'll take a vodka soda to salute the *old* man we're celebrating this weekend."

Logan leaned across the back of Tate's seat and flicked Robbie in the shoulder. "I'm still your boss, remember?"

To which Robbie replied, with all the sass and attitude he possessed, "Not this weekend, you're not."

Once they all had their drinks in hand, Tate looked to Logan. "Lena and Mason are meeting us there this afternoon. Lena had to work."

"Meeting us *where*?" Logan asked, but Tate just wagged his finger. Logan was loosening up, and Tate knew by this afternoon he would be having a blast.

Replacing a bad memory with a good one...

He watched Logan down his drink in one gulp and then lean over and kiss Tate's lips. "Okay, Morrison. Do your worst, and if you're lucky, there'll be enough alcohol in this limo for me to forget how underhanded you were about this."

Tate thought of their final destination and kissed him back. "Somehow, I'm not too worried, Mr. Mitchell. You just sit back and relax. It's time to celebrate."

Chapter Twenty-Four

AROUND FORTY MINUTES—not to mention several drinks—later, the limo came to a stop and Logan tried to shift around Tate to get a glimpse out the window.

"Stop it." Tate put a hand to Logan's shoulder and slowly pushed him back into his seat. "For someone who put up such an argument about even coming today, you sure are eager to see where we are."

Logan leaned in to Tate's side and twisted one of the curls peeking out from his beanie around his index finger. "You know me. I can't stand to be the only one who doesn't know what's going on."

Tate arched an eyebrow and shook his head. "I'm not going to tell you, even with you looking at me like that."

"And how am I looking at you?"

"Like you're thinking of ways to persuade me to do what you want."

Logan removed his hand from Tate's hair and brought it down to cover his heart. "You wound me. I would never do anything so underhanded. If I wanted something, I'd just pin you down and *make* you talk."

Tate scoffed at the arrogance in that comment. "I'd like to see you try."

"Oh, I'm sure you would." Logan ran his eyes over Tate's outfit and trailed his fingers down the side of his scarf. "Where you're taking me, do we have to spend all our time with this bunch of yahoos? Or do we have a…private area?"

"We have a private *suite.*"

Logan's cock jumped at that new piece of information as he tried to work out where the hell they were. They'd been on the road now for some time, and he'd tried his best to get details out of the other occupants of the car, but so far no one had budged.

"Leave Tate alone," Cole said from where he sat with an arm slung around Rachel's shoulders. Logan didn't let go of Tate's scarf but looked over his shoulder at his brother, trying to decide if his attire gave anything away about where they were headed—it didn't.

Cole was in dark blue jeans and a light grey turtleneck—nothing out of the ordinary.

"I don't *want* to leave Tate alone, and since this is my day, you can just deal with it. It's not my fault you all invited yourself along to wherever it is we're going."

"Tate invited us," Shelly said from beside a chuckling Rachel, and Logan aimed his eyes her way. "And I, for one, am going to enjoy myself, whether *you* are being petulant or not." The blond bombshell raised a second glass of champagne to her lips and swallowed it down. Logan noted she was wearing knee-high brown leather boots with a cream woolen dress, and was pleased by the prospect that whatever they were doing, the good doctor could obviously accomplish it in heels.

"I'm not being petulant. I've decided to embrace my weekend even *with* friends and family along." Logan scanned everyone in the limo. "But if any of you mention the B-word, the O-word, or a particular number to me, I don't care who you are, by tomorrow morning the rest of us will be playing How to Host a Murder with you as the victim."

Robbie snorted. "God, you're not that ol—"

Logan pinned him with a fierce glare. "Says the young whippersnapper in the car who is all of twenty-nine."

"Huh." That came from Priest, and had everyone looking in his direction.

"You got something to say over there?" Robbie asked.

Priest shook his head, his hunter-green sweater making his auburn hair look extra fiery today. "No. I just thought you were much younger."

When everyone in the car fell silent, Logan looked between Priest and Robbie and noticed Robbie's eyes had narrowed to slits. "What's that supposed to mean?" Robbie demanded.

Priest finished the vodka he'd been sipping for the last fifteen minutes and shrugged. "Just that you act younger than your age."

"You insufferable assho—"

The door to the limousine opened, and Larry announced, just in time to prevent an all-out war, "Okay, everyone, we're here."

* * *

TATE WAS STARTING to second-guess how wise it had been to invite Priest *and* Robbie along with them this weekend as everyone began to climb out of the Hummer.

Once they were all out and standing in front of a large house covered in ivy, Tate took Logan's hand in his. "This is Lynley Winery Bed & Breakfast." Logan looked at him, and Tate arched an eyebrow. "You know, one of those places for you fancy wine-tasting types."

Logan angled his body into Tate's and grinned. "I might be familiar with those."

"Yeah?"

"Yeah," Logan said as he looked back to what Tate knew was the "old house" of the property. That's where he'd been told they needed to check in. "This place is beautiful."

"So...good surprise?" Tate asked as he watched everyone else head over to the wide set of stone stairs that led up to the front door.

"A very good surprise." Logan walked alongside Tate as he led them toward the rest of the group. "And you said we have a suite here tonight?"

"We do."

"So that means we get to taste *all* the wine we want and neither of us have to drive anywhere?"

As they took the stairs up under a second-floor balcony, Tate nodded. "None of us do. And I was thinking I might put in an order for some new wines. I'd love them to be local. So what do you say? Up for a little taste testing with me?"

Logan's eyes lit as Tate opened the main door, and as he walked past, Logan said, "I'm up for tasting anything you want me to tonight."

Tate chuckled and pointed inside. "Go, troublemaker. Your guests are waiting on you."

Logan strolled in through the gift shop and under an arched hallway to where they were to check in, and as Tate came around the corner and saw how Logan had neatly situated himself between Robbie and Priest, he couldn't stop the laugh that bubbled up.

Damn, he loved that man. Logan was intuitive as hell. And as he stood there with their family and friends, Tate took the time to really drink in the sight of the people in their lives.

Cole, Rachel, and Logan were all laughing at something Robbie had just said, while Priest merely looked on like the silent observer he was. Shelly and Josh were at the main desk talking to a woman with a friendly grin, and as she nodded and gestured to a hall to her left, Shelly looked over her shoulder and said, "Okay, are you guys ready to go and get plastered on Logan's dime?"

"I believe, actually, that Tate's paying," Logan said.

Shelly smiled and gave Tate a flirty little wave. "That's what you think, handsome."

They all laughed and started off after her, but when Logan realized Tate wasn't over there yet, he looked over his shoulder to seek him out. As his eyes came to a halt on him where Tate stood leaning against the archway, Logan walked back in his direction.

"You coming?" Logan asked.

Tate nodded and pushed off the wall. "Yeah. I was just taking a step back to watch."

"Oh yeah? And what did you see?"

"You," Tate said, and cupped Logan's chin. "I always see you."

"Hmm, well, I'm not going to complain about that."

"No, I didn't think you would."

"Want to show me our suite? I think you'd be able to see me *much* better there."

"No," Tate said. "You have a bir—"

"Uh ah." Logan put a finger to Tate's lips. "I have a *wine* tasting to go to."

Tate's lips twitched. "You do know you never have to worry about your age, don't you? You get better looking with every year that passes."

"You have to say that. You love me."

Tate took Logan's wrist and drew his hand away, lacing their fingers together. "I'd say that even if I were a straight man and we were just friends."

Logan's eyes widened, and he looked horrified.
"Don't even joke about that. Why would you say something
so heinous to the birthday boy?"

"I'm sorry, what did you just call yourself?"

Logan opened his mouth, but when he realized
exactly what he'd said, he pointed an accusing finger at Tate.
"That's cheating."

"No, it's not."

"Yes, it fucking is. Going around calling yourself a
straight man to get a reaction out of me *is* cheating. That
word was banished from our lives years ago." Logan
sounded so put-out that Tate couldn't stop himself from
laughing.

"I didn't say that. I said *if* I were a straight man…"
Tate lowered his eyes to Logan's mouth. "Which clearly I'm
not, with what I'm thinking." When Logan remained
stubbornly quiet, Tate grinned. "I'll make a deal with you.
Later tonight I'll take the *birthday boy* back to our suite and
prove to him just how crooked this *straight* tree's roots have
become over the years."

As his words penetrated Logan's irked attitude, Tate
saw the instant he picked up on them and realized they were
the same words he'd used back when he'd been trying his
hand at convincing a very straight man to give in
and…experiment.

"You know," Logan said, "it's kind of rude to use my
own arguments on me in such a sneaky way."

"After years of living with you, I've had to adapt to

ever have a chance of coming out on top." Tate winked at Logan, who just grumbled some more, and then tugged on his hand as they headed toward the hall to go and track down the others.

Chapter Twenty-Five

AS IT TURNED out, Tate had rented the Founder's Room, a private function room that could be booked for small gatherings or larger, more corporate affairs, and today / tonight, it was all theirs.

Their bags had been taken off to their individual suites. Logan had been informed they were staying in the Italian Suite, and they were all now relaxing in front of a fireplace with several bottles of wine on the table, a port bottle that Logan had wanted to try, and a couple of sideboards packed with apple slices, grapes, fine and hard cheese, and fluffy homemade breadsticks.

There were a couple of small tables that sat four over by the windows, where Lena and Mason had just taken up a seat after finally arriving, along with Shelly and Josh. And over at the other table were Robbie and Rachel, who were talking about what color one of them—Logan wasn't sure who—should color their hair. Cole was over on one of the two leather couches talking to Priest, and Logan had taken up a spot as close to Tate as publicly acceptable on the other couch.

Now that everyone had arrived, the sommelier, a

middle-aged gentleman with a thick head of salt-and-pepper hair who introduced himself as Dave, came out with a tray full of empty wine glasses and instructed them each to take two. Then he went back to the private bar around the corner of the room and quickly returned with four port snifters.

After handing those to Cole, Priest, Tate, and himself, Logan settled back in his seat and begrudgingly admitted that an afternoon/evening at a winery where he didn't have to drive anywhere was really the perfect birthday present.

If he were into birthdays...which he was not.

"Okay, everyone, if I could get your attention. First, let me start off by saying welcome to the Lynley Winery Bed & Breakfast. We're delighted that you've chosen to come and taste a few of our wines and, I see, some of our ports, as well as spend the night on our property. We have several tours that are offered daily, should you wish to take one tomorrow before you head home. And if I may be so bold as to recommend my own personal favorite, that would be the cellar tour, which will take you down under the property to where we keep all of the wine bottles and barrels."

Logan leaned into Tate. "Maybe you and I could go and get lost down there now. Think anyone would miss us?"

Tate bumped his shoulder into Logan's. "Behave, would you, *birthday* boy."

"I will if you promise to stop calling me that."

"Looks like I'll have to keep you in line, then, because *that* is your name until tomorrow."

Logan rolled his eyes, but then settled back into his

spot and returned his attention to the man now holding up the first wine bottle.

"Tonight we'll be starting with our ice wine. It has a tropical feel to it, and is for someone who likes something sweet on their palate."

"Ohh, that sounds delicious," Shelly said, and Robbie turned around to tell her, "I've had some *amazing* ice wines. This one sounds to die for from the description on the menu."

"How about you just take that bottle over there?" Cole said, pointing toward the table where Robbie, Shelly, and Lena sat.

Rachel and Mason both turned their noses up, and Mason covered the top of his glass. "I'll pass, thanks. We've got a few of those at Exquisite, and they're a little too sweet for me."

"Me too," Rachel said, as she looked over the menu card in front of her. "But I'd love to try the Cuvée White. Does it really taste like buttered popcorn?"

Tate screwed his nose up in disgust. "Okay, you don't even have the excuse that you're pregnant for that oddball choice."

"As far as we all know, anyway," Logan said, aiming his eyes in Cole's direction.

"Do you really think we'd come to a winery if Rachel were pregnant?" Cole asked.

"Can you please stop saying the P-word?" Shelly raised her glass and took a sip. "The children were all left home tonight for a reason. Except for Logan, but we needed him for the free food. Hmm, I just might need another bottle of that."

"Certainly, ma'am," Dave said as he hurried off to the bar area, and Shelly looked over to Logan. "So you turned, what? Forty-five this week?"

As Rachel laughed, and Shelly gave Logan a flirty wink.

"Fuck you, Dr. Monroe," Logan said, and aimed a fake smile her way.

"Aww." Shelly slipped off her chair and dug into her handbag for a small box before crossing over to Logan. "You wish you could've been lucky enough to experience that, Mitchell."

Shelly handed him a beautifully wrapped box and kissed him on the cheek. "Happy birthday, you pain in the ass." She turned to Tate with a devious smile on her face. "I mean, with an ego the size of his, I figure that nickname would be accurate, right? He's got to have the equipment to match. My condolences."

"*Shelly*," Josh said.

"What?" she said, glancing at her husband before turning back to look down at Tate. "Did I offend you?"

Tate started laughing. "Not at all."

"I figured," she said, and then gestured to the box with her head as she took another sip of her wine. "Open it."

"Geez," Logan said, and looked around her toward Josh. "She always this bossy?"

"You don't need to ask *him*. I'm right here."

"*And* there's your answer." Josh chuckled. "You know Shel."

"That I do," Logan said as he looked up at the blonde who had, once upon a time, been his lifeline through a trauma he'd never imagined he'd have to deal with. And seeing her here like this was always such a kick, knowing how serious she was when it came to her job. "Okay, okay. Am I going to regret this?"

"No. It's just a little something I saw, and thought of you."

When she grinned at Tate, Logan let out a groan. "Yeah, I'm totally going to regret this."

After he pulled the silver ribbon off the box and dropped it in Tate's lap, Logan slipped off the lid and looked inside. There, nestled in black satin, were two sterling silver rectangular cuff links with something engraved on them. He reached inside, and when he pulled them out and read them, he groaned and glanced up at Shelly, who blew him a kiss.

"Imagine wearing those in a courtroom. You'd totally distract your opposing counsel. They'd be so curious."

"*Or* they'd ask me on a date."

"What do they say?" Tate asked, and Logan handed them over.

As soon as Tate was done reading them, he started laughing and held them up to read out loud the first one: "Mine's twelve inches." And then the second: "But I don't use it as a rule."

"You can thank me later after you start winning all your cases," she said as she headed back to her seat.

"Yes, because that's been such a problem for me lately," Logan said. "Winning cases."

"See?" Shelly said. "There's that big...*ego.*"

Just as she sat back down, Dave came back with her bottle of wine and uncorked the Cuvée White for Rachel. He then came back around to where he'd put two bottles of red and picked up the first.

"Okay, who'd like to try the Sangiovese 2007 Reserve? It's a rich, bold flavor of mocha and figs, very nice for the sophisticated palate."

Logan glanced at Tate. "Better count you out, then, huh?"

"Oh, that's nice."

"Aren't you the one who told me you didn't know anything about all that fancy wine stuff?"

"Maybe," Tate said, his eyes alight with humor.

"Then you better go and sit over there at the kiddies' table," Logan said, indicating in Robbie and Rachel's direction with a tilt of his head. "This stuff is for the adults."

Tate took hold of Logan's chin and kissed his smart-talking lips. "You really want me to go and sit next to *Robbie* instead of you?" As Tate scraped his teeth over Logan's bottom lip, he groaned.

Cole coughed from somewhere behind them, and when Logan waved him off, his brother said, "Uhh, do you two need a room?"

Tate's eyes sparkled, and Logan wondered how long they had to wait before it was considered appropriate to leave. "No. Your voice was enough to dampen even my rampant desire, brother."

"I'm so glad to hear it," Cole said as Logan reluctantly turned away from Tate to face Dave, who was holding up the wine bottle and looking down at the two of them.

"Would you both like to try a glass?"

Logan smiled and then reached for his and Tate's glasses. "We would, thank you."

Dave poured two servings and then went around the room to fill glasses for Cole, Priest, Mason, and Josh.

As it turned out, the Sangiovese 2007 Reserve was by far the crowd favorite, and by the end of that second bottle, Tate had ordered a case for The Popped Cherry and Mason a case for Exquisite.

And if things kept up like this, Logan had a feeling there'd be many more winery trips in their future—only without the entourage, if he had any say.

* * *

SOMETIME LATER, EVERYONE was well on their way to being relaxed, and Tate was pleased to see that Logan had forgotten somewhere along the way to be annoyed about the whole birthday shindig.

They'd all moved out to the balcony for a little bit and taken up seats around a fire pit. There were a couple of outdoor heaters also, so even as the night took over from the day and the chill tried to chase them back inside, the alcohol and heaters were warming them all enough for now to enjoy themselves a little longer on the privacy of the deck.

Mason and Lena had said their goodnights around ten minutes ago, both tired after working all day, but the rest of them lounged around chatting about anything and everything—how Logan and Tate were finally settling into their new home, how Priest was getting ready to move into their old condo—and then Rachel decided to drop the mother of all bombs into the casual and friendly conversation just to make things…interesting.

"Okay, *Priest*. Since you're the new guy and all, I think it's time to fess up. Did you leave a girlfriend back in L.A.?" she asked, and then giggled. "Get it? Priest? Confess?"

Rachel had pretty much finished that bottle of buttered popcorn wine alone, since she was the only one who actually liked it, and it had left her more outgoing than usual. And, Tate had to admit, ridiculously amusing.

Cole wrapped an arm around her and kissed her cheek, and when she blushed like a schoolgirl and leaned in to deepen it, Logan held his port snifter out to Tate and said, "Can you please refill this before I lose my buzz? My eyesight is starting to come back, and I don't really like what I'm seeing."

Tate laughed, and as he reached for the bottle of
cherry port they'd all gotten stuck into when they'd come
out here, he felt Logan's fingers trail up his leg. He turned
back not seconds later, bottle in hand, and poured some of
the *Cherrivino* into the snifter and then snuck a kiss from his
lawyer. "You're going to be the one who tastes like a cherry
tonight."

Logan sipped at the port and then waggled his
eyebrows. "There's a first time for everything. Want to suck
on my seed?"

Fuck yes, I do, Tate thought, loving this flirtatious side
of Logan even as his hand slipped higher up his leg, making
it difficult for Tate to sit still. "You know I do."

"Mhmm. Good. Then make sure you buy a couple of
bottles of that for home, and one for later. It's fucking
delicious."

And so are you, Tate thought, but then made himself
turn back to the previous conversation before he lost all
thread of it.

Rachel had just sat back and touched her fingers to
her lips, but before a lawyer also distracted her, she turned
to Priest and zeroed in on him again. She crossed her legs,
rested her elbow on her knee, and said, "I'm not trying to be
nosey or anything…"

"Yes, you are," Cole said, and then laughed. "Just
excuse her, she's—"

"Curious," Rachel interrupted. "I'm *curious* about the
new guy to the group, that's all. Everyone else I know

about."

"You don't know about Robbie." Priest's voice was so cool and calm, you never would've known he'd drunk just as much as the rest of them.

"Well…" Rachel said, and then swung her gaze over to Robbie, whose face had turned the same shade as his scarlet vest. He looked as though he wanted to strangle Priest. "That's not really true. I've been talking to him all night. But you," she said, circling her finger in the air at Priest. "*You* are a mystery."

"Am I?" Priest said, and Tate was close to backing Rachel up by agreeing, but he didn't want to piss the guy off, so he stayed silent.

Rachel flashed a smile and then nodded. "Yep, totally mysterious. He used to be like that," she said, gesturing with her thumb over her shoulder at Cole, and Logan let out a boisterous laugh.

"Ouch, brother," Logan said, and Cole pinned him with a *shut the hell up* look, which only made Logan laugh louder.

Disregarding the two brothers, Rachel continued, "You have this"—she waved her hand around—"air about you."

Priest downed the last sip of his wine and then said, cool as a cucumber, "The answer is no to the girlfriend back in L.A."

"Like that's a surprise." At Robbie's mumbled response, Priest turned in his direction, as did everyone *else* on the balcony. "Sorry, did I say that out loud?"

Shelly leaned over to Robbie, patted him on the thigh, and said in a stage whisper, "Yeah you did, sweet cheeks."

"Shit," Robbie said, and Logan singsonged, "*I told you before...* Thou dost protest too much."

As Robbie glared daggers at Logan over the inside joke, Tate caught Shelly's eyes narrow before Rachel went right back to grilling Priest.

"So no girlfriend?"

"No."

"Wife?"

Priest screwed his nose up. "No."

"*Ohh.*" Rachel held her finger up. "Boyfriend?"

Priest looked around at everybody staring at him with the best poker face Tate had ever seen, and he was around Logan and Cole weekly, so that was saying something. Then the guarded bastard turned back to Rachel and shook his head. "No."

A frown hit her forehead, and she cocked her head as she regarded him for several beats. "Okay, I give up. Are you really a priest, then?"

Priest's lips curled up on one side, and as he reclined in his chair, he shook his head and said, "Definitely no."

"Ugh." Rachel slumped back against Cole, who laughed and kissed her temple.

"Well, you tried."

"I did," she said, sounding utterly defeated. "He's a

fortress."

That he fucking is, Tate thought. *What did Logan call him? A vault?* Tate wrapped an arm around Logan's shoulders and saw Shelly look over at Priest and then back to Robbie before she aimed a cheeky wink at him and Logan. *Oh shit, here comes trouble.*

"Well, you know what I think?" Shelly said, and took a sip from her port glass. "Robbie's single and you're new in town, so maybe he could show you around. You know, since you aren't seeing anyone."

Robbie's head snapped to the right so quickly that Tate was surprised he didn't get a crick in his neck.

"I am positive he could find someone other than me to show him around," Robbie said. "In fact, I'm thinking anyone *other* than me would fit the bill."

"Really?" Shelly said. "But you're so nice, and he's—"

"Not," Robbie ended for her.

Logan actually snorted as he laughed at Robbie's reaction, and when Tate looked down at him and caught his eyes, he noticed they were slightly glazed as the birthday boy then switched gears, checked Tate out, and subjected him to an intense eye fuck.

Christ, he really wanted to get him back to their room—like, now.

"Aww, Robbie," Logan said as he peered around Tate's shoulder, the alcohol definitely making his words a little lazier than before. "You don't have to sound so horrified by the prospect. Priest's really a good guy."

"Sure he is."

"You do know I'm right here, don't you?" Priest said from across the balcony.

Robbie gritted his teeth and aimed his eyes at the man sitting as casual as you please under the curious surveillance of, well, everyone.

"Yes, trust me," Robbie said. "We all know you're here. Your stony silence is louder than anyone else in the room. But don't worry; I have absolutely no problem telling you what I think of you—trust me."

Priest shrugged as though he wasn't fazed in the slightest, and the action only seemed to infuriate Robbie even more. "No skin off my nose," Priest said. "You're not my type anyway."

"Uhh, vice versa," Robbie said, as he tipped his chin so high in the air that Tate thought he might get a nosebleed. "I don't like assholes."

"Really?" Priest said, and this time got to his feet. Tate's eyes widened slightly as he looked over to see Cole and Rachel watching on with caution, and Shelly and Josh sitting wide-eyed at the show unfolding. And when Tate went to stand to intervene, Logan placed a gentle hand on his leg, stilling him as Priest said, "And here I'd heard the exact opposite about you."

Robbie, oblivious now to anyone else, as far as Tate could tell, marched across the space and aimed his eyes up at Priest, who merely looked down, unperturbed by

Robbie's display.

"I hate you."

Priest tossed the napkin in his hand down on his seat, and then he gave an insolent laugh. "Oh, I know, princess. I know." He then stepped around Robbie and walked over to where Tate sat with Logan's hand resting on his thigh, and said in a tone that was as polite as ever, "Thanks for inviting me tonight, Tate, Mitchell. I had fun."

"Wait a sec..." Logan said as he sat up straight and swayed a little. "You're not staying?"

"No. I have a good friend here in town, and I'm going to catch an Uber over there now."

"Ahh... Okay," Logan said, and held his hand out. "Was good of you to come up here with us."

Priest shook Logan's hand and then looked to Tate. "Good luck with him tonight."

Tate laughed and shook Priest's hand firmly. "Thanks. He can still walk, and he's still awake, so he's not that bad."

Priest laughed then waved to everyone as he pulled out his cell phone and headed inside with it glued to his ear.

As silence descended on the balcony, Robbie seemed to realize he was still standing in the middle of everyone, and shook his head. "Have you ever met anyone so infuriating?"

"Yes," Rachel said, and pointed to Cole. "He was totally infuriating."

Robbie gave her a meek smile and headed over to the

doors that led inside. "I'm going to go to bed. Suddenly I
feel...nauseous. Happy birth— Thanks for inviting me. This
place was awesome, and *most* of your friends are really
cool."

Tate nodded and Logan waved, and then Robbie
disappeared inside, no doubt running away in case Shelly
started in on him again or Priest decided he'd forgotten
something.

When Logan yawned, Tate took his cue and got to
his feet. There was no way he wanted Logan to fall asleep
before he got back to the room, so he stood and held a hand
out.

"Ready for bed, then?"

As Logan placed his hand in his, Tate tugged him to
his feet and pulled him in to kiss him lightly.

"Mhmm," Logan said against his lips, and Tate
glanced over his shoulder and grinned at the four who
remained on the balcony.

"That's my cue, guys. Thanks for being here tonight.
And even though Logan was a total pain for the first half of
it—"

"Hey."

"I think we can safely say he's thoroughly enjoyed
himself, the wine, and the port."

Logan ran a palm down Tate's chest. "*Annd* soon
you."

"Take him away, for God's sake," Cole said.

Tate wrapped an arm around Logan's shoulders.

"Yep, going now. We'll see you in the morning."

"See you then." Cole waved and Rachel blew them both a kiss. Then Shelly stood and gave them a hug each and wished them good night, and as Tate led Logan down the hall to their room, Logan leaned up and put his lips by Tate's ear.

"God bless Shelly and her troublemaking ways."

Tate chuckled and stopped by their door. "Yeah. It was rather entertaining."

"Uh, that's one way of putting it."

Tate inserted the keycard in the lock and then kissed Logan on the mouth. "It is. But I don't want to talk about anyone else other than us for the rest of the night, if that's okay with you."

Logan ran his hands down Tate's chest to his waist and then nipped at his lip before nodding. "That's more than okay with me."

"In that case, then," Tate said as he pushed down on the handle and opened the door. "After you."

Chapter Twenty-Six

LOGAN LOOKED AROUND Tate and inside to the suite, and when he remained where he was just outside the door, Tate cocked his head.

"Not afraid to come inside with me tonight, are you, counselor?"

Logan's buzzed brain had him sidling up close to Tate where he stood with his back to the door, keeping it propped open. "I'm not afraid of coming inside of you *any* night."

Tate pushed off the door, making Logan take a step back inside. "Way to mix up my words there."

"I thought so." Logan turned around, a little faster than he intended, and as the room tilted slightly to the left, he started to laugh. "Ohh, this is nice." He heard the door shut behind him, and as it clicked and locked, he decided he was suddenly a little hotter than felt comfortable.

Logan shrugged out of the coat he'd been wearing on the balcony, tossed it over the end of the bed, and then walked through the room, checking out the small kitchenette that had two more bottles of wine and a set of wine glasses on it, and a platter with an assortment of fruits and cheese beside those. He made his way down the hall to the bathroom and stopped dead in his tracks as he peered at what was in a small alcove on one of the walls.

He called out to Tate, "Hey, did you book this room because there's naked men sculpted into the walls?"

As a rumbling laugh made its way through the suite, Logan grinned and reached out to run his finger over the marble statue, liking the idea that maybe Tate *had* booked it for that reason.

If I were a straight man indeed, Logan thought, remembering Tate joking with him earlier. This bathroom looked like the inside of a bath*house. No straight men allowed tonight.*

The sound of a bottle being uncorked had him turning around to go and track Tate down, but before he did, he ran a finger under the collar of his sweater. He needed to get out of his damn clothes. He wasn't sure, but he was positive it was getting hotter in there by the second.

After stripping out of his sweater and the shirt he'd had under it, Logan tossed them haphazardly on the floor and sighed at the relief of the cool air hitting his flushed skin. *Ahh, that's better. Now, where's Tate?*

He carefully made his way back toward the bedroom, trailing his fingers along the wall to make sure he didn't stumble, and then laughed at how unsexy that would be if Tate were to walk in and see him flat on his ass.

When he walked past the kitchenette to see Tate had poured them both some wine and was now over by the bed removing his clothes, Logan leaned against the cabinet.

Tate glanced over his shoulder as though he sensed Logan there, and when he spotted him, that pearly grin Logan loved appeared.

"You're drunk," Tate said, and laughed as he straightened and came around the end of the bed. He'd taken off everything, minus his jeans, which were undone and hanging around his hips.

"Not drunk, buzzed. But inebriated or not, I know you're seriously fucking hot." Logan tracked Tate as he walked over to him, and felt his cock throb in anticipation.

"Did you really just use the word *inebriated* in your state?"

"Yep." Logan tapped his fingers to his temple. "Nerd, remember?"

"Sexy nerd. Did you have fun tonight?" Tate asked, and when Logan nodded, Tate ran a finger down the center of his naked chest. "Stripping out of your clothes, huh? I'm glad I got you back here before you decided to do that in front of our friends. I'm not sure I would've been able to hold Robbie back."

Logan swayed forward, closer toward Tate, and gave him a lazy smile. "Was hot. Don't care about Robbie. But you…" Logan drawled as he put both hands on Tate's tanned skin and smoothed them down over his abs to his unbuttoned jeans.

"What about me?"

"Mhmm," Logan said, and turned one of his hands

around so he could dip it inside Tate's jeans. "I've wanted to get my hands inside these jeans ever since you put them, and *only* them, on in front of me back at home." When he wrapped his fingers around Tate's erection and tugged it upright, freeing it from its confines, Tate groaned, and Logan bit his jaw gently. "That was *very* bad of you, Mr. Morrison."

"Maybe," Tate said, not sounding the least bit repentant. "But it worked, didn't it? You're in here and have your hand around my dick."

Logan's lips curved against Tate's cheek, and then he pulled back a little, the alcohol swirling around inside him making him feel nice and relaxed. "Would've done that anyway. And *more*. Just ask."

Tate licked his lips, and the sight of his tongue had Logan leaning in, wanting a taste, and then he stumbled slightly, and Tate laughed. "Okay, birthday boy. How about we take a minute or two to sober you up a little before you fall over and damage part of yourself—or me, for that matter."

Logan frowned, not liking the idea of stopping. But Tate reached for his wrist and stilled his determined hand.

"I'm going to go and run a bath in that room with all the naked men."

"I didn't see a bath in there," Logan joked, as Tate moved past him and headed down the hall.

Tate called over his shoulder, "Why am I not surprised? Strip, Logan—I want you wet and naked and in that bath with me in the next five minutes."

Well, Logan thought, *not gonna argue with that.* Then he leaned his back against the wall for some extra support, and went about unzipping and shoving off his jeans, more than happy to follow orders for the night.

* * *

TATE HAD JUST turned the faucets off when Logan walked into the bathroom bare-ass naked, and hard as the marble that made up the opulent space.

Logan hadn't been wrong about the sculptures being one of the reasons Tate had picked this place. When he'd been researching the wineries and come across the themed bed and breakfast here, and the bathroom that came with this suite, Tate hadn't cared how much it cost. He wanted Logan naked and in that tub with him, and it appeared he was about to get that wish. And thank God for that, because Logan looked mouthwatering.

He was confident without the aid of alcohol. The port and wine Logan had consumed tonight had done nothing to dampen his confidence, instead only serving to enhance his arrogance and sex appeal.

With not one shy bone in his body, Logan sauntered over to the four steps that led up into the recess, and peered into the whirlpool tub big enough for two grown men.

The tiled room had been set up much like a Roman bathhouse, but instead of a pool, the tub had been built into

a tiled niche with a sculpture of a very well-endowed man
above it.

Tate shoved his jeans off and then kicked them aside,
just as Logan turned around to look at him. Logan took his
sweet time running his gaze down over Tate's body, and by
the time that heated gaze climbed back up to his face, Tate's
cock was standing at rigid attention. The man was pure sex
right now.

"So," Logan said, "just gonna take a bath, are we? I
think your body has other ideas..."

Tate swallowed and walked forward, not about to be
sidetracked by the arrogant man subjecting him to a once-
over that had Tate's temperature well above average.

As he climbed up the first two stairs and tilted his
head back to look up at Logan, Tate raised an eyebrow.
"Considering you can barely stand up without the very real
chance of falling, I'd say getting you on your ass is a step in
the right direction."

Logan's lips curled, and then, bold as ever, he
reached down to start stroking his cock. "I'm okay with that.
My ass. My back..." he said, and a wicked glint sparked in
those eyes. "Just tell me how you want me, Tate. I'm yours."

Though Logan meant his words in a completely
sexual way, they suddenly thrust Tate back to the last few
weeks and all that had happened between them, and again
he wondered, just as he had since the night Logan had
proposed, why had he become so troubled by the notion of a
piece of paper that meant forever, when forever was exactly

what he wanted?

Just tell me how you want me, Tate. I'm yours...

Tate knew those words to be true as they stood there naked in front of one another. Just as they had been that night, clothed and surrounded by candles. And as he looked up at Logan with his hand wrapped around himself and a cocky smirk on his face, Tate waited for the anxiety he'd felt that night to hit him—but it didn't.

As that reality sank in, he walked up the rest of the stairs so he could take Logan's face in his hands and kiss him with all of the emotions that were slamming into him.

Lust. Want. Need. And desire. They all coursed through him as Logan grabbed his waist, and then, suddenly, the kiss changed direction.

There, in a bathroom that was built for sin, the passion eased and the fever simmered until the deeper, scarier feelings began to consume the two of them. Tate opened himself up to the onslaught as Logan wove his fingers through his hair and cradled his head, seeking more. Tate gave it without any conscious thought, just handed it over as he would his last breath, should Logan require it, and then he was falling all over again.

Falling for the charm of the silver-tongued lawyer who'd picked him to sit down opposite that first night.

Falling into a relationship he'd always wanted but never dreamed he would have.

But most of all, he was falling in love with Logan all over again, just as he'd done every day since he'd known him.

"Logan..." Tate eased away from him, and as
Logan's eyes focused, much more aware now than they had
been minutes earlier, they had that expression Tate had seen
lately. The new one Logan had whenever he looked at him
and *now* Tate understood.

I dare you to try.

I think you're my truth.

Terrify me.

Marry me.

No.

As that final word mocked Tate over and over,
memories slammed into him, brought on by the one whose
life was so intimately entwined with his, and he almost
stumbled down the stairs as his stomach knotted and his
hands began to shake.

"Tate?"

Oh God, how could he have been so stupid? Why
had he let fear of change win out between them? And how
in the world would he *ever* get Logan to say yes to what he
now wanted more than his next breath?

As he slowly backed down the stairs and out of the
bathroom Logan remained where he was, naked and
curious, looking at Tate as though he'd lost his damn
mind—and all Tate could think was, *Maybe I fucking have.*

* * *

NOTHING WAS MORE effective at sobering a person up than watching the one you love run from you. Logan wasn't quite sure what had just happened there in the bathroom, but the look on Tate's face as he'd left wasn't one Logan had ever seen before.

Anger, confusion, and love had all been there. But if Logan's addled brain wasn't mistaken, so was a heavy dose of disgust—at himself.

But what spooked Tate? What had him running?

One minute they'd been naked and well on their way to what Logan had been hoping would be some wet and slippery sex in the bathtub. And the next, Tate had hightailed it out of there like the room had caught on fire.

Logan scrubbed a hand over his face and headed down the stairs to grab a towel, and after wrapping it around his waist, he walked out of the bathroom to hunt down Tate.

When he got to the bedroom, he noticed the room was empty, and cursed and wondered where the hell Tate had gone off to. Not far, obviously, Logan was pleased to note, when he spotted Tate's wallet, phone, and keys sitting on the bedside table.

After dropping the towel to the floor, Logan pulled on a pair of black and white checkered lounge pants and a black t-shirt, splashed his face with some frigid water, and then scooped up the extra keycard sitting on the bench. With a quick glance in the mirror, he rubbed at the stubble on his chin and then opened the door, heading out to find Tate.

He walked down the main corridor toward the bar and balcony area they'd all left earlier, and as he turned the corner and stepped inside, Logan spotted him.

Tate was sitting over at a small table for two by the fireplace, and with only the soft glow of the flames and the small candle on his table, Logan could barely make out his features or what kind of mood he was in. If he were to go by body language alone, Logan would hazard a guess that the slumped shoulders were a good indicator that whatever had happened back in the bathroom was definitely still on Tate's mind.

As he walked past the bar and the bartender looked his way, Logan held a hand up and shook his head. He'd had far more than his usual intake of alcohol tonight, and he had a feeling that whatever he and Tate were about to discuss now would be best done with his brain in a somewhat functioning state.

When he reached Tate's table and he looked up, Logan was blown away by the sadness in his eyes. All night Tate had been nothing but laughter and happiness as they'd sat amongst their friends, and when they'd gotten back to their suite, there'd been no hint of this emotion anywhere.

Logan pulled out the chair opposite him and reached across the table to take Tate's hands in his. "Hey."

"Hey," Tate replied, and lowered his eyes to where their fingers were joined.

Logan squeezed his around Tate's, waiting for him to say more, but when it was clear he wasn't going to, Logan said, "What are you doing out here?"

"I, uhh…"

"Tate?" Logan said before Tate could give him some half-assed response. "*What* are you doing out here?"

As Tate withdrew from him and sat back to run a hand through his hair, Logan immediately knew that Tate was nervous or upset about something, and if he had to guess, the way Tate kept worrying his lower lip made Logan think: *nervous.*

"Back there in the bathroom…" Tate started, and then stopped. But Logan waited, knowing there was more coming.

"I had a thought. It was more of a moment, I guess. A flash of us. Of all we are and will be and— Shit, I sound crazy, don't I?"

No, he didn't. Tate sounded reflective, introspective, and Logan wanted to know what had brought it on. What had made Tate go from carefree to so serious? "You don't sound crazy. But you are freaking me out a little. Were the things you were thinking good things, at least?"

Tate frowned and then shot Logan an apologetic look. "Yeah, of course. I should've probably started with that. Everything about you was good. Perfect, really, but me…"

"What about you? You're pretty fucking perfect from where I'm sitting. And back there in that bathroom, trust me, you looked better than any of those naked statues on the wall."

Tate's lip curled up on one side, but when the humor didn't quite reach his eyes, Logan asked, "What is it, Tate? Come on; you know you can tell me anything."

Tate swallowed and then shifted in his seat as he looked over to the flickering fire, and the light from the flames made his tanned skin glow before he turned back to Logan and asked, "Am I too late?"

Logan gave him a quizzical look, not understanding what Tate was asking. But then he reached into his pocket and pulled out a crumpled piece of paper. Tate unfolded it, put it on the table, smoothed his hand over it, and then spun it around and pushed it over toward Logan.

As Logan stared down at what was in front of him, he took in the date and saw his handwriting and remembered the exact day he'd written out the words below.

William Tate Morrison

William Tate Morrison-Mitchell

William Tate Mitchell-Morrison

. . . .

William Tate Mitchell

As Logan looked up, Tate asked again, "Am I too late?"

Logan tried to keep his erratic heart from stopping right then, but when his brain was pretty much short-circuiting, it was hard to keep everything else from going haywire. When all he managed was to shake his head, Tate pulled a pen from his pocket and leaned over to circle one of the names.

Logan looked down, and when he saw which one now had a bold circle around it, a huge grin split his lips as he looked up and Tate said, "So what do you think? Can the world handle *two* Mr. Mitchells?"

Special Thanks

I don't think it would be an Ella Frank book if at the end the first person I didn't have to thank was Brooke Blaine. This woman is not only my BFF and co-author, she is also my writing compass when I go out on my own. She makes sure I never steer too far off course, and if I do, she's right there to tell me how to get back on track. Thank you for being my trusted guide. <3 Also, this time around, I feel the need to apologize to you, Brooke. I think there's only been one other time where I have received so many I HATE YOUS. WHY DID YOU DO THIS TO ME? YOU'RE AN A**HOLE comments in my crits, and that had to be in *Trust* (and you can all understand why). Just know that Brooke goes through all of this alone for you months in advance, and feels your pain and need to kill me.

I would be remiss not to put Fred Goudon, Clement Becq & Shanoff Formats next for creating this sexy and intense cover for *Tate*. I was immediately drawn to this

image for several reasons. But hands down the main
one was for that fierce, bold stare and those curls—I
know that's what you were looking at too, right?
Arran, thank you for always finding the time for me
(even when I change the dates or have last-minute
requests). Feel free to edit this special thanks to say
how wonderful you are also. Wonderful, a smartass,
and truly a great editor. I hope you were able to keep
that guitar amp after all. ;)

Thank you to the creative and super-awesome women
over at Social Butterfly PR. Jenn Watson, Sarah
Ferguson, and Shannon—you give great eye candy for
everyone to see months in advance, and you organize
my ass so I don't have to. Without you guys, things
wouldn't run half as smooth, and I can't wait to hit you
in October.

To Shannon Gunn. Thank you for bringing Logan and
Tate to life in the first three installments of this series,
and for coming back to us to continue their journey in
these next three. You captured the personalities of these
two men in ways I didn't even write down on the page,
and both I and the listeners can't tell you how amazing
it is to feel as though these two men are real and in our

lives. And you gave us that.

Judy at Judy's Proofreading, you and I have been together now since the beginning in some form or another right? Reader, blogger, proofreader. You're a lady of many talents, and you are an awesome human being. Thank you so much for finding the time to feast your eyes on my guys, and for always finding the things I inadvertently miss. I can't WAIT to see you in Orlando. <3

And to my wonderful, fabulous readers who have followed Logan and Tate along their journey. I hope you enjoyed this chapter of their lives as much as I did, and know that I can't wait to bring you the next in 2018!

Xx Ella

About the Author

Ella Frank is the *USA Today* Bestselling author of the Temptation series, including Try, Take, and Trust and is the co-author of the fan-favorite contemporary romance, Sex Addict. Her Exquisite series has been praised as "scorching hot!" and "enticingly sexy!"

Some of her favorite authors include Tiffany Reisz, Kresley Cole, Riley Hart, J.R. Ward, Erika Wilde, Gena Showalter, and Carly Philips.